tasty MANGO

By JJ Knight

USA Today bestselling author of

Single Dad on Top
The Accidental Harem
Big Pickle
Hot Pickle
Spicy Pickle
Uncaged Love
Fight for Her
Reckless Attraction

Want to make sure you don't miss a release?
Join JJ's email or text list.

ABOUT THE PICKLE-VERSE

★★★★★

"OMG I was snort laughing by page 2!" ~ Judy Ann Loves Books Blog

★★★★★

"It's laugh-out-loud, snort-your-drink, absolutely-do-not-read-this-book-in-public hilarious, with this crafty writer's clever wit creatively showcased on every page." ~ Book Addict Book Blog

★★★★★

"The poster child for how a romantic comedy should be written. I dare you to try and not laugh or fall in love with this book!" ~ Dog-Eared Daydreams

★★★★★

"You know you are in for a whole lot of fun." ~ Life, Books, and More Blog

★★★★★

"The puns, the innuendos, the hot pickles...I loved it all!" ~ Kay Reads Romance

★★★★★

"This series has so much hilarity that I can't stop laughing about it." ~ Southern Chics Lit

★★★ **TASTY MANGO** ★★★

Ladies, you've never had a first date quite like this.
He's a billionaire.
Desperately handsome
Wildly charismatic.

In fact, a certain article of clothing of mine has gotten quite damp.
Except…
It's not the good kind of damp.
In fact, I'm suddenly very, very wet.
Oh no.

I've left out something important.
I'm nine months pregnant.
Don't ask about the father.
I'd rather forget.

But I'm sitting in the fanciest restaurant you can imagine.
Opposite the man of my dreams.
It's our first time alone together.
The start of something spectacular.
And…
My water just broke.

———

Tasty Mango is a standalone romantic comedy about

going into labor on a first date with a billionaire, the
ensuing hilarity (and pushing) in a very expensive limo,
and trying to manage a new relationship with the
world's most eligible bachelor while cleaning spit up out
of your hair.

Edition 1.0

Casey Shay Press
PO Box 160116
Austin, TX 78716
www.jjknight.com

Paperback ISBN: 9781938150937

1
_____

HAVANNAH

I've always pictured this moment.

Me, in a little black dress.

My hair swept into a perfect chignon.

An exclusive restaurant filled with elegant diners.

China clinks. Crystal glasses gleam on linen tablecloths.

Seated opposite me is the ideal man. Tall, dark, handsome.

Custom suit. Gold cuff links.

He's charming and witty.

Wildly successful in business.

And he only has eyes for me.

It could have been the greatest first date of my life.

Except.

My belly is too big to let me pull up to the table properly.

The baby is kicking like crazy for me to eat something—*now*.

And a funny trickle of wetness is forming deep in the recesses of my panties.

And *not* the good kind.

Am I peeing myself?

"Havannah, are you okay?" Donovan McDonald pauses, his water goblet halfway to his lips. He's a gentleman, so he's not drinking wine, since I can't.

His eyes are on me, his thick brows knitted in concern. His gaze dips to the table's edge, where I'm hunched, trying to hide my bump. I'm desperately trying to appear like a normal date from the chest up.

"Perfect!" I say, keeping my voice as chipper as possible, wondering if a wet spot will show on the dress. I really want to sneak away to the bathroom to see what's going on.

God. This is horrible.

Of course, it's mid-June, so I don't have a wrap to tie around my waist. Just my foolishly tight dress that fit fine at six months pregnant but is snug at nine.

I shift on the chair, making sure my legs are hidden by the tablecloth. I spread my knees in hopes that I can air-dry.

Pregnancy is a beast.

Donovan takes a sip of water, watching me.

I flash him a bright smile. "I'm so glad we got to do this!"

He nods. "Me too. How has the first week of the new deli gone?" This question isn't random filler. He wants to know. Donovan and his brother Dell Brant have been our mentors as my sister and I launch our restaurant, the Tasty Mango.

I wave my knees back and forth beneath the table in hopes of drying the errant pregnancy pee. "Your advice helped. We've exceeded our sales expectations for the grand opening."

"That's great," he says. "I was hoping to stay the whole week, but duty called."

"You did so much. And you were there to cut the ribbon." I abruptly shut off the conversation when his expression shifts.

He's remembering the awkward hauling of the pregnant chick to the car. He *had* helped carry me when I panicked right after the ribbon cutting, thinking I was in labor.

I wasn't.

So humiliating.

Then I didn't see him again, as he was off to New York by the time my lack of labor was sorted.

But two days ago he called, saying he was going to drop into Boulder between his meetings in California and Chicago.

And would I like to have dinner?

I squealed so loud that my sister Magnolia raced into the bedroom with towels and my overnight bag, sure I was in labor for real this time.

But I have a few days to go until I'm due, and I hear first babies are always late. I've vowed to be nothing but chic and put together on this date. He'll see my elegance, my poise—

Uh oh.

Another squirt of wetness slips out.

How can this be? I peed right before I came. I'm not coughing, or laughing too hard, or sneezing.

I push my cloth napkin under the tablecloth and shove it up my dress. Sorry, fancy restaurant. I'm stealing this. It's an emergency.

The waiter approaches. "Your salads."

He sets two perfectly arranged wedges in front of us, artfully cut on a square plate with a fan of tomato slivers.

At the smell of bleu cheese, Junior kicks hard enough to make my belly jump. Another bit of water slides out. He must be aiming for the bladder. So that's what's happening.

I let out a sigh, relieved to have figured it out. I squeeze my thighs around the cloth napkin and pick up my fork.

"This looks amazing," I say.

"You look amazing," Donovan says.

Our gazes meet over the vase of roses in the center of the table. He is such a hunk. His dark eyes sparkle. His beard is neatly trimmed. Everything about him is absolutely perfect.

And he's here with *me*.

Everything is fine. We'll have a lovely dinner. Then he'll leave again and think about me on his travels.

This will work.

"How is the new financial manager working out?" he asks.

I cut off a sliver of lettuce, despite Junior's insistence that I eat the entire thing whole. I'm a *delicate flower*, baby. Don't make me look bad.

"Magnolia says he's great. I'm more of the branding expert." I slip the tiny bite in my mouth.

Donovan's grin disarms me completely. "I guess we shouldn't talk shop on a date."

A date.

It hits me one more time.

I'm on a date with a billionaire.

Junior kicks again. He couldn't care less about the man. He wants the food.

Despite the distraction, I give Donovan a dreamy smile. "What do you do back in New York for fun?"

Another grin. "I have a collection of classic cars. I like to work on them myself. Get my hands dirty."

Okay, *that* bit of wetness is for real.

"What kind of cars?" I cut another tiny bite, if only to keep Junior pacified.

"Two Mustangs. A 1986 yellow Camaro. A 1952 Jaguar. And a 1963 Porsche."

"Dang. Are they all in good shape?"

"I've had them restored, but the motors require some upkeep." Donovan's eyes light up. He enjoys talking about the cars. I could listen all day.

"Do you drive them?"

"Not often. I don't store them in the city. I bought a property in upstate New York with a garage to hold them all." He tilts his head. "I hope you can come see them sometime. It's quiet and peaceful up there."

Junior thumps, as if to remind me that traveling isn't going to be on my life agenda anytime soon. But I say, "That would be lovely."

I go to stab more salad, but my plate is empty. I've

inhaled it. My bites must have gotten bigger while Donovan talked.

A waiter rushes by, the white cloth tucked into his belt flying behind him. His movement disturbs the candle near my water glass, and a waft of smoke reaches my nose.

Oh, no.

The tickle is small at first, and I try to suppress it.

Not a sneeze. No, no, no. Not when I'm already leaking.

Donovan's gaze is resting on me. He's smitten. I can see it.

But he's also paying close attention. I can't squeeze my nose or take preventive measures. That wouldn't be elegant *or* chic.

The tickle becomes an itch, then expands to a burning need to sneeze. My eyes water slightly.

Donovan's hand snakes across the table, heading toward mine. "I thought about you a lot in New York."

The moment is here! We're connecting! Me and this perfect man! I reach for him as well.

But I can't hold back the sneeze.

It takes over my face, my lungs, my upper body. I inhale in a big "Aaah" then release in an alarming "Choooo!"

The candle goes out.

Several diners turn.

But Donovan's hand doesn't move. His lips quirk with a smile he's trying to hide. "Bless you."

He might say something else, but I can't pay any attention whatsoever.

My legs feel warm and wet. *Really* wet. Like, to my ankles.

A weird sound sets off a panic. What is that? Rainfall? Water spilling?

My glass is still beside my plate.

Then realization dawns. It's water hitting the floor below the table. Below *me*.

I'm soaked. My legs are drenched. I can feel it in my *shoe*.

I can't seem to stop myself from abruptly standing up. My chair kicks back, then falls behind me.

Donovan leaps from his seat. "Havannah?"

I stare down at my bare, dripping legs. The soggy cloth napkin falls to the floor with a *splat*.

There's no hiding it now. I have to say it.

"My water just broke."

Pandemonium ensues. Several waiters rush forward to drop pristine linen towels on the floor. Diners crane their necks to watch.

Donovan rounds the table to put his arm around me. "Should we call an ambulance?"

I'm in shock. Not that I'm in labor…again. I've already done this whole routine, a week ago. But that something hasn't bent to my will. I wanted this date. This dinner. This man.

And I'm not going to get it.

I shake my head. I'm crying, and I hate crying. But emotions are taking over. "I'm not even having contractions."

"But your water," he says.

I nod. "I know. We have to go. But we can drive. It's no rush."

Donovan whips out his phone and punches a button, then tucks it in his pocket again. "Let's get you out of here."

I take several mincing steps, hating the sloshing feeling of walking in the wet pumps. But then the next stage begins. A long, slow contraction, tightening in my belly like a giant fist.

"Oooooh," I say. "Oooooh."

I can't move, breathing in and out. More water falls to the floor. More waiters drop their linens.

"Breathe," Donovan says, gripping my waist.

I nod, focused on his chiseled, glorious face. Couldn't I have had just one date with him?

As the contraction slows, I try to take a step forward, but I slip in the wet shoes.

Donovan catches me. "Here." He lifts me into his arms. I'm airborne, his arms securely beneath my back and knees. "Let's get you to the limo."

I wrap my arms around his neck, breathing slowly, trying not to think about how my wet dress is probably getting him soaked.

As we hurry out of the restaurant, I close my eyes to avoid seeing the alarmed looks of the other diners as a soggy pregnant woman gets evacuated from a restaurant.

Instead, I pretend I've been *swept off my feet.*

2

DONOVAN

W hen I make it outside with Havannah, the valet looks at us with alarm. "Shall I call your driver?"

"I already did," I tell him.

The night is warm. Havannah has buried her face in my neck. Despite the pregnancy, she's easy to carry. But I'm not sure she'll manage this position if another contraction hits. I don't know much about labor and delivery, not more than I've seen in movies.

The long, sleek limo pulls up to the awning. I hired a service, since I don't travel with a driver, so he's unfamiliar. But at least he's prompt.

The valet ushers us inside. "Good luck," he says, tipping his hat.

I duck down, no easy feat with a pregnant woman in my arms, and lay Havannah on the long leather seat. "You okay?" I ask.

She nods. "I'm in between the pain. Just wet."

I sit opposite her as the car moves forward. She tries

to sit up, but her eyes go wide and she lies down again. "I think I'll stay right here."

The driver rolls down the glass partition. "Everything okay?"

"What hospital?" I ask her. I don't know my way around Boulder.

"East Side," she says.

I turn to the driver. "You know it?"

"Of course," he says, and turns back to the wheel. Then he whips around again. "Does that mean she's—"

"Yes, she's in labor."

"Oh, geez," he says. "I just had the car cleaned."

I'd like very much to crack his jaw for that. "Just get to the hospital."

He nods, and the limo jets forward.

Havannah presses a palm to her forehead. "I can't believe this is happening."

I reach over and take her hand. "Maybe it's me. Twice now I've visited Boulder, and both times you ended up in the hospital."

She laughs, the sound vibrating through my chest. "I do seem to have a terrible habit of needing medical assistance when you're around."

I lift her fingers to my lips. It's early for such an intimate gesture, but it feels right. "Should I call someone?"

Her eyes go wide. "Oh, right! I guess this is the real deal, if my water's gone. Yes. My sister. My mom. And — Ooooooh!"

Her hand grips mine like a vise. She huffs, sweat popping on her brow. I push her hair off her forehead where it's sticking to her skin. She rolls on her side, sucking in air, then huffing it out again.

"Another one?" I ask. I'm not a man to panic, but this situation has me concerned. I picture the baby coming out on the seat. Should I catch it? Do they still smack them on the bottom to make them breathe?

"Seems…sorta…fast…" she says.

"Should I time them?" They always talk about timing contractions in movies.

"Yessss. Try."

She won't let go of my hand, so I use the other to tug my phone out. I glance at the driver. "How far?" I ask him.

"Downtown traffic is a bit locked up. I'll go around."

"There's…a…festival on Pearl Street," she gasps. "Lots…of…people."

"Right!" says the driver. "That explains it." He makes a quick right, and my phone clatters to the floor as I press my hand to Havannah's belly to hold her in place. It's as hard as a rock.

"Does it always feel like that?" I ask.

"Only…during…a…" She gives up talking to squeeze her eyes shut and breathe in short, rapid-fire huffs.

"I understand." I reach around on the floor for my cell. "Take it easy up there!" I tell the driver.

My fingers finally locate the phone. "What's your mom's number?"

She holds up a finger, then lets out a long, slow breath. "Use my phone," she says. But we both realize at the same moment that she left her purse behind in the commotion.

"I'll call the restaurant and have it sent," I tell her quickly. "Do you know the numbers?"

"Who knows numbers anymore?" she cries. "It's all in speed dial."

"Dell will have them," I say. "Or at least he can call Anthony, and Anthony can call Magnolia."

She nods again, then sucks in, her face red, more huffing breaths coming. "Why is this one so looooong?" She lets go of me to grip the edge of the cushion.

I don't even try texting, but put a call straight through to Dell. It goes to voicemail.

Damn it!

I leave a curt message: "Call the Pickles as soon as you get this. Havannah's in labor and doesn't have her phone. Get one of them to tell Magnolia so she can notify the family. We're headed to East Side Hospital." I hang up.

Surely I talked directly to the Pickles at some point. Or Magnolia. Havannah grips my hand as I scroll through my call list.

I see the name Boudreaux and click on it.

It buzzes before I realize, *Oh.*

It's Havannah's. Right. When I asked her on this date. This wild, ill-timed date.

Havannah's hand stops squeezing mine, and she relaxes on the cushion. "Okay. This one's over."

"Now I should time it?"

She nods, brushing a long tangle of hair away from her face. Her updo has come down. Little wire pins are scattered across the seat. "My hair is driving me crazy. I need something to tie it back."

I start a timer on my phone and glance around for something to tame her hair. There's nothing in the limo. I strip my tie from my shirt. "Will this do?"

She nods, taking the silk Hermès tie and sliding it under her hair. She shifts it so the wide part is on top of her head, then knots the ends at the back of her neck. The effect is cute and very sixties.

"It's a good look," I tell her.

She closes her eyes. "This is not how I pictured the night going."

When I don't have a response to that, she opens one eye. "Say something."

I shrug. "After the last time we were together, I considered this as one of the possibilities."

She props herself up on an elbow. "Really? And you came anyway?" She seems stricken, her chin jutting out.

I'm not generally at a loss for words, but how do I explain her predicament is part of her charm? I haven't asked any questions about the baby, or the father, or how she got in this situation. It's simply part of who she is. She comes with a baby. I knew that from the moment I saw her.

And I can't forget that moment. Dell and I arrived at the empty deli about a week before opening day. My brother was laughing over some joke he'd told. We opened the door. The inside of the place was already set up, orange tables scattered through the open dining area.

And seated at one of them was a goddess.

Her long blond hair was a tangle of curls. She wore white pants and a pale green T-shirt with the restaurant logo.

Her eyes were crystal blue, and when they met mine, I felt absolutely sunk.

When she stood up, I saw she was pregnant, of course. My heart crashed completely. The lack of a ring meant nothing at first, because probably her fingers had gotten too swollen to wear it.

But later that day I learned that she lived with her sister. And on day three of our mentor sessions, when Magnolia suggested we all go to dinner, and Anthony came along but Havannah had no one, I suspected she was in this alone.

I asked Anthony discreetly about her situation. He only said she was single and the father was not in the picture.

"Uh, oh," Havannah says, gripping my arm in a tight squeeze. "I think another one's coming. How long has it been?"

I glance at the phone. "Just over three minutes."

"That seems fast."

"Is it?" I have no idea.

"Google it," she says. "I think under four is when they think it's imminent."

Imminent?

I shout up the driver, "How close are we?"

"Five minutes!"

Five minutes. "We'll make it," I tell her. "Don't worry."

"Just Google it!" she says through gritted teeth. "If

I'm going to have a baby in the back of a limo, I want to know!"

"Don't have a baby in my limo!" the driver shouts. "I just cleaned the seats!"

"I'll have your damn car cleaned!" I shout back. I could *purchase* this limo a million times over. *Jesus.*

I fumble with my phone to Google "timing of contractions."

Havannah lets out a long, guttural moan. I'm feeling the uncomfortable, slow rise of panic. I thought I was unshakable. I've sat in board meetings with angry CEOs, entire rooms shouting at me.

But this a hell of a lot more stressful.

I find a good link. "It says here less than five minutes apart and lasting a minute or more is active labor."

"I think we're beyond that," she says. "How much longer until he comes?"

"We should have an hour. You're not in transition."

This calms her, and while her breathing continues in short, huffing spurts, she relaxes on the seat, eyes closed, hand on her belly.

"We'll make it fine," I tell her.

One of her shoes has partially come off, so I pull it away, as well as the other, and set them on the ground. "Should we call your doctor and let him know?"

"I would," she says. "But no phone, remember?"

"I can look him up."

"The hospital can do it." Her shoulders relax. "That one's done. I'm so tired."

She has a long way to go, though. I pocket the phone. "What can I do?"

"I'm super thirsty."

I sort through the cabinet. Beer. Wine. Finally I locate a bottle of water and unscrew the cap. "Here you go."

She props up on her elbow again. "Thanks."

Her smooth throat bobs as she chugs half the bottle. I take it from her. "Next round will be soon."

"I'll probably puke this up, actually," she says. "Are there any towels?"

Folded silk napkins are tucked inside a row of chunky crystal highball glasses. I pull one out. "I'm not sure this will help much, but I'll give you them all." I tug out all the napkins and spread them along the seat near her head.

"Maybe a plastic bag?" she suggests.

I sort through the cabinets and locate a small trash can. I pull it out. "How about this?"

"Good." She drops her head.

"Anything else?"

Havannah shakes her head, eyes drooping. "We wait."

She looks exhausted and forlorn, her tiny frame with its basketball belly curled on the long leather seat. I scoot close to her, sitting on the floor, my arm bracing her so she doesn't shift with every movement of the car.

"We're here!" the driver calls. A big red sign penetrates the dark tint on the windows. The hospital.

"You ready for this?" I ask her.

She nods, and I help her sit up. "Thank you."

The driver throws open the back door. "Woman in labor!" he shouts.

Havannah looks up at me. "Did he really do that?"

"He did."

After a moment, a medic peers inside. "Can you walk?" he asks.

Havannah nods. We help her out of the car, and the team loads her on a rolling stretcher.

"Should I come with you?" I ask, suddenly unsure.

But at that moment, Magnolia runs up. "We made it." She glances at me. "Dell called Anthony."

Then her mother is there. And her father.

"Thank you, son," her father says. "We'll take it from here."

"Her phone is at Julio's Bistro," I say. "We forgot it in the race here."

John Paul nods, following his daughter through the sliding doors. "We'll handle it. Thank you!"

The driver ducks to peer at the interior of his car, sighing in relief that it isn't whatever he pictured. "Where should I take you?"

"Back to the hotel, I guess," I say.

I head inside the car and wait for the driver to walk around.

Havannah and her family have already disappeared inside the hospital. As we pull away, I pick up the pile of silk napkins and set them on the bar.

A sparkle catches my eye.

On the floor of the limo, gleaming like Cinderella's slippers, are Havannah's fancy shoes.

I'll have to bring those back to her sometime.

3

HAVANNAH

Having a baby is the worst!

The ER doc decides I'm not in any imminent birthing stage, so the staff leisurely sends everyone but my sister out to wait until a labor and delivery room is ready for me.

"Make that doctor get back in here!" I tell Magnolia. "I'm going to have this baby any second." I huff my way through another contraction.

Magnolia bites her lip in a way I know means she's trying to figure out how to be tactful. She looks a mess. Her hair is in a loose, twisty bun that doesn't look intentionally tousled. She's wearing sweatpants and a Boulder Pickle T-shirt. What was *she* doing on a Saturday night? Eating ice cream and watching Hallmark movies?

"What?" I finally say when she doesn't speak up. "What is that face for?"

She straightens the paper sheet covering my knees. I'm still in the black dress, inched up to my waist. Am I going to deliver Junior in a cocktail gown that's two sizes too small?

I fling my arm over my face. This is too much.

"You're only three centimeters dilated and your contractions are irregular," she says.

"They were three minutes apart in the limo!" I've been saying "limo" every other sentence. I don't know why. To brag, I guess. Like I have anything to brag on, knocked up with a deadbeat dad and unable to finish a first date with someone normal.

Tears leak out of my eyes and I dash them away. No time for a pity party.

"That can happen as things get started," Magnolia says gently. "I think you probably have hours to go."

"So I could have finished my date?"

Yeah, yeah, I know it's an irrational thought. Hush.

She shrugs. "I guess if you'd thought to wear an adult undergarment." She turns to a steel cabinet, the only furniture in this curtained space. "I think there might be an extra in here. Want me to fetch one and we'll call back the limo?"

I can't help but laugh. "Why is this happening?"

She leans her hip against the bedrail. "Because you're one wild and crazy chick, and you were destined to live a hot-mess life."

A nurse in pink scrubs arrives with two young men in blue. "Havannah, I'm Nurse Cindy. These two gentlemen are going to wheel you to labor and delivery. We've got a room all ready for you." She holds up a white plastic band. "Can you verify this is you?"

I peer at it. Havannah Boudreaux. DOB April 17, 1994. "That's me."

She fastens it to my wrist. "You'll have a matching one for your baby when it's time. Do you know if it's a boy or a girl?"

"A boy," I say. I'm already feeling calmer.

"Nice." She nods at the two men, and they bend down to unlock the wheels to my bed. "Have you picked out a name?"

I shake my head. I have a list, but the arrival of the baby has been hard to picture. I've put all my energy into our new deli. Until now, the baby has been a rather fuzzy idea in the far-off future.

Magnolia walks alongside us as we navigate the sectioned-off curtains of the ER. "I brought the name book. It's in the bag."

I glance at her. "Where's the bag?"

"With Dad."

"Will you tell him to head to the maternity floor?"

"Your parents are already there," Cindy says. "They seem to have quite a setup for you."

Oh, right. I vaguely remember a big rant about the perfect birth. The music, a silk robe, lavender-scented handkerchiefs. I might have asked for a gurgling fountain.

The reality of labor makes my suggestions seem silly. A real-life baby is coming.

We enter an elevator. "I take it this is your first," Cindy says.

I nod.

"Are you expecting any other arrivals?" I figure this is her tactful way of asking about the father.

"I don't think so." The familiar sinking feeling takes over. The real-life baby isn't going to have a real-life father.

"Grandmama will certainly come later," Magnolia says. I know she's trying to make my mind shift gears. I can't go spiraling down a pity hole.

It's taken a lot to convince my family not to ask about the baby's paternity. But Magnolia knows. She's sworn to take the secret to her grave.

Not that I'll leave him out of the picture forever. But right now, he's in jail, and since I didn't even know his last name when we did the deed, I'm sure I'm only the vaguest memory to him.

If he ever gets his life together, I might tell him. Or if Junior ever needs him, like for a kidney transplant or whatever, maybe I'll track his awful ass down.

But for now, he's out. He's a horrible person and deserves to be where he is. I don't think they let you out of jail to attend your baby's birth even if you do know one's coming.

I'm on my own.

Magnolia squeezes my arm as we exit the elevator to the happy colors of the maternity ward. I'm not entirely alone. I've got my sister. And my parents. And the Pickles have been extremely involved since Magnolia and Anthony got engaged. In fact, the only reason I have a nursery is that Anthony's family keeps sending gifts.

Our family is stretched pretty thin with the second

deli so new. But we have hand-me-downs they saved. And I have a beautiful new crib, courtesy of Anthony. A ton of baby clothes. All the necessities.

I'm fine.

It's going to be fine.

The orderlies push open the door to my room. Mom and Dad are there, as promised. The music is playing, the air smells of lavender, and a tiny rock fountain gurgles on the side table.

Tears prick my eyes again. "You did it all!" I say.

Dad leans down to kiss my head. "Anything for our baby girl."

"And our grandbaby!" Mom says.

The two men lower the rails to the bed. "Can you stand?" Cindy asks.

I nod. I haven't had a contraction in a while. They were right. This is the beginning of a long night. I swing my legs over, keeping my paper sheet wrapped around me, to move to the larger bed.

Dad heads out so the nurse, Mom, and Magnolia can help me get changed and settled. I have my cotton gown, my silk robe, and a pillowcase embroidered with stars.

Mom's eyes glisten as she adjusts the pillow. "You were born with this pillow on the bed," she says. "And your sister." She swallows. "I'm pleased it's here for our first grandchild." She holds my hand.

Magnolia goes to fetch Dad. The next contraction hits, finally, and I breathe through it.

"Good girl," Mom says.

The anesthesiologist arrives, and we talk about

options. I choose an epidural, and everyone leaves while he sprays my back and sticks me.

Something icy flows through my veins. At first I don't think anything is different, but when the next contraction hits, mercy me. It's better. They dialed it down.

My family returns, and we settle in for a long, crazy night that will change my life completely.

4

DONOVAN

After leaving the hospital, I head back to the restaurant to fetch Havannah's bag myself.

Then I text my brother, asking for numbers so I can directly contact a member of the family. He comes up with Magnolia's.

I send her a message saying I have Havannah's bag and shoes, and I can bring them by tomorrow before my flight.

It's almost an hour before I hear back.

Leave them with your hotel desk in the morning. Dad can fetch it tomorrow.

I'm not clear if she is keeping me away or being courteous.

After a few hours of fitful sleep, I wake up, immediately wondering how Havannah might be faring. I have no way of knowing. Her phone is with me.

By morning, I'm not going to wait one minute more. I tell my assistant to have the pilot submit a new flight plan and delay all my meetings in Boston. I pack up my suits and put on a casual cotton Henley and a pair of jeans, and make a stop by a baby store for an appropriate purchase.

If they think I'm going to avoid Havannah, they can forget it. I've never met anyone like her. And I don't care about her predicament, dating while pregnant.

I care about *her*.

I feel completely lost in the giant baby store. There are aisles of things I can't even fathom the use for. A baby butt fan? To air-dry a baby?

I turn to a clothing display and spot leopard-print baby high heels. For infants.

I'm totally out of my element here. I text my brother.

What should I take to the hospital as a gift? Bottles? Diapers?

I know he might be in a meeting. It's nine a.m. in New York. But he texts me right back.

No, no. Flowers. Something for the mother.

Damn. I've taken a completely wrong tack. But I'm already here. Might as well get something.

A young saleswoman in bright pink overalls approaches. "Looking for a gift?"

"Yeah. A…friend had a baby."

"Is she registered?"

"I have no idea."

After we check the listings and don't find Havannah, the woman leads me to a display of elaborate wicker baskets surrounded with cellophane and topped with bows. "These always go over well. It's a layette."

Looks like a bunch of clothes to me.

She tilts a basket so I can see inside. "It has all the

essentials for the first weeks. Bibs. Sleepers. Onesies." She's speaking Greek, but gamely continues as I stare. "This pink one is for girls and blue for boys."

I ignore the gendered choices and choose the pale green set. "Thanks."

I pay for the layette and have the limo driver stop at a florist. The amount I pay for a normal bundle in New York creates an obscene bouquet in Boulder. When the woman returns from the back, I almost ask her to cut it in half. But I'm anxious to see Havannah.

I'm quite the spectacle walking through the lobby of the hospital with my explosion of flowers and giant basket, but the woman at the desk smiles at me. "Maternity floor, I take it?"

I nod. I don't know what the rules are in this hospital regarding visitors, so I smoothly say, "I'm the proud uncle."

I had a thousand uncles who weren't actually related. In Alabama, everybody's your uncle.

"Who's the patient?"

"Havannah Boudreaux."

"Oh, yes, I saw her famous sister in the cafeteria this morning."

Right. I forget that Anthony and Magnolia were quite the talk show darlings for the better part of last year.

The woman clicks on her keyboard. "She's in 743."

"Thanks."

I wind my way to the elevator. I'm not sure how my presence is going to be taken, but I have to see her. First date or not, it's almost impossible to drop off a woman at a hospital and let it go.

My accessories get even more smiles as I walk down the hall. It's midmorning, thirteen hours since Havannah's water broke.

No doubt by now she's curled up in her bed with the baby at her side. She'll be the picture of maternal bliss.

I knock on the door, but a guttural scream from inside drowns it out.

What was that?

Then a raspy voice that could only come from a middle-aged chain smoker shouts, "Stop saying that!"

I check the door number again. It's the right one. Did the woman downstairs get it wrong?

The door flies open and John Paul Boudreaux barrels through, almost knocking me over.

He halts, staring at me a moment. "You're still in town?"

"I am."

He glances behind him at the open room. "I wouldn't go in there if I were you." With that ominous remark, he takes off down the hall.

Oh, boy. I'm intruding. The baby hasn't been born yet after all.

But as another keening cry comes from the room, my protective urge takes over and I dash inside, flowers, basket, and all.

I'm not prepared for what I see. Havannah, grasping the bedrails with both hands, red-faced, sweating, her hair everywhere. Her sister, mopping her forehead with a cloth. Her mother Malina, standing in the far corner, looking up at the ceiling, tapping her face with her hand in agitation.

And a broad, serious nurse, standing at the foot of the bed, red-faced herself. I pause just in time for the woman to say, "Havannah, you have to calm down."

I make sure my gaze goes nowhere near Havannah's bare knees or anything below. That's way too much for someone at my level of acquaintance to see. It takes a moment for anyone to notice me, even with my giant flower arrangement.

But when Havannah's eyes lock on me, they go wide. She sucks in a breath. "You came back?"

This was a mistake. A terrible, terrible mistake.

"I have your purse and your phone. And I brought these." I hold out the flowers and basket.

I look around but don't see anywhere to set them. Each surface is covered with clutter. A silk robe thrown over a table. Some knitting, probably the mother's. Cups. Wrappers. And…a fountain? I place my offerings on the floor.

Both Magnolia and Malina stare at me.

I take a step toward the door. "I'll see myself out."

But the nurse holds up her hand. "Wait."

I'm not ordinarily a man to take orders from anyone. But this woman stops me cold.

"What?" Magnolia asks.

"She's calmer. Her blood pressure has improved." The nurse faces me. "Who are you? Dad?"

"I, uh…"

The nurse's gaze fixes on me. "It's about time you got here."

Everyone turns to Havannah. Her face does seem less red. She's still heaving air, but it doesn't seem much more than what she did in the limo.

"Stand over there," the nurse orders me, pointing to the head of the bed on the opposite side from Magnolia.

"Take her hand," the nurse says. "We've been within an inch of an emergency C-section with her stress levels. Her blood pressure skyrocketed. We could have used you before now."

"Sorry," I mumble.

"Well, hold on to her," the nurse says. "Don't take all day."

I lean down to Havannah. "Should I go?"

She doesn't answer, another keening wail coming out of her.

"Take her bloody hand!" the nurse shouts.

I pry Havannah's hand off the rail and hold it.

"That's it. See? Her blood pressure dropped again." The nurse bends down over Havannah's knees. "Havannah Boudreaux, it's time to get this done. Hold on to your man and push."

Havannah glances up at me. Tears are streaming down her cheeks.

"I'm here," I tell her. "You're going to be okay."

She nods.

Magnolia looks exhausted, dark circles under her eyes, sweat stains on her shirt. "Sit down," I tell her. "I've got this."

In truth, I don't have anything. But I'm here. A pinch hitter.

"Scoot her back a little. It will be more comfortable," the nurse tells me.

Havannah tries moving backward, but she's pretty spent. I lift her up and shift her until she sits up, knees high.

The nurse's face is less scarlet now, too. "Breathe, Havannah. Let's see if we can get that baby to crown."

Havannah sucks in a breath, then lets it out with a long groan, her eyes squeezed shut.

The nurse actually smiles. "Good, good. Dad, you want to feel the baby's head?"

"Noooo," Havannah says, keeping a vise grip on my hand. She doesn't have to tell me twice.

"Now we're talking." The nurse pulls out her phone and taps on it quickly. "I'm paging the doctor."

"I guess I got here right on time," I whisper in Havannah's ear.

She huffs out a laugh. "Are we calling this a second date?"

"Head is coming," the nurse says. "Slow it down. Pant your way through this one. Don't push."

Havannah glances up at me. I stick out my tongue and pant like a puppy.

She laughs again. But she mimics me and we pant together.

This is the wildest moment I've ever had with a woman, hands down.

A tall blond man in blue scrubs enters the room, snapping on a pair of gloves. Havannah relaxes immediately upon seeing him. "Dr. Briggs!"

"I hear we're about to have this baby," Dr. Briggs says. "I appreciate you waiting until I could get here."

The relief on Havannah's face is clear.

The doctor glances at me, his eyebrow quirking. I wonder if he thinks I'm the missing dad as well. But he doesn't comment, pulling a small stool out from the bed. He positions herself at Havannah's feet. "I'm sure you're ready to get this done. Ready to push?"

"I'm so tired," Havannah says. "How do people do this?"

"To end their suffering," he says with a grin. "Let's all rally around Havannah for this final stretch."

I hold Havannah's arm close against my chest. She and I have very little shared history, but I can pull from what we do have.

"Picture a cantaloupe down there," I say. "Imagine popping it right out of your nether regions and smacking into that evil nurse."

Havannah laughs.

"She'd go down like a bowling pin," I say.

The nurse raises an eyebrow at that, but she's probably heard worse.

Havannah's grip tightens on my hand. Her face turns red again.

"Watch her blood pressure," the nurse says. "We almost called it ten minutes ago."

"I see it," the doctor says. "Havannah, let's get this baby out right now. Count with me while we push to ten. One, two, three, four…"

I focus on Havannah's face while she concentrates on pushing down.

"I have a head," the doctor says. "Now for the shoulders."

They repeat the sequence of pushing. Havannah seems too tired to scream. Or maybe she's calmed down because of the doctor. But she lets out a low, raspy hiss.

"Nine, ten," the doctor finishes.

For a moment, there is utter silence in the room, and then, a cry.

"I've got him," Dr. Briggs says. "A perfect baby boy."

The doctor suctions the baby's nose, and my body prickles all over. I had nothing to do with any of this, other than to show up in the ninth inning.

But the sight of that baby, red and squalling and attached to Havannah with a cord, is unbelievable. Dr. Briggs lays him on Havannah's chest. She lets go of my hand and curls the baby up to her neck. "He's here," she whispers. "Mom? You can come back."

Malina springs to action from her corner. She kisses her daughter's forehead. "You did it."

Dr. Briggs leans in. "Let me take a quick look." He presses his stethoscope to the baby and nods. "All good."

The nurse tugs a stretchy hat over the baby's head and lays a blanket over them both. "Keep him warm. We'll do the assessment in a few minutes."

Magnolia heads for the door. "I'll go get Dad. He's no longer banished, right?"

Havannah nods. "It's all good. Why don't you both go?"

Malina looks from me to Havannah for a moment. "All right."

The doctor continues to do something near Havannah's knees. Havannah's eyes are only on the baby's face.

"Look at him," she says. "Just look at him."

I touch his little head. We remain there for long moments.

"No stitches." The doctor stands up. "We'll be back very shortly to assess the baby and get him cleaned up. You guys take a moment."

The nurse follows him out. We're alone.

"Should I be here?" I ask.

Havannah looks up at me. "I don't know. You just are."

"Should I leave you two?"

She shakes her head. "I know we only had a single date. And maybe we won't see each other again. But I like you being here." She lets out a shaky laugh. "Besides, I sent the others away and I'm terrified to be by myself."

Her arm starts to shake, so I shift the baby to the center of her chest to relieve the pressure. "You want a picture?"

She nods.

I pull out my phone. "I'll send it to you. Your phone is in your purse. I brought it. And your shoes."

She glances over at the pile I left by the wall. "Thank you for the gifts." She waves her hand at the room. "Your tie is…somewhere."

"I don't need it."

I smooth her hair back and step back to take a shot. She looks ethereally beautiful, light from the window on her blond hair, her cheeks rosy from the strain. The baby's face is right below her neck. I snap a few more and AirDrop them to her phone. "I just sent them."

"Thank you."

I tuck my phone away. "I certainly didn't expect this when I showed up this morning."

"I bet. I thought you were supposed to be in Boston by noon."

I shove my hands in my pockets. "My meeting was an hour ago."

"Oh no!"

"It's fine. We rescheduled everything. But I will have to leave this evening. I couldn't leave Boulder without knowing you were okay."

Havannah's eyes rest on my face. "Thank you. I'm not sure when I'll be able to see you." Her gaze skitters down to her baby again. His little eyes blink and blink as if he can't figure out what's happened.

"Text me. We can FaceTime. You can show me this little guy once he's more used to the outside world."

She nods. "Let's do that."

The door opens and suddenly the room is full. Magnolia. Malina. John Paul. Even the grandmother has arrived.

It's time for me to go.

I lean down to kiss Havannah on the head and touch the baby's cheek. "Good luck."

My presence and then my departure is scarcely noticed as the family circles the bed to get their eyes on their newest member.

I head out to the hall, my feeling of elation at being there for the baby's birth quickly sliding down into hollow emptiness. In a few hours, I'd be back to my own grind. Travel. Meetings. Business dealings. An endless routine where the only things that change are the numbers on the contracts and the faces around the conference table.

But, for a little while, I've seen exactly what it might be like to live a completely different life.

5

HAVANNAH

It's time to name this baby.

They've brought back the drill sergeant nurse because I haven't been cooperating. My parents exchange a nervous glance as she smacks a form on my over-the-bed tray.

"No name, no going home," she says. "And your insurance stops paying for you in precisely one hour."

The baby stirs against my chest. "Shh," I tell the woman. She doesn't scare me, not after what I've already been through. "You'll wake him."

But the woman doesn't budge. "I'm not moving until you put a name on that form."

I look over to my father for help. Normally he would take on Godzilla for me, but he shrugs. "The baby needs a name."

Mom is no use, busying herself by packing all the flowers and gifts I've managed to accumulate since I got here two days ago.

I turn to my sister. "Mags?"

"Havannah, we have a great list. Let's go over it one more time." She pulls up a chair and cracks open the baby name book. "Aaron."

"He'll think he has to play baseball."

Magnolia rolls her eyes but keeps going. "Bernard."

"Bookworm. What if he's more like me than you?"

A sigh this time. "Constantine."

"I liked that one before?"

"You thought it sounded classic."

"They'll call him con-man!"

"She's not wrong," Dad says.

I glide my fingers across the baby's cheek. To be honest, I thought seeing him would make his name obvious.

But nope. The only thing that pops into my head when I look at him is *perfect love*. Can't name him that.

"Dennis," Magnolia says.

"The menace?" What was I thinking?

"Fergus."

"I was smoking something. Give me that book. You're making stuff up now."

Magnolia passes it over. I shift the baby into the crook of my elbow as I flip through it. Actually, I *did* highlight those names.

Gary. Hastings. Jericho. Liam.

Okay, those are better.

"Liam," I say to the baby. His face scrunches. "Okay, maybe not."

Magnolia's exasperated. "You're letting the baby judge?"

"It's the cosmic energy!" I say.

"The baby's more decisive than she is," Dad says.

The nurse nods. "Ain't that the truth."

"Here, take him." I hold the baby out to Magnolia. She clucks over him as I go through the book. "How permanent is this choice today?"

"You can change it," the nurse says.

I sigh. "Great."

"In court," she adds.

"Oh."

Back to the book. Morty. Paul. Ranier.

"Say Ranier to him," I tell Mags.

She takes in a long breath, like she's trying to stay patient. But she whispers, "Ranier," next to his ear.

He doesn't move.

Hmm.

Stefan. Xander. Zeke.

Crap, I'm at the end.

I lean back against the pillows. "Why is this so hard?"

"It's a big decision," Mom says.

"Right! So why am I being pushed?"

"Hospital rule," the nurse says. "It's for the social security forms."

"Maybe we can be rebels," I say.

"You already are," the nurse says.

Mom pops her head up. "That was my father's middle name."

Dad snorts. "He was definitely a rebel."

Mom punches his arm. "No, I mean for real. His name was Gustave Rebel."

"Rebel. Rebel." I hold my arms out for the baby. "Let me have him back."

I pull up my feet to make a ramp with my thighs and lay the baby there, jiggling him until his slate-blue eyes open.

"What do you think of Rebel, little man?"

He gives a big yawn, then thrusts out a tiny fist.

"It's a yes!" I say.

The whole room whoops.

"She did it!" Mom says, hugging my father. "And for Dad. It's perfect."

Magnolia nods. "It's a good choice. And undoubtedly, it's going to be true as heck."

"Give me that form," I say, passing the baby to Mom. I pull the page to me. "Uh oh."

Everyone looks to me. "What?" Dad asks.

"He needs a middle name, too."

When I bring Rebel Zachariah through the door of the two-bedroom apartment I share with my sister, I have to stop three steps in. The living room is an explosion of balloons, gifts, and unopened boxes.

"Where did all this come from?" Mom asks.

"It's been coming in for a while," I say. "Looks like the landlord stuffed more in while we were gone."

Magnolia scoots aside three boxes of diapers so we can walk through. Dad stacks containers of baby wipes and three unopened packages on the floor so he can plunk down on the sofa.

Mom sets Donovan's flowers on the coffee table. "You're going to need more room!"

I shimmy between the armchair and the TV, the bucket car seat heavy in my arms. When Rebel is safely in the corner, still snoozing, I plop onto the floor beside him. "We'll get it all put away. It's fine. I'm not expecting a magazine shoot in here."

Dang, I'm tired. With all the noises, beeps, and nurse checks during the nights in the hospital, I haven't slept more than six hours total since my date with Donovan. I lean my head against the wall. *Sleep when the baby sleeps,* more than one nurse told me. I could use a nap.

"I'm going to unpack the kitchen things, bottles, pump parts, brushes, and all that," Magnolia says.

I give her a weak thumbs-up.

"Havannah, why don't you go rest?" Mom says. "We'll bring you Rebel if he wakes up hungry. John Paul, you start rearranging the boxes so we have some semblance of a walkway in here."

Dad lumbers up from the sofa. For a moment, I'm too tired to even stand. I contemplate crawling to my bed, but Mom leans down and extends a hand. "Come on, baby girl."

I stumble to the bedroom. Abandoned dresses are strewn across my bed from my indecisiveness before going out with Donovan. I shove them aside and collapse on the rumpled sheets.

I swear only seconds have passed when a cry startles me awake. Mom stands in the doorway. "I've got him," she says. "Magnolia assembled the pump so that after this feeding, you can express some, and next time you can sleep a little more."

She sits next to me on the bed. Rebel squirms in her arms, his mouth opening and closing like a bird's.

I scoot back so I'm sitting up against the wicker headboard. That's uncomfortable, so I pile the pillows behind me. "Pass him over."

Mom hands me the baby and glances around. "Would you like me to pick up in here?" She lifts one of the discarded dresses to reveal a red lace bra and matching thong. She sets the dress down again as if she hasn't seen.

I don't feel a lick of mortification that she saw my sexy undergarments when I just had a baby. That's who I am.

I shift Rebel and squeeze my boob in hopes he'll latch easily. Sometimes he does, and other times, it's a struggle.

After some tussling, he's on, and I let out a sigh. Mom waits at the end of the bed. When I look up, she says, "So, you want to tell me about Donovan? We didn't expect to see him at the birth."

"He's not the father," I say quickly.

"We assumed." She folds her hands carefully in her lap. The room is dim, the filtered light from the window outlining her mop of light curls. Neither Magnolia nor I got the texture of her hair, only the color. "It appeared as though you two only met when he and Dell came down for the mentoring meetings."

"We did. That's it."

"We noticed he was smitten. Everybody did."

I stare down at Rebel. He's already fallen asleep. I shift him, and he resumes sucking. "Me too. But I ended up in the hospital on ribbon-cutting day."

"That's right. And he left town. He came back to see you?"

Wow, this is the nosiest she's been in years. Does the baby mean she feels like she needs to know everything about my life?

"He wanted to go on a date. I thought I had time. Then my water just…broke."

She glances back at the dress that covers the lacy underwear. "When your waters ruptured, were you…"

"What? No! We were at a restaurant. I had been leaking a bit, but thought maybe it was pee."

Oh, why am I telling this story?

She waits for me to keep talking. Ugh. Fine.

"It all gushed out after a sneeze. The waiters dropped napkins at my feet." I'm hoping that detail convinces her I was not banging Donovan when my water broke.

Her eyes meet mine for a moment. "Are you going to continue to see Donovan?" Her gaze drops to the baby's head. "Even now?"

"I have no idea." I don't even know why Donovan was willing to ask out a massively pregnant woman. A sloppy, milk-dribbling new mother is even less appealing.

"Maybe he has a pregnancy fetish."

"Mom!"

She shrugs. "It's a thing."

"Mom!"

She stands up, picks up the dress again, and this time

hangs it in the closet. Then another and another. She opens a few drawers, locates the underwear, and tucks the lacy ones inside. "I assume they were clean."

"Yes." This is the absolute worst. It was bad enough I was hanging out for all the world to see in labor and delivery. But this is too, too much.

"Can you send Magnolia in?" I ask her. "I can talk with her about where to put all the new stuff."

She hesitates, clearly knowing I've found a tactful way to kick her out. "Sure. Your dad is arranging boxes and assembling a swing that came in. You sure you don't want to live with us for a while? We have more room."

"I'm sure. We'll come over a few nights a week, especially if I feel Magnolia needs a break from us."

She nods. "All right, then."

When she's finally gone, my head falls back against the headboard. That was mortifying. But with Rebel here, there's probably plenty more prying to come. A single mom with no father in sight is always going to be the source of speculation.

It's probably best if I leave Donovan alone.

I gave it a shot.

My priorities have to change.

6

DONOVAN

For the three weeks following the epic date with Havannah, I'm less focused than usual. I attend meetings, consult with lawyers, review business agreements. But my head isn't in the game.

Havannah texts me in random spurts, sometimes not responding for days, then writing a string of messages at two in the morning. It's clear her life is challenging, and she longs to get a sense of normalcy back. I'm not sure what role I can have in that. Between the distance and her new status as a single mother, the gulf feels impossibly wide.

My niece Grace turns five, so Dell messages me with the date and time of her party. He and Arianna are expecting another baby themselves.

I enjoy hanging out with them on weekends. It gives me a sense of what ordinary lives are like, when I'm not traveling nonstop.

The party is at a children's boutique designed for

such occasions. The front is a store filled with all manner of sparkle and bling. When I arrive, I'm ushered to a back room where a dozen little girls are seated at a circular table outfitted with lighted mirrors.

All are dressed in Disney princess frocks, and several hair and makeup artists work on them, completing their looks.

Dell stands in the corner with a high-end camera. I set my gift on the table piled high with boxes and bags and join him. "That looks above your pay grade."

He fiddles with several of the buttons. "You say that as if we're not at the top of all pay grades." He turns the camera over to peer at the lens. "Arianna insisted I stop using my phone to record Grace's life. With the new baby on the way, I decided to level up my documentation game."

I take the camera from him. "If you leave it on auto settings, you're better off using your phone. It never picks the right choices. You're supposed to be the brain."

"You know how to work this thing? I didn't think it would be so challenging."

"I took two photography classes in undergrad." I flip the camera to a program mode. Dell won't be able to use full manual, but I can improve his likelihood of good shots. "If you're outdoors and there's lots of action, like a playground, use this S mode."

"What does S mean?"

"Shutter priority. But don't worry about that. Think of it as *S for speed* mode, for fast things."

"Got it."

"If you're indoors and it's mostly shots of them posing, use A."

"And A is…"

"Aperture. But think of it as *A for alone*, a person sitting there ready for a shot."

"Okay."

"I'm going to put both modes in basic configurations that will cover most things. Don't mess with them until you know what you're doing."

I shift a few settings and hand the camera back to him.

He clicks a shot. "Hey, look at that!" He's chuffed with this image and wanders away to show his wife.

I lean against the wall and watch the girls giggle and ooh over each other. They ham it up for Dell as he takes each of their pictures. I'm glad I could help.

Grace spots me and flies out of her chair to run my way. "Uncle Don!" She's dressed as Moana, her long, dark hair crimped and fluffed, the orange top and textured skirt a perfect fit for a girl who is equal parts princess and wild child.

I lift her up. "Dang, you've gotten heavy now that you're five!"

She giggles. "You picked me up last weekend."

"And you're bigger!"

"You're so silly."

She presses her cheek to mine, and I flash with the image of Havannah in the hospital bed, her baby nestled against her neck. My family was wildly disjointed for most of my life. Dell took off and left me with crazy parents. Then, after I graduated college, he showed up and decided to play big brother.

I resisted at first, resenting the hell out of his changing his name and acting like none of us existed, but Arianna changed him. They went through a lot after baby Grace was left at his penthouse with the note "Do the DNA, she's yours."

By the time they were engaged, Dell was willing to make amends. And with his time devoted to family, he brought me into his business.

I do the lion's share of the traveling, being single and enjoying the hustle. But with my niece so close, smelling of hair spray and childhood, I can see why Dell switched priorities.

"Time for our fashion show!" a bubbly woman with shining black hair announces, clapping her hands for attention. "Princesses and wildlings, come behind the stage so we can all see your final looks!"

Grace wiggles down. "Are you going to watch us, Uncle Don?"

"Of course!"

She looks up at me. "I sure could use a Maui to go with my Moana!"

"You mean the big demigod guy?"

"Yes!" She looks up at me, eyes sparkling.

I can't even imagine having to do that. "Too bad I don't have a costume!"

The perky young woman who has been managing the party sidles up. "Of course we have a Maui costume!"

What?

Grace jumps up and down, clapping. "Yay! Uncle Don is going to be Maui."

Arianna catches on and hurries over. "Oh, Grace, you can't ask Uncle Don to do that in front of everyone!"

The party handler sizes me up, pausing on my arms and chest in the low-key polo I'm wearing. She's deadly beautiful with her long, spiraling curls and rich brown skin. "I think he'll do fine," she says.

"Please, please, please, Uncle Don?" Grace beams up at me, her hands clasped.

And so, I find myself escorted to a changing room bearing only a skirt made of leaves and a bone necklace.

Thankfully, my boxers are black and fitted. They hide beneath the skirt well enough. The bright over-head light falls on my bare chest. The things we do for kids.

"Ready?" calls the woman.

I push back the curtain. "I guess so."

Her eyes linger on my skin. "Works for me." She hands me the tall hook Maui carries. "Break a leg."

I pad barefoot across the empty room.

The parents have settled into rows of chairs set up on either side of a long catwalk on the far side of the room.

Grace runs up to me. She has a flowered wreath on her hair. "Uncle Don! You're perfect!" She smacks my belly. "Could use a tan, though."

From the mouths of babes.

Arianna approaches and punches my arm playfully.

"Look at you. The young ladies are going to swoon, and probably half the married ones, too."

I run my hand around my neck. "Sure."

We stand on the side stage as the girls line up. I spot Dell in the front row, fiddling with the camera.

Arianna leans in. "Thank you for helping him. I would have hired a photographer, but I made such a fuss about Dell learning how to take a real picture, I got trapped."

"No problem. It's kind of nice knowing something he doesn't."

"Oh, you should have been there when Grace first arrived. He didn't know squat."

"I bet."

The music begins pulsing, and the first girl, dressed as Lilo in her floral recital dress, holding a stuffed blue Stitch, walks shyly down the walkway.

Her feet shuffle until the cheers erupt from the parents. "Go, Shila!" someone yells.

She warms up to the attention, and by the time she arrives at the end of the walk, she's doing a hula dance and tossing Stitch in the air. A million cell phones lift, documenting every moment.

I tug on my grass skirt. What have I done?

The next girl takes off down the runway. She's Tiana in the full-skirted green dress and carries a stuffed frog. Every girl is seriously decked out.

Each one takes her turn to great cheers. Grace is last in her Moana outfit.

She takes my arm. "You ready, Maui?"

"As ready as I'll ever be." God, I'm about to be on

every one of these parents' social media feeds. I draw in a breath. Good thing she's so cute.

The announcer's deep voice comes over the speaker system. "And now, the star of the day, our birthday princess, Grace Brant as Moana with her uncle Maui!"

We head out onto the stage to an incredible eruption of cheers.

"Let's show 'em!" Grace says.

Why not?

I lift Grace onto my shoulder and slam the hook onto the ground. Above us, confetti canons pop, and the birthday girl is showered in bits of color.

Yeah, that's going to go viral.

"I know the Rock," one woman says. "I'm going to tag him."

Great.

But I smile, turning left and right so everyone can get a good angle on Grace. I'm here. Might as well own it.

The woman in charge comes out again. "Parents, I encourage you to come up on stage with your princesses. I'm happy to take your picture with your phones."

Cool, my duty is over. I set Grace back on the ground to be surrounded by her friends.

"Oh no, Maui, you have to stay!" one girl says.

"Stay, Maui!" they chorus.

I guess I'm still on.

I tower behind the line of girls. Then I'm asked to lift each one on my shoulders for individual shots.

Finally, someone announces cake, and the party

moves back to the main room. I rotate my aching shoulder. I think I've completed arm day.

The party planner approaches, her eyes on me, and I see the spark of interest. "Mom, Dad, the caterer is all ready with cake and treats." She hesitates. "Does the cool uncle want to change?"

"Yes, please."

"I'll take you back."

I follow her through the door to the changing rooms. She turns in front of the curtain. "The kids will have some finger foods, so don't worry about missing the cake."

"Thanks."

She hesitates. "Need any help getting out of that grass skirt?"

Now that's a proposition if I've ever heard one.

But first I think of Grace. Uncle Don doesn't need to be getting action at her party.

And second, I think of Havannah, home with her baby.

So, yeah. That's a double no.

"I've got it. Thanks."

She smiles. "See you out there." And then she's gone.

I refocus my brain. I have about an hour before I need to call my assistant to review the flight plans. I have a meeting in Milan on Monday, so I'll be flying out later tonight, prepping for a round of meetings over a fraught takeover.

I quickly step out of the skirt and place it with the necklace on a hook. Maybe if I'm far, far away, I won't see any of the pictures of me dressed as a Disney character.

When I get back out to the party, Dell claps me on the back. "You're a real champ, Donovan. I wouldn't have thought you had a costume walk in you."

"Anything for Grace." I lift her up in the air until she lets out a squeal.

"I'm taller than everyone!" she cries.

"Tell them all to come over here so we can eat cake," I say.

She stretches out her arms, her flower wreath tilting on her head. "Cake! Cake! Cake!"

The other girls take up the chant, and I set Grace back on the ground to be surrounded by her friends.

I swipe the camera from Dell and take some shots of her blowing out the candles so he can focus on his daughter.

I return to my corner while they settle at the round table, the mirrors and lights gone, now outfitted with tablecloths and place settings. This place is slick.

When I pass the camera back to Dell, I realize I have a text from Havannah.

I'm sure your life is way more sophisticated than mine.

An image follows. It's a selfie, her hair a wild twist on top of her head, the baby on her shoulder. She looks at the camera soulfully. She's incredibly beautiful.

But I'll show her.

I elbow Dell. "Show me what you took of me."

He scrolls through the images. They aren't half bad. When we find the one of me with Grace on my shoulder, I snap a shot of the screen with my phone.

I text Havannah. *You mean as sophisticated as this?* I attach the image.

I get a reply right away, which is unusual. *I love it so much! Is that your niece?*

Yes, she is five today.

And you're there! Dressed as Maui!

I chuckle. *Anything for Grace.*

I love it! I bet all the women are swooning.

I want to text her that the only one I care about is her. But I resist. Instead I ask, *How are you and Rebel?*

Baby is sleeping. Grandmama did all the laundry, and Mom did the dishes. I'm practically a free woman.

I clamp my jaw, suddenly wishing we were in the same city. I could see her then. But I'm hours away by plane. Hours and hours. I type, *Enjoy it.*

I will try! Probably sleep right through it.

The party manager approaches with a slice of cake. She seems completely fine about our moment in the back. "Something sweet for Uncle Don?"

I shove the phone in my pocket. In other circumstances, I'd be very interested. But I simply accept the plate. "Thank you. It's a great setup."

She looks over the party. "It takes up all my weekends."

"I bet that's tiring."

She glances back at me. "I can manage. Our last party ends at six. The perk of catering to children. I'm finished early enough to have a night on the town."

There it is again. She's suggesting she's available.

"You've done a wonderful job with the party," I tell her. "Excuse me. The birthday girl awaits."

I don't look back as I head over to Grace. Dell has already wrecked his camera settings again, so I set down my cake to help him.

I might be technically single. And I might not have any idea of how to have a relationship with Havannah right now.

But I do know where my interests lie.

7

HAVANNAH

I'm officially jealous of my sister.

She's currently raiding my closet for a wedding outfit.

"Don't you have all those fancy dresses from when you were on the talk shows?" I whisper.

Rebel is asleep on my shoulder. Six weeks old and he's decided sleeping vertically is where it's at. But as a bonus, I'm getting cut deltoid muscles from holding him in place for hours a day. I'm going to look killer in a sundress.

If one ever fits me again. I don't understand how two hundred gallons of water poured out of me in a restaurant, then eight pounds of baby, but I weigh almost exactly what I did at my last prenatal checkup.

I may or may not have dropped our bathroom scale off our second-floor balcony into the dumpster behind the building. The crunch may have been pretty satisfying.

Magnolia doesn't answer until she's close enough to whisper. "Most of those were borrowed from designers and had to be returned. I need something Anthony has never seen."

I can't argue with that. I've been known to buy new dresses every weekend when dating someone amazing so he never sees me in the same outfit twice.

Of course, ninety percent of those cute purchases may never fit me again.

"You might as well take 'em all," I say. "I've got a mom bod."

Mags bends down to kiss Rebel's noggin. "And totally worth it." She straightens. "But I don't want to hear a word of it. Most people would kill for your mom bod."

"You haven't seen the stretch marks."

She returns to the closet and pulls out a red dress with an asymmetrical neckline. When I wore it, people compared me to Alexis from *Schitt's Creek*.

Mags holds it up, her golden hair flowing over the shoulder. "Tell me the truth. Can I pull this off?"

Of course she can. She looks amazing. One thing the talk show stylists did for her last year was give her confidence. "You'll knock everyone dead."

She turns to the full-length mirror on the back of the closet door. "I'm nervous. This wedding supposedly has four hundred guests."

"Wow." My sister is engaged to the youngest Pickle brother, and the middle brother Max is marrying his girl Camryn next weekend in the South of France.

They've rented a friggin' *castle*.

Everyone's going. Mags. Her fiancé Anthony, of course. He's the best man. Even Mom and Dad are flying out, both as a vacation and to spend quality time with the future in-laws.

Grandmama is staying behind to help me with Rebel, although we have a decent routine. She's also watching over the delis. She's had a bit of a rebound in her energy levels since Mags and Anthony got so much publicity last year, and we opened the second deli.

She's been fired up by the renewed success of her franchise. Instead of hanging out at her retirement community, she's taken over greeting customers, alternating delis for her shift.

Thankfully, we have solid staffs and great managers at both locations. The family sees this trip as a trial run for when Mags and Anthony have their own wedding. They haven't set a date or a place, but it's bound to be a production that takes all our attention.

And I'll be involved, as well as Grandmama. The Tasty Pepper and Tasty Mango delis will have to run on their own for a few days.

Magnolia pulls out a pale yellow sundress. "This is lovely. Looks like France."

She has to keep saying that. France, France, France. I've never been out of the country. I've barely been out of Colorado. I stuff down my jealousy. "It is. Take it. You can't have too many pretty things."

She sets it on the stack at the end of the bed. "I'm grateful, H. You sure you don't want to come? There's a spot for you and the baby in my room."

"Twelve-hour plane ride with a newborn? Even I'm not that brave."

She sits close to us on the bed, running the back of her knuckles across the baby's wispy hair. "I'm going to miss this little guy."

"We'll be fine."

It seems like she's going to say something else, but she only presses her lips together. She's about to stand when I throw out my hand to stop her. "Say it."

She folds her hands in her lap. "Donovan's coming. He and Dell and Arianna and Grace." She bites her lip like she's divulging some big secret.

"I know that. Donovan is already in Europe. He's planned several business meetings around the wedding."

"So you're still talking to him?" She settles beside me, leaning against the headboard. "You haven't mentioned it in a couple of weeks."

"There isn't a lot to tell." And there isn't. I get occasional texts with pictures of clouds from a plane window. He likes to send food images, too. Sometimes there's a selfie from an exotic location. I save those.

"He must travel a lot."

"He does." Rebel stirs, and I stop talking to see if he is going to wake. He settles back in.

"Are you going to see him again?" Mags can never hide her emotions. Her worry is all over her knitted brow, her lips pulled into a frown.

"I have no idea. Look, I know he's not a real boyfriend or anything. We text occasionally."

"But you wish he was?"

"Of course!" I say, too loudly, and Rebel makes a soft whine. I pat his back. "Of course," I whisper. "He's gorgeous and thoughtful."

"And rich."

I smack her lightly with the back of my hand. "So's Anthony."

"I'd only call them very comfortable. It's not like Donovan and Dell. They have a jet!"

"I know." I close my eyes and tilt my head to the ceiling. "I daydream about it. Me and Donovan, heading up the metal stairs, my scarf flying behind me. We fly to Italy or Paris or a Swiss chalet."

"It could happen. He's certainly not dating anyone else."

I pretend not to know what she's talking about. "Really?"

She squints an eye at me in suspicion. "You telling me you don't have a Google Alert on his name?"

I sink onto the pillows. "I don't have time for random Internet searches."

She stares me down a moment more, then apparently decides to believe me. "Well, he made a gossip rag last week." She wriggles her phone out of her jean pocket. "Here, see?" She turns the screen.

New York's most eligible bachelor off the market?

I know the headline. *Of course* I have a Google Alert on Donovan. I won't admit it, though.

"What's it say?" I ask, as if I don't know.

She reads it aloud.

. . .

Financial magnate Donovan McDonald has been buying tables at all the best charity events, as usual. But instead of attending, he has donated the pricey tickets to lucky volunteers working at New York's soup kitchens, homeless shelters, and refugee houses.

The dashing billionaire is known for his relationships with powerful femmes fatales, including actress Heather McCabe, district attorney Angela Lisbon, and a string of socialites and prominent family heiresses.

But this year, his splashy arrivals with beautiful women have been notably absent, even for the causes he personally supports. Where is Donovan McDonald, and has some lucky lady taken this favored bachelor off the market?

I can almost recite along. I've read the article a thousand times, not even daring to hope that Donovan's disappearance from big events has anything to do with me.

"He's traveling like crazy," I say. "He hasn't had time. They needed a story, and speculation is fun to them."

Mags turns off the screen. "Maybe. Seems interesting he had time for them before, though."

I shrug, holding on to Rebel's back so I don't disturb him. Mags starts pulling hangers out of the dresses she's chosen.

"What time is your flight?" I ask her.

"Eight. So weird to leave at night."

"I suppose so you can sleep on the way."

"We'll see." Her eyes are bright as she collects the dresses in her arms. "I guess I better pack these. Only a few hours until we head to the airport."

When she's gone, I slide down the head of the bed until I'm lying down, Rebel tucked in my arm. If I'm going to go it alone with the baby for a week, I better sneak in a nap while I can.

8

DONOVAN

My life consists of airports, cars, and conference rooms.

I'm accustomed to the grind, traveling from one continent to the next, ushered into one boardroom after another.

But lately, it's been getting to me.

I'm not sure if it's seeing Havannah's birth, or going to Grace's fifth birthday party, or if it's simply time. But this life that many would envy has gotten old.

Today I'm spending my time in a chilly gray meeting room trying to maintain a calm demeanor while the founder of a failing company rails at me for buying out the majority of shares.

Never mind that, had I not done that, he would've been in liquidation in less than a year.

Everyone always wants someone to blame when things go wrong. When the day finally ends, I shove it from my mind as a porter unlocks the door to my suite, and a bellboy pushes a rolling cart with my bags inside.

I've brought more luggage than usual because this stretch of travel will last so long. Max Pickle's wedding is in four days. We've scheduled meetings leading up to it, although tomorrow should be the last one. I've been asked to attend the rehearsal dinner, as well as a low-key beer tasting, and I aim to enjoy a small break in the madness to take in some scenery.

As I often do when I arrive at a new location, I take a quick shot of myself with the view through the open windows behind me and send it to Havannah. Even though I haven't seen her in a month and a half, she's become part of my routine.

I've begun to figure out her schedule as well. She usually texts me during the baby's morning nap, and she responds again around two a.m. Colorado time when the baby wakes up for a night feeding.

She's settling in and claims she's getting enough sleep. I don't know much about babies or their schedules, but it's interesting to watch how her sporadic responses have become more measured and regular. I assume that means all is well.

She has sent many pictures of the baby, but only a few of herself. I tend to picture her as I remember her the night we went out to dinner, and how she looked right after the baby was born. I have, of course, that first glowing image of her and the newborn, the one I took and sent her when we were alone that day.

I often take it out and look at it. Her hair is pushed back where I smoothed it with my own hand. She is at peace, the calm that can only come after a great storm.

She's ethereally beautiful.

It's impossible, though. Our timing could not have been worse.

The buzz of her reply arrives while I'm getting ready the next morning. It's her usual middle-of-the-night feeding, but the time difference makes it a normal hour for me.

It's quiet in the apartment with Mags gone. She should be landing in France in about a few hours. Not jealous at all.

I swiftly finish shaving so I can write back before my car arrives to take me to today's meeting. *I wish you could come. It's going to be a great party.*

The baby must be quiet, as she responds quickly. *Me too. But I can't leave Rebel. The flight is too long. Everyone on the plane would want to kill me.*

My hand stills as I adjust my tie in the mirror. The phone sits on the bathroom counter, Havannah's message staring up at me like a dare.

An idea starts to form. So I ask her the question on my mind. *Is it the commercial aspect of the flight that's the problem? Can the baby fly otherwise?*

The row of dots precedes her reply. *He could fly. You just have to nurse or bottle-feed them through takeoff so their ears can pop from the pressure. He's kind of little to be around all those germs, though.*

So it *is* the commercial nature of the flight that's knocked her out. My heart beats faster as I conjure a plan.

Are the delis relying on you being there?

I can almost hear her laugh in the reply. *Oh, heck no. Rebel is way too hard. Grandmama is taking care of all that. Until I decide I'm ready to get a nanny, I'm stuck.*

I drum my fingers on the bathroom counter. Could this work? Or would Rebel be too hard for this, too?

A second message pops up. My car is ready downstairs. I snatch up my phone and pull my suit jacket off a hanger as I pass through the living room of the suite.

But even as the driver takes me across town to the office building, my mind keeps turning. Is there a way to get Havannah here?

What will it take?

I have no idea what's about to happen.

I sit in the limo for a full five minutes on the street in front of Havannah's apartment complex before I work up the nerve to tell her I'm here.

This driver is more professional than the last, keeping his face forward and asking no questions about why we're parked on a random street.

I try to remind myself that I have flown all the way from Europe to Boulder, Colorado, just for a chance at a yes. But if she says no, if I have misjudged her completely, it will be fine. We can go back to the low-key texting relationship we had before.

But I have to try.

Courtesy would normally dictate you tell a lady you're coming. But this is no ordinary request. If I asked her over the phone, a woman like Havannah would say no. She'd be practical.

I want her to be impractical.

So I took the wild risk of flying here. I need to be right in front of her when I put in my request.

I scroll to the end of our conversation. My last text from her arrived while we were flying.

It's a selfie this time, Havannah dressed and carrying Rebel in a sling. She's wearing her Tasty Mango shirt. I can tell from the logo next to Rebel's head.

She told me she was stopping by the deli for a while. With the picture are the words *I doubt we make it thirty minutes. But I'm going!*

That was four hours ago, and the deli closed about half an hour before I touched down.

Havannah should be home. Fate has smiled on me— I'm not catching her in a position where she will be completely upset to see me. She's been out in the world, gotten dressed. I know that some days, even a shower is a luxury.

I text her.

Look at that kid already representing your brand!

The three dots appear immediately. This is good.

Her words pop on screen. *We made it almost two hours before I had to come home and feed him. It was a great day.*

I wonder if it's about to get even better, or if she'll be upset.

I step out of the limo and close the door, leaning against its gleaming black side. Then I put through a voice call.

She doesn't pick up right away, and suddenly I worry she's having to scramble to get to it. Maybe she's changing the baby. Or feeding him.

But I'm committed, so I wait. The call rolls over to her voicemail. What do I do now? What do I say?

I have no time to think. I just talk.

"Havannah. It's Donovan. I wanted to put through a quick call to congratulate you on getting back to the deli."

Okay. That was good.

"But I can text you," I add.

Right as I'm about to hang up, another call beeps in. She's returning the call in the middle of my voicemail.

I hang up and switch to the new call. "Havannah!"

"Donovan! You're calling. You're going to have to turn in your Millennial card!"

I laugh. "I do a lot of phone calls for work. It's natural to me."

"I only talk to Grandmama on the phone." She laughs, and the sound is like music.

"Well, I have a proposition for you. It's not an indecent proposal. I promise. But it might sound like one."

"Now you have my attention."

"Can you see Maplewood Street from your apartment?"

"What?"

"Maplewood Street. It's in front of your apartment complex. Can you see the street from where you are?"

"Sure, if I go to Magnolia's room." Her voice has a suspicious note in it.

"Well, go to Magnolia's room!"

There's silence for a moment, then some rustling, then a sharp inhale. "Is that your limo?"

"A rental, but yes, it's mine."

"Is that you?"

I look up at all the windows I can see on my side. I have no idea where her apartment might be. I've never been there, as she met me by the street for our one and only date. But then I see movement, and Havannah leans out the window and waves.

"Is that really you?" she yells, forgetting the phone. I have to pull it away from my ear.

I kill the call and hold out my arms. "In the flesh!" I shout.

"Well, come up! I'm in 208. Go straight down the pathway, then turn left two staircases down."

I follow the directions. The apartment complex is a lot like the one where I lived in college, tan brick with faded brown siding. Metal and concrete staircases lead to doors with gold numbers and twenty layers of paint.

I knock on the door, and she opens it, looking exactly like her picture from a few hours ago. Her long golden hair flows down her back.

She's perfect.

"You're here," she says, sounding breathless.

"Pretty crazy, right?"

She backs into the apartment to let me in.

A floral sofa dominates the room, the arm piled high with white cloths. There's a baby swing in the corner, slowly undulating back and forth. Rebel is inside, asleep.

"We should whisper," I say.

"Let's go to another room," she says.

I follow her down a short hall to a bedroom. It's messy, the bedspread rumpled. A small bassinet sits at the foot of it. The dresser is strewn with colorful bits of baby items. Cardboard boxes of diapers fill the corner.

"I'm not even going to make an excuse about the mess," she says. "I'm doing good to keep us both bathed and fed." She sits on the edge of her bed.

I lean against the doorframe. "Don't sell yourself short. I'm not sure I could keep a small human alive, much less take him to work."

She smiles, her eyes on me, and that electric charge I felt when I first met her two months ago zips through me as if no time has passed.

"So, I thought you were in France," she says. "I don't understand why you're here."

It's do-or-die time.

"I have a proposition for you."

"Right." She tilts her head, her expression wary. "You mentioned an indecent proposal."

"Come to the wedding."

Her eyes go wide. "How? Everyone's already gone. I could never get a flight. And there's Rebel. The plane would be full of people."

"I brought my own plane. It'll just be us." I long to reach out and hold her hand or make some small gesture, but I'm not sure where we stand. We have, after all, had only one date. I've never even kissed her.

"There will only be the pilot and two crew members. The flight attendant is the mother of three. We'll have help."

Havannah runs her hands over the bedspread, smoothing out wrinkles. "This seems sudden."

"There's a place for you. You'll stay with your family."

"I can't bring Rebel to the wedding. He might make a fuss. He's so little."

I anticipated this. "Dell and Arianna are bringing an *au pair* from her daycare business to come with them. I checked with her. The woman is happy to watch Grace and Rebel during the ceremony. She and the kids will be on-site at the castle for the entire ceremony and reception."

"You thought of everything."

Even as she says it, she stares at the floral pattern on her bedspread.

So it's a no. I'm not going to push.

"I understand it's too much. I thought I would take a shot."

When she finally lifts her eyes to me, I say, "I knew I didn't have a chance at all if I texted you. I wanted to make a real go at it by flying here to ask you in person."

I never took Havannah to be shy, but the way her gaze returns to the floor makes me wonder if I have misjudged her. Maybe it's her new role as a mother that's made her cautious.

I've overstepped. "I apologize for putting you in this awkward position," I say. "I'll head out."

I take a backward step through her doorway, but she holds up a hand.

"No, wait. Maybe you're good at snap decisions, but I'm not. Especially now. I have so many things to factor in."

So there's hope. "Is there any concern I can

alleviate?"

"I guess I won't worry too much about the baby. The flight will be like a bedroom in the air for him, as long as I help him through the takeoff."

I chuckle. "A bedroom in the air. That's quite a picture."

She tilts her head with the warning look, and that's the Havannah I remember.

"That's a great segue into the next part of this conversation," she says. "What are we doing here? You're a world traveler who owns a jet. I'm a single mom barely keeping her head above water. What's in it for you?"

I close the distance and sit next to her on the bed. When her hand is in mine, that electric thrill returns. It's rare for me to feel it, even with the actresses and heiresses and power players I often find myself out on the town with.

But I say none of that. I run my thumb along the inside of her palm. "It's simple, really. Your family is in France. It's going to be an amazing wedding, and I have the ability to get you there."

"So it's all honorable." Her tone tells me she doesn't buy it. Damn, I like her.

"Oh, certainly not. But I don't meet a woman like you very often. I'm looking to mitigate the obstacles to be near you. And this wedding is a significant carrot."

"A carrot."

"You want to go, right? You said yourself you were devastated to miss out."

"But a carrot. Like I'm a horse." She jerks her hand

out of mine.

"No! Not a horse. I needed a way to draw you out."

"Like the stable. I'm a broodmare you find more challenging than the society girls you normally run with."

"It's not that."

Her ire is rising, her face and chest bright with color. I love it even more.

I draw upon everything I know about managing difficult circumstances. I'm not out of my depth here. At least, I don't think so.

"I knew it would take a lot to get you to come. Rebel is your top priority. I admire you for that. But I want to be your knight in shining armor. I want to take the princess to the ball. Baby and all."

Her chin drops out of its defiant jut. "I see. Why this princess? There are real ones to be had where you're headed."

This is it. My last shot. "Because I look forward to our text messages. Even when I'm in the most intense meetings, I find my thoughts drifting to you. I have to fight the urge to check my phone when I know you're up with the baby. I've put his feeding schedule in my phone so I know when I might catch you." I tug my phone from my pocket and light up the screen.

She reads it aloud. "'Five a.m. feeding. Seven, nap, about an hour. Second feeding midday, another nap around two, but she sleeps, too. Feeding around five, then nine. Don't bother her until she texts at two a.m.'" She looks up. "You do know it."

"You've only settled in the last two weeks. But that's

how I knew this could work. The flight might mess him up, but if we keep him on the schedule he's used to, he'll be sleeping during the ceremony."

When I look up after putting the phone away, her eyes are misted with tears.

"How can you know so much about me when we've only met a few times?" She seems incredulous.

"Because everything about you is worth knowing," I say.

We're close, the mattress tilting us toward each other. It's not how I pictured kissing her for the first time. Normally I make it memorable. A quiet balcony at an elite restaurant. A snowy walk. A frenzy on the plush seats of a limo.

But when my lips meet hers, surrounded by laundry, diaper boxes, and scattered clothes, it isn't any less perfect.

It's the kiss of *let's try*. Of *I want this. I'm ready.*

Her mouth is warm and inviting. She tastes of stolen chocolate and smells like fruity shampoo and baby powder. My hand slides beneath her hair to the back of her neck. She leans into me, a small groan in her throat.

Her lips part and the kiss goes deeper, honeyed, desperate. I draw her close, her body pressed to mine. We kiss like teenagers, like star-crossed lovers, like a long-parted couple reunited at last.

It's impossible. I barely know her. But I feel it.

When we gasp apart, her hair is mussed, her lips pink, her eyes bright.

"All right," she says. "I'll come with you."

I squeeze her hand. "Good. Let's pack."

9

HAVANNAH

Holy baloney, this private jet is something else.

I step outside of the limo directly onto the airfield. Like, literally, planes are going down the runway a couple of football fields away.

The wind is high with so much unbroken ground. I hold Rebel's baby bucket car seat in my arms and take it all in. The airport control tower, off in the distance. The plane, long and sleek and silver, right in front of us. The driver asks if I would like him to carry Rebel up the narrow steel steps leading to the jet door.

Uh, no way. Nobody's carrying my baby up those stairs but me.

"No, thank you," I say. "But I'll give you this." I pass him the diaper bag, my purse, and the sling I expect I will need on board.

"Very good, ma'am," he says, and adds my items to the pile of luggage moving from the trunk to a rolling cart.

Man. One baby and you go from a miss to a ma'am.

Donovan walks around the car from where he was directing another man to handle the bags. "You got him okay?" he asks.

I clutch the handle of the bucket seat closer to me. Do I look too pathetic to carry my own baby? Geez. "I'm fine."

It might be my outfit, though. I've really done it up.

I had to do it. Big black movie-star sunglasses. A bright gold scarf wrapped around my head and a second one tied around my neck, left long to fly with the wind. Ankle-breaking gold heels. Finally, my feet aren't swollen anymore, although it was a bit of a squeeze. I have a feeling I might be a permanent half-size bigger, which sucks for my stiletto collection.

I poured myself into shaper lingerie I bought when I was first pregnant and trying to control my bulge.

I outgrew it within a month, but it's coming in handy today to keep all the jiggly parts reined in.

At first, I regretted letting Magnolia borrow so many of my great dresses, but quickly realized that the ones that fit her weren't going to work on postpartum me.

Thankfully, my entire wardrobe isn't made of skintight hooker dresses. Today's outfit is a loose-fitting sheath that hits just above the knee.

I'm going for an Audrey Hepburn vibe, despite the weather pushing ninety degrees in the shade. If the paparazzi were here, I'd look like a million bucks.

Donovan takes my arm and leads me to the stairs. "I'll follow close behind. If the baby gets too heavy, say the word."

I nod. I'm about halfway up the steps when my arm

starts to shake, but I grit my teeth and keep going. Still, when we reach the inside of the plane, I'm relieved to set the baby down.

A cheerful mid-fifties woman in a smart slate-blue pencil skirt and cardigan approaches. "You're here!" She looks down at Rebel. "Oh, what a precious little boy!"

Okay, I already love her.

She shows me where we can lock his base onto a long padded bench. "We have a spot here to strap in his car seat so he's good and safe. Looks like he's out like a light."

He snoozed through the car ride, which is typical. The motion soothes him. Only when he's strapped safely in do I turn around and look at the interior of the jet.

Two rows of wide leather seats fill the part of the cabin closest to the front wall, which I assume leads to the cockpit. On the far wall, a beautifully appointed dining table with a tablecloth and crystal goblets awaits by a window

On my side, two swivel chairs take up the corner, then the padded bench holding Rebel's seat.

Donovan glances around and nods. "Everything looks perfect, Bianca. Thank you. I'm going to speak with Simon about the flight plan. Show Havannah around so she knows where everything is should she need something for the baby."

Bianca smiles. "Of course. Looks like he's going to sleep for the moment. Let's take a tour."

Donovan heads to the front of the plane. Bianca presses a button on the back wall near the swivel chairs, opening another compartment. "Through here," she says.

We pass through a small galley with a sink, microwave, and refrigerator. Clearly this is where the crew stores food and things.

"If you need to warm up a bottle for the baby, let me know. We can do it in the microwave, or I can boil a pan of water and set it inside. Whichever you like. Do you have some refrigerated things?"

"I brought some breast milk."

"Very good. We'll get it stored."

"I'm not sure where they put the diaper bag," I say.

"It will end up here, I'm sure." She presses a button, and the back panel opens to another room about a third of the size of the first one. "This is the bedroom. The leather sofa folds out into a queen."

Everything is luxurious and spotless. The air smells like the inside of a freshly filled linen closet.

Bianca says, "Let me know if you want me to turn down the bed for you and Rebel. Donovan will sleep up front. The bench Rebel is on also can turn into a bed."

"Oh, should I take that one instead?" I ask.

Bianca shakes her head. "You should be back here. You'll want to be next to the bathroom." She presses one more button, and another panel slides open.

How long is this jet? But I can tell by the shape of this room that we're at the end. It has a glass and steel shower, a toilet, and a gleaming steel sink.

"We don't have a changing table, but I'm guessing any surface will do," Bianca says. "I'll make sure some small plastic bags are around for the diapers. Are you cloth or disposable?"

"I brought disposable for the trip," I say.

She nods. "That's easy, then."

We head back to the bedroom. "I do hope I get an opportunity to rock the baby," Bianca says. "My children are that age where they are grown, but I'm still quite far from grandchildren. I love getting to steal someone else's."

I laugh. "I'm sure you will get your chance."

I take the sunglasses from where I pushed them up on my head and unravel the scarf. I feel silly, all gussied up, when I should be more practical. As I pile the items on a small table, the limo driver enters with the diaper bag, my purse, and the sling and sets them on the bed.

As we pass back through the galley, I ask Bianca, "Will you be traveling with us once we get to France?"

She shakes her head. "Sadly, no. Donovan's brother Dell will be coming from New York. So as soon as we land and the pilot gets a good night's sleep, we'll be heading right back to New York to fetch him."

"Oh. I got the impression they were already in France."

"Arianna and Grace are. She wanted to take her time. She's pregnant, you know."

I vaguely recall Dell mentioning that during our mentoring sessions two months ago. "When is she due?" I ask.

"Not until November."

"So she's in the easy phase," I say.

Bianca nods knowingly. "She's quite energetic still. We can't wait to find out what they're having."

I'm glad Bianca is here. It will help with the awkwardness of traveling with a man I barely know.

In the main section of the jet, Donovan waits by the baby. Rebel's eyes are open, and he's looking around with interest.

"We were having a little man-to-man," Donovan says. "I'm teaching him the finer points of jet ownership."

I laugh. "I'm sure that will come in handy with our humble lives."

Donovan's face gets serious. "Dell and I grew up mucking out greyhound stalls as kids. It can happen to anybody."

"Oh. I see." I realize how little I know about him.

The cockpit door opens and a friendly man with an orange-gray beard peers out. This must be Simon, the pilot. "We'll be taking off in T-minus Starr's arrival."

"Thanks," Donovan says. "Though I might leave her this time."

Simon laughs. "You always say that." He ducks back into the cockpit.

Rebel starts to fuss, so I unbuckle him and cradle him on my shoulder. "What did he mean by that?"

"Starr is the other member of the crew. She's an assistant pilot, whip smart, but terribly tardy."

"I wouldn't have thought you or Dell would allow anything but perfect, impeccable staff."

He laughs. "Starr is worth it. She can do anything.

Fly a plane. Jump from a plane. She's a bodyguard, too. She should be in an action movie."

Bianca approaches. "Havannah, would you like me to warm up a bottle, or do you plan to nurse him through the takeoff?"

I glance at Donovan. I didn't think some of this through. Getting Rebel to latch is often a tussle of boy and boob.

"We can start with the bottle," I say.

"Would you like your baby sling?" she asks.

I nod, and she heads back to the galley as I settle in one of the swiveling chairs. "I like her," I tell Donovan.

He moves to the seat beside me, kicking up the footrest and leaning his head back in his hands. "We all do. She takes good care of us." He yawns. He's probably been going nonstop since leaving France to pick me up.

A noise beneath the plane startles me. Rebel senses my sudden lurch and lets out a cry.

I pat his back. "I'm sure we're going to be in for some tears as this gets going."

"No worries," Donovan says. "We have everything well in hand." His eyes are already starting to droop.

So the man *is* human.

Bianca returns with the bottle and sling. "Let me help you get settled. Give me that sweet baby so you can buckle in. Simon takes off smooth as glass, but sometimes we hit some turbulence."

I set the bottle on a small table bolted between our chairs and pass her Rebel. The seatbelt is smooth leather, unlike the merely serviceable ones on regular planes. I pull it around my waist and tighten it. The sling goes across my shoulder easily, and I open it wide.

Bianca nuzzles Rebel. He's stopped crying. "All right, I'll give you up," she says, and passes him back.

When he's settled in the sling and quietly slurping the bottle, I relax.

"Anything else before I strap myself in?" Bianca asks.

"I'm good," I say. I glance at Donovan. I think he's out cold. "Does he always fall asleep this easily?"

"Not always. But he was in an anxious state flying over here to get you." She walks to a cabinet over the padded bench and extracts a pillow and a blanket. "But I can see why it was so important."

She sets the items on the cushion with a wink and heads back through to the galley.

A long minute passes. Rebel drinks greedily. He's always fast on the bottle. I wonder if the other pilot is going to show.

But as Donovan said, right as it seems everyone's ready to go, boots clang on the metal steps, and a willowy young black woman bursts through the doorway. "I'm here. Don't leave me."

Donovan opens an eye. "Glad you could make it, Starr."

Starr whips around to close and secure the door behind her. She stops short when she sees me. "Now I see why we flew back to the States."

Something metallic clangs right outside the door. I assume that's the stairs being disengaged and moved aside.

"I told you," Donovan says.

Starr gives me a nod and a grin. "Don't put up with any of his smart-aleck remarks. I don't." She disappears into the cockpit. Shortly after, the engines start up with a rumble and whine.

I look down. The baby has already slurped almost all of the bottle, and we haven't even taken off. Uh oh. I glance at Donovan. He's belted into his seat, eyes closed again. I don't know if he's asleep.

I guess if the boob comes out, the boob comes out. He saw a lot more of me when Rebel arrived, if he was looking.

Whew. This is a lot.

I realize I've told no one I'm coming. Not even my sister. As the plane starts to taxi, I fumble to pull my phone out of my bra, the only place I had to stash it.

I quickly tap out a text to Magnolia. *Donovan came to fetch me. Headed to France. See you tomorrow. Talk more later. About to take off in his jet.*

I lean down to kiss Rebel's head. He's fallen asleep. "Now this is a story to tell my grandchildren," I whisper.

I tuck the bottle into the folds of the sling and lean back in my chair.

As the plane goes airborne with both the boys asleep, I can't even believe where I am right now. I don't know how I've managed it, but I'm on my way to France with a billionaire by my side, and a baby in my arms.

10

DONOVAN

I jolt awake to the darkened interior of the plane.

Damn. I must've been exhausted.

I rub my eyes and look around. The chair next to me, where Havannah and Rebel were when I fell asleep, is empty.

I listen carefully. The engine drones. Starr and Simon are certainly in the cockpit.

The sliding door to the galley is closed. I assume Havannah is in the bedroom portion. Bianca probably turned down the bed for her and the baby.

A blanket drapes over one of the seat rows in the front of the plane. I unbuckle and creep up there to see who it is.

Bianca. Back-to-back overseas flights have gotten to her, too. I've asked a lot of her in the last couple of days. I won't wake her.

Havannah must be in the back. The double doors seal the noise from the front of the plane to the back pretty effectively. She and the baby could be either asleep or awake. I wouldn't have heard them.

I press the button, and the first panel slides open. The second panel is already open, showing me that, indeed, the bed is turned down.

I can see Havannah's legs at the end of the bed.

I'm about to creep back to my chair when Havannah sits up, her golden hair shining in the half-light.

"You're awake," she whispers.

I move carefully into the room. The baby is asleep in the center of the bed.

"You doing okay?" I ask.

She pushes her hair back. It's fallen from the elaborate updo she had when she got on the plane.

"I'm a little milk sticky," she says. "I'd love to clean up."

I glance down at Rebel. He's totally zonked. "Take a quick shower. Whatever you need. I'll hang out here with the baby."

"You sure?" she asks.

"Definitely. I'm not scared of him."

She smiles. "If he wakes up and cries, absolutely come get me."

"We'll be fine. You go on."

"Thank you." She leans over and kisses my cheek. She does smell milky. I feel a wave of nostalgia, not so much for my own mother, who was probably putting whiskey in our baby bottles by the time we were six months old. But for family. Home. I'm not immune to the idea.

It's a far cry from my normal life. But it feels good. Real.

She glances around the room. "Do you know where my luggage is?"

"Bianca should've placed the small one on the shelf underneath the sink in there."

"Great. Thanks. I guess I've taken all your usual spots."

"It's for a good cause."

Her teeth flash white in the half-dark, then she heads for the bathroom door. Her dress is wrinkled, and her hair cascades down her back in a tangle.

But I like this version of Havannah. If she's anything like me, very few people get to see this side of her. The less-than-perfect, not-made-up version.

She closes the door and bumps around a bit, moving her luggage. Then the water turns on.

I shrug out of my suit jacket and set it on the end of the bed. The baby sighs in his sleep, and I freeze. When he's quiet again, I carefully sit on the corner, trying not to rock the mattress beneath him.

I've never slept on this bed. Never even seen it pulled out. Most traveling jaunts are spent working or talking on the satellite phone in the main cabin. The bed creates a nice setup. I like it.

The shower door slides on its rails in the room next to us, and I become acutely aware Havannah is naked on the other side of the wall. I remember our searing kiss before she decided to come with me on the trip. A test drive for her, maybe. I intended to keep it light. Failed at that, for sure.

I've never dated a mother before. Particularly one so new. I don't know how that will impact our ability to spend private time together. Or if she's even ready for that.

She makes no mention of the baby's father, ever. No one did, not even the hospital. When the nurse thought it was me, no one corrected her.

I assume Havannah will reveal the story when she's ready. It's not time. We're still in the early getting-to-know-you stage.

A giant thud breaks the quiet. Then a muffled curse. Havannah must've dropped the shampoo bottle.

I smile to myself until I realize the baby's eyes are open. His mouth pinches in a line, then a grimace.

Uh oh.

His tiny cry strikes me straight in the heart.

I scoot closer and place a hand on his belly. He quiets for a moment, then the howling grows in intensity.

"No, no, Rebel," I say. "Let Mom take a shower."

Clearly he doesn't understand my message, because the cry rises in volume.

Oh boy.

Havannah probably won't be able to hear us in the shower. If I can figure out what's wrong quickly, she won't be interrupted. I pick up the baby and hold him on my shoulder like I've seen Havannah do.

For a moment, this placates him. I hum, trying to keep the peace.

But then the cries are renewed. I pat his back, suddenly realizing there is a smell coming from him.

"You have a bad diaper, little bloke."

I jiggle him more intensely, wondering if we can make it until Havannah is out.

The cries so close to my ear sound like his soul is tearing. I have to do something.

The diaper bag sits on a small table beside the bed.

"How hard can this be?" I whisper in his ear as I place him back on the bed.

Being put down gives his misery new vigor. I glance through the galley to the front of the plane, wondering if Bianca will save me.

But I don't want to wake her. I don't want to admit defeat.

I quickly close the doors to the galley so the sound will be contained to our part of the cabin.

"Let's do this, baby," I say. "Work with me."

For some reason, my plea helps. Rebel quiets down, waving his arms in the air.

"I'm glad we understand each other. You know I've got to do this and do it properly."

He tries to get his fist in his mouth, but only bonks his eye. His mouth opens for another shriek. I tap his nose. He's shocked into silence at the touch. "Give me a minute. We'll get this done."

I rapidly sort through the diaper bag. There's a mat that folds out. I bet this is what you change him on. I place it on the bed and move Rebel over to it.

He remains quiet, and I assume this means he understands I am doing the right thing.

"I got this," I tell him. "I won't steer you wrong."

Except Rebel isn't so sure. His eyes squeeze tight,

and he cries again. I go back to the bag and find a nubby thing. A pacifier!

I hold it for a second. Which way does it go? The plug part is symmetrical, but the piece that goes against his face is not. I turn it so it's shaped like a smile. That makes sense. I put it up to his lips, and he sucks on it, hard.

"See? I'm a quick learner."

Rebel continues to suck as I dig through the bag.

I pull out a diaper. At least I recognize those. There's a small plastic case next to them. I open it, and yes, soft wet wipes.

"Crackerjack," I tell him. "You're as good as done."

His pacifier pops out, but before he can cry again, I pluck it off the changing pad and stick it back in his mouth.

"Work with me here."

His arms wave as I examine the outfit he's wearing. It's all one big piece that snaps down the front. Why would anyone put a child in this when they need diaper changes? Why not pants?

Nevertheless, this is what I have to work with. I begin unsnapping at the neck and go down, exposing his round belly and the top of the plastic diaper.

The one I've chosen is a match. I'm doing this right. The snaps go all the way down both legs. I pull them all open with flourish, then realize maybe I should have looked at how they went together.

I have to push on. His legs come out, and I realize his outfit will get soiled when I remove the diaper.

Naked it is.

I pull one arm out a sleeve, and the pacifier flies again.

I snatch it up and plug it back in, but by the time the second arm is free, it's rolled across the bed.

"Nope, nope, nope. No tears," I say, plugging it in again.

Good grief, a job that should take three minutes is going to take twenty.

The water still runs in the shower. I've got this. I'm determined to change this baby and dress him before Havannah can come out. If she has any doubts that I can handle anything, this will show her.

Finally, the complicated outfit is off. The baby lets out a shiver.

Oh. He's cold. How can I keep him warm and change his diaper simultaneously? I can't return a block of babysicle to Havannah.

I hurry. Little tabs on the side of the diaper are made of Velcro and pull off easily. But as soon as the diaper falls away, I'm met with a sight I could never have imagined.

The baby's poo is mustard yellow and oozing every-where. What's wrong with him? Poo should not be this color or consistency!

Is he sick? Is flying on a plane doing something terrible to his insides? Do we need to doctor? An emergency landing?

I'm sure we're over the ocean.

Oh God.

I snatch up a wipe and begin cleaning up the mess.

It's sticky and wet and everywhere. It quickly gets all over the changing pad. I use the wipe to clean it up.

The diaper's overflowing with it. No wonder he was so upset.

I don't know what to do. I set the diaper aside, but as luck would have it, it flops over and the yellow poo smears all over the sheets.

I'll deal with that later.

I go through two wipes. Three. Four. There seems to be an endless amount of the yellow poo. I don't know what to do with the dirty wipes, so I stack them on top of the diaper.

Rebel kicks, and his foot catches the pile of wipes, scattering them on the bed and streaking his knee.

This is a nightmare.

I move the entire stack away from him, and my hand is also covered. I grab another wipe, trying to clean his knee and my hand.

I can't believe it's come to this. The child is clearly ill. The sheets are covered in runny yellow poo. And I'm down to the last wipe.

I take it out of the pack, hoping Havannah has more stashed somewhere. I wipe and wipe until it seems the child is clean.

I place it on the stack with the others.

"Okay. Are you better?"

The pacifier falls out again, but Rebel no longer cries. In fact, he almost looks like he's smiling.

"See, all better."

But even as we speak, another ooze of yellow comes out of his parts.

"What?" I grab the least-messy wipe and clean it up. "How much more is in you?" What if it's serious? Should I get Havannah? Will she panic? Am I panicking?

I am. I poke my phone and call my brother. He has a baby. Surely he knows about these things.

It's almost one a.m. in New York, but I know my brother when his wife is away. He'll be burning the midnight oil.

He picks up on the second ring. "Why are you calling me on the satellite?"

"I'm in the air."

"You're supposed to be in France."

"I came back to the States."

"Just to go back again?"

I need stop this line of talk. "Dell, shut up and listen. I fetched Havannah and the baby. We're going to the wedding."

"She agreed to that?"

"She's in the shower on the jet."

"What do you need me for? You need a big brother talk about women? See, Donovan, when a man loves a woman very much, and they—"

"Dell. Shut up. This is serious. I have baby Rebel here. I'm in charge of him while Havannah takes a shower. I think he's sick."

"Did he spit up? That's normal."

"No. His diaper is full of yellow sludge! Something's wrong!"

Dell laughs so loud and for so long that my whole body flushes hot. "What the hell, Dell? This isn't funny!"

He continues laughing. I consider hanging up, but I need his help. "Dell! Do I need to find a way to land this plane? I don't know how far we are out. I'll have to ask Simon for the closest landmass with a hospital."

He manages to rein it in. "Donovan, new babies don't have the same color…" He dissolves into laughter again.

"Same color what?"

"Poop. Theirs is yellow. That's normal. It's because they don't eat solids. Grace had yellow poop until she got real food. The baby only drinks milk. That's what it looks like on the other end."

I let out a long breath. "Okay. I get it."

"So you're changing your first diaper?"

"I am."

"Did you find the wipes?"

"I did."

"Did you memorize how to put the outfit back on?"

"Negative. I realized my error after unsnapping it all."

"I'm not going to be able to help you there. It's like the worst kind of puzzle to solve. You should get him some stuff from Arianna's baby line."

"Fine." I hesitate. "How do you know which way the diaper goes?" I lift the baby's legs again. "Do the tabs go from back to front or front to back?"

"Find the cute pattern. That goes in the front."

I turn the diaper around. There are dolphins on one side. I shift those around to the front.

"Lift him up by the legs to slide the diaper under,

then bring the front up so it's about the same height as the back. Then stick the tabs."

I lift Rebel's legs and slide the diaper under him. "Got it."

"One thing different about boys than girls," Dell says, "is you need to cover their—"

I stop listening as an arc of pee straight from Rebel shoots through the air. It lands on the clean diaper, the sheets, and my hands. "Fuck!"

Dell dissolves into laughter again. "You didn't cover the important bits."

"I did not."

"The cold air often makes them go," Dell says in between laughs. "Arianna has gotten hit many times when changing a kid in her daycare."

I'm barely listening. I'm out of wipes. I decide to hell with it and grab a corner of the sheet to dry off my hands and wipe off Rebel.

I place the once-clean diaper on the stack with all the dirty stuff. "At least it's all out," I say, just as the second round spurts into the air. "Seriously!"

I grab another section of the sheet to wipe my hands and the baby again. This time I tuck the sheet over his parts as I rummage around for another diaper. I pull it out, quickly lift his legs, slide the diaper under him, move the sheet, and press the front down before he can pee again.

When the tabs are set, I finally relax.

"It's done," I tell Dell.

"The outfit too?"

"I'm going to wrap him in a blanket and call it a day."

Dell continues to chuckle. "Next time, call Bianca. She's more qualified than you."

"Shut up, Dell."

He laughs again. "See you in France." He ends the call.

I survey the bed. One corner is covered with yellow sludge, wet wipes, and a leaking diaper. Two sections are wet with pee. This is a disaster.

Rebel wriggles on the changing pad, naked except for his diaper. I pick him up and put him on my shoulder. There's a small blanket inside the diaper bag, so I cover him with it.

"Baby, I know when I'm beat."

I move the diaper bag and my phone to a side table so I can roll everything up in the soiled sheet. "Remind me to give Bianca a hazard bonus for this trip."

I use my free hand to ball up the sheet and shove it in the corner. By the time Havannah comes out of the bathroom, smelling of shampoo and floral soap, Rebel is asleep again, wrapped in the blanket on my lap. "How'd it go?" she asks.

"Just fine," I say. "I had to change him, so I wrapped him in a blanket."

"You changed him?" She lifts Rebel into her arm and tucks the blanket around his sleeping form. "Good for you. I guess there's nothing you can't do."

I shrug. "Some things come naturally."

11

HAVANNAH

We touch down at the Paris airport around six in the morning. I've mostly stayed in the bedroom area with the baby. Donovan started making phone calls at the table in front starting around three.

I'm not sure what to think. When we set out on this journey, I had a vision of a coed slumber party. We'd talk and laugh and get to know each other better.

But I didn't count on how tired I would get or how hard it would be to manage the baby in a new space. We slept most of it. So by the time Bianca restores the bedroom to its normal configuration, and the metal stairs are rolled up to the jet, I'm not sure I know anything more about Donovan than I did when he came to get me.

Other than he's super handsome when he sleeps.

But also, I guess I know he cares what I think about his ability to handle the baby. I totally noticed the missing sheet, the damp spots where he pulled off only the top layer without realizing the telltale line of baby pee had soaked through. Every time I picture Rebel going boy fountain on a billionaire, I have to hold in the eruption of giggles. Oh, to have seen that.

Bianca returns the hand-washed onesie and the wiped-down changing pad to me as we pack. "Looks like Donovan tried to help."

We both get a good giggle out of that.

When I stand at the top of the exit stairs looking down, I decide maybe this time I don't want to carry the baby myself. Going down looks a lot scarier than climbing up.

Donovan solves the problem by going down several steps ahead of me and letting me pass the bucket seat to him, and then he passes it down to the driver. I hold my breath until Rebel is safely on the ground.

The limo waits on the tarmac. When we're seated in the back, Rebel strapped in, I say, "So isn't Paris pretty far from the wedding?"

"Two hours by train. No closer airports. Plus I need to get the jet back to Dell so he can make it here in time."

"We should have picked him up!"

"He wasn't ready to go. Big meeting this morning."

As we leave the airport, I press close to the windows to see everything. It's my first trip to France.

At first, it's only a tree-lined freeway that could be anywhere. But then buildings begin appearing, industrial, but with a different character than ones you see in the States.

"How far is it to the city?" I ask.

"For the things you might think of, like the Louvre or the Eiffel Tower, it's about an hour from the airport."

"Oh. That's far. Are we going directly to the train?" I try to hide my disappointment that I will be so close to Paris but not get to see it.

"I thought we could spend the night in Paris, and then leisurely take the train tomorrow to the castle. We'll be there in plenty of time for the rehearsal dinner."

"So we're going into Paris?" I can't contain my excitement.

He grins, and I'm reminded again how handsome he is. "Yes, we are. We'll take a drive around, settle into the hotel, and work around Rebel's schedule as we think about shopping or sightseeing."

I can barely contain myself. "I can't believe it!"

Even as this fantasy comes true, something prickles at the back of my mind. Why did he come and get me? How is this happening?

But he's staring at his phone with a frown, so I return to the window to take it all in.

Soon the character of the buildings begins to change. Everything seems so old. Stone cathedrals. Towering archways. I realize this is what it looks like for a city to have history. Everything in America is so new by comparison.

We come to a giant circle, and I squeal as the limo dashes into the wild churn of cars making the loop. "I could never drive in this!"

Donovan tucks his phone away. "It does take some mettle to manage a roundabout in the heart of Paris.

We're coming up on the famous Rue de Rivoli. You'll see mostly tourists here. We'll pass the Louvre."

The street is wide, with a bus lane and a tiny divider down the middle. The buildings go unbroken for blocks and blocks, arches all across the bottom floor, and narrow balconies lined with metal rails.

I've never seen anything like it. I press my fingers to the glass like a kid.

"Here comes the Louvre," Donovan says. He's not looking out the window, but at me.

I can't stop staring. The museum isn't open yet, and the walkways are quiet. We pass by, and I look ahead at another stretch of arches and classic buildings. "Do you come to Paris a lot?"

"Every few months." Donovan sits back in the seat, his hands interlocked behind his head. It's becoming the posture I recognize most in him. He wears a suit, as usual, but his white shirt is unbuttoned at the throat.

Damn, he's brutally gorgeous. Bits that haven't thought about anything more than pregnancy pee leakage and recovering from birth start to tingle. *Hey-o, girl parts. Simmer down. Don't get ahead of yourself.*

"We're coming up on the Champs-Élysées," he says.

The streets are lined with cafés. My stomach grumbles. "I've always dreamed of sitting at a café and having a croissant and a bit of coffee in Paris."

"Consider it done."

He rolls down the window between the back of the limo and the driver. "Can you pull over at your first convenience?" he asks the driver. "We're going to pop into one of the cafés. We can walk."

I glance down at Rebel. He's sleeping. He usually does in cars. I dig through my diaper bag for the sling. I don't think I want the bucket seat for this excursion.

"This is exciting," I say as I unlatch the harness on Rebel's car seat. He stirs sleepily as I lift him out, but when I tuck him into the sling on my chest, he's out again. Good thing I fed him right before we got off the plane.

The limo turns a corner and stops. Donovan picks up the diaper bag. "Anything else you need?"

"I don't think so." My excitement is growing as we step outside. The air feels different here. Heavy, like it might rain any moment. The light is blue, golden on the edges. It's magic.

We walk along the sidewalk, pausing to peruse the menus at a couple of the cafés.

"I can vouch for this one," Donovan says. "Perfect pastry and strong, aromatic coffee."

"Sounds heavenly." The outdoor tables are surrounded by a low wrought-iron fence. Donovan opens a small gate and ushers us inside.

We find a table in the far corner near the street. I hold Rebel close to my belly as I settle on a small wooden chair. The café table is barely large enough for two. Cars roll by, swishing in wet parts of the street.

I can't believe I'm here.

A young woman in a short skirt and perfectly braided bun approaches. "*Bonjour*," she says. Then I lose it all in a stream of French. My anxiety prickles.

But Donovan smoothly returns her "bonjour" and

asks several long questions. He turns to me. "How hungry are you?"

"So hungry."

He nods and gives an order. I pick out *fromage* and *croissant* and *café noir*.

When she's gone, Donovan sits back in his chair with a sigh. "I love it here, too."

"What did you order?"

"Meat and cheese, pastries, coffee, and juice."

"Cheese for breakfast?"

"Cheese is around the clock here."

"Sounds lovely." Rebel stirs, and I glance down at him. He opens his eyes for a moment, then falls dreamily back to sleep. Good boy.

"He's doing well," Donovan says.

"So far." I sigh. "I can't believe that at this time yesterday I was putting a load of burp cloths in the wash."

"I'm glad I could make that happen," Donovan says. "Weddings are important, and you're about to be part of the Pickle clan. Have your sister and Anthony set a date?"

"Not yet. We're getting used to having a second deli, and that's a big event that will knock out the whole family. That's one thing about a business like ours—when something happens to one of us, we're all involved."

"I can see how that will be a concern when their big day arrives. Even your grandmother will be away."

"I guess it's different for you and Dell? It's the same business, right?"

"We're not a business so much as a conglomerate. These days, Dell seems happy to work on Arianna's dream school for kids. He doesn't do as much buying and reselling of businesses as he once did."

The woman delivers our coffee. I pick up my cup and inhale the heavenly French roast. I blow on the surface. The first sip is like an orgasm.

Okay, not quite, but given my love life lately, it's close.

"So is that what you do?" I ask. "Buy and sell businesses?"

"Mostly. And often in difficult circumstances. I had a particularly thorny meeting two days ago."

This is the most we've talked about his life since we met. "What happened?"

"The founder didn't appreciate being bought out, even though it's the only option the board had left."

"Did you restructure and lay everybody off?"

He picks up his cup and breathes in the smell. This makes me smile. Even billionaires have simple pleasures.

After he takes a sip, he says, "I try to avoid it if I can. The dynamic is different depending on the country. I'm always about trying to retain the heart of a place. But businesses have to change with the times. Their unwillingness to pivot is often what got them into dire straits."

"Oh, that's like us when we opened Tasty Mango," I say. "The original was based on my grandparents' tradition, but ours needed to be more modern."

"Exactly," Donovan says. "And you did it. You kept some of the old feel but appealed to a new demographic."

The woman returns and sets so many plates on our table that I don't think they will fit.

But she works jigsaw magic, leaving us a basket of croissants, pats of butter, a plate of meats and cheese, and an array of colorful jams in white dishes.

"This looks amazing." I pick up a croissant. The first bite is all buttery layers that dissolve before I can chew.

I want to swoon. The food. The just-after-a-rain air. The sleeping baby. And Donovan.

This has to be a dream.

Donovan pinches the end of a croissant. I watch him eat, realizing we never got past the salad course of our dinner date. "Do you only go to fine restaurants, or are you down for fast food?" I smile over my croissant. "These are the important questions, no?"

His grin is infectious. "I've traveled across the world, and I'm pretty sure the only place I'm completely happy with my food is Milo's Burgers."

"I've never heard of it—are they fast-food burgers?"

"You bet. Only in Birmingham, Alabama."

"That's where you grew up?"

"Yep."

"Why do you think fast food is so good, even when your tastes change?"

Donovan takes another bite of the croissant while he ponders. "I think it's because you're always starving when you go to a place like that."

"Genius. Of course that's it. You go to fast food when you're dying and in a hurry to get something to eat. So naturally it tastes like heaven."

I fill my plate with meat and cheese. I want to try everything.

But when I lift a small square chunk of soft cheese to my nose, I have to immediately jerk it away. "Oh my gosh! What is that?"

Donovan leans in, and I hold it up to him. "Camembert," he says. "It's a popular French cheese, but it's an acquired taste." He grins, then moves lightning fast to bite the cheese right out of my fingers. His lips close over my skin and slide down the tip.

I pull back, astonished. My heart is hammering. Him snatching the cheese with his mouth is literally the sexiest non-sex thing I've ever done.

He sips his coffee, watching me over the rim. His eyebrows are raised. I can barely calm myself. Everything is sparking. I'm thinking wild thoughts. Mouths. Fingers. Body parts. Sweat.

Slow your roll, Havannah Boudreaux.

I've kissed this man exactly one time, and here I am alone with him in Paris. Where is this going to go? Time to ask more questions.

"So you could have asked me out when we were mentoring that week. But you didn't. Why did you wait?"

He watches me a moment. "You want an explanation?"

"I do." It's not like I can do anything if I don't like the answer. I'm stuck in Paris with him. "Was it because I was pregnant?"

"Not really. You were still very pregnant when I came back to Colorado."

"Then why?"

Donovan picks up his mug and takes a sip. I have a feeling it's a common tactic he uses to gather his thoughts. He's not the type to speak rashly.

"I wasn't in a relationship, if that's what you're thinking. I'm known for my avoidance of entanglements."

I tug apart another croissant. I'm not going to starve while he takes his time explaining.

"But I had been on a couple of dates with a woman in New York prior to flying with Dell to meet with you and your sister. I already knew there would be no more, but I hadn't spoken with her about it. It seemed wiser to ensure I spoke to her myself before she caught a photo or online mention of me with someone else."

I pick up a different piece of cheese, sniff it, and set it on my plate. "That sounds fair. Did she take it well?"

"I spotted pictures of her with someone else before we even had the conversation."

Ugh. "Did that upset you?"

He sips his coffee. "Not in the least. Quite a relief, actually. Anything else you want to know about my personal history?"

About a million things. "Have you ever had a relationship longer than a couple of dates?"

"Sure. I was with the woman for almost a year during undergrad. She got a job in California, and I moved to New York to work with my brother. We mutually agreed that was for the best."

"And since then?"

"I travel a lot. It's hard to build a relationship. But I

like to have a date for fundraisers and society events. I find the evenings go faster."

I want to ask him how fast he goes, but instead I say, "I've seen pictures," and shove a piece of cheese in my mouth.

"I bet. Some of the press I can control. But not always. Photographers like to suggest I'm involved in a torrid love affair so the price of the images goes higher. It's just commerce. I don't take it personally."

I glance around as if expecting the paparazzi to show up. "Do you expect them here?" My hands move to my hair subconsciously. It's not particularly styled after the rushed shower on the jet. I did manage to get makeup on early this morning. But I'm wearing one of my loose floral dresses, and the striped baby sling clashes completely. The *National Enquirer* would love that headline:

Hot-mess baby mama attempts to entrap billionaire.

"The wedding should be private, but still, we will want to decide how to present ourselves if we find ourselves in a more public social event."

I shove another piece of cheese into my mouth. This one is not smelly, and as creamy as milk. "I guess you're not sure if we should be seen seated together? Or dancing?"

"I can mingle. Or I can be all yours."

The words make me freeze. Donovan McDonald. All mine. I have to gulp to swallow my mouthful. "I see."

"No reason to decide that now. I'm not exactly

followed like a Hollywood actress. Oh look, he's awake." His eyes are on the baby sling.

I look down. Rebel is gazing up at me. Then he turns to my chest, his little mouth opening and closing.

"Chap looks hungry," Donovan says.

He is. I have a few bottles packed in ice in the bag. I could ask the waitress to warm it, or I guess Donovan could. I should probably learn a few French phrases. "I was going to save the bottles for sightseeing," I say. "I doubt I will have much time to pump."

"The French women have no problem nursing in public," he says.

I glance around. Most of the tables are empty. It's early.

I unbutton the front of my dress. Donovan busies himself with the jam and bread, giving me the tiniest bit of privacy. My fantasy of pastries in Paris didn't involve tussling with an infant in a sling. The only time I've nursed him outside of my own home was locked in the office of the Tasty Mango yesterday. It didn't go well.

I've never done it in public.

I arrange the sling so I'm not totally out in the open and tilt Rebel toward me. *Come on, baby, latch on easily.*

At first, his face screws up in confusion. He's not used to this position. But his mouth finds the nipple, and soon he's sucking happily.

I let out a breath. I did it. I really did it.

I glance at Donovan. He's watching the baby, then his gaze moves to my face.

"That's the most beautiful thing I've ever seen," he says.

My whole body flushes. "I think so, too."

Our gazes hold. He's unbelievable. His eyes are chestnut with flecks of gold, like the night sky dotted with stars. He smiles and his attention returns to Rebel, my swollen breasts, the expanse of skin visible only in his line of sight.

And something turns in me, a slow shift of feelings. It's not a hot night or a wild chase, like most of the men I've dallied with. And it's not the aching love I feel for Rebel either.

It's something new. Something unexpected.

And I'm ready to explore it.

12

DONOVAN

While Havannah and Rebel settle in at the hotel, I make a few calls.

We don't have a lot of time in Paris, but I can see by the stars in Havannah's eyes that she is smitten by the city. And who wouldn't be? All the times I've visited for work, and I am always struck by the city's beauty and style.

Havannah wanders into the living room of the suite, this time wearing a pale blue sheath dress that coordinates with the striped sling holding the baby. Her hair is twisted high, sunglasses atop the sleek updo. Her makeup is neutral, other than a dash of eyeliner and long lashes. She looks like she stepped out of a magazine.

"You will have all the other Parisian mothers positively green with envy at your style. Will you be comfortable enough?"

She kicks out a leg, showing off her chunky sandals. "I could walk twenty miles in these."

"Good. It might feel that way by the end of the day."

She picks up the diaper bag from the coffee table. It is out of sync with her chic outfit. I take it from her. "You have enough to lug around."

"Thank you," she says. "Hopefully I have stashed away everything we might need today. Where are we going?"

"Shopping first. Then lunch. Maybe a bit of sightseeing."

"For as long as we hold out," she says.

"For as long as we hold out."

We head down the elevator. The car is ready for us outside the massive entrance of the hotel. As we drive along the Parisian streets, it's more entertaining to watch Havannah than the sights. Rebel is back in his bucket seat, and she sits on her knees, turned toward the window, not missing a thing.

"It's so much more touristy than I thought it would be!"

"It's Paris in the summer."

"So many trinket stands everywhere."

"We're in the thick of the best sightseeing. We can escape it and go to more far-flung parts of the city if you like."

"Not this time. If I'm only here for a day, I would like to see all the things you think of when Paris comes to mind. And shop!"

"The stores we're visiting won't be very busy with the traditional tourists. They're too exclusive."

She turns to me. "I'm quite sure I won't be able to afford a thing. But it will be great fun to look."

"The day is yours, my dear. Choose what you like on me."

Her eyes meet mine for a moment. "I might feel like I'm in debt to you if too much is exchanged."

I shrug. "I'm not a man to call in a debt like that. But I do enjoy having people indebted to me. I hope you'll do me the honor of allowing you to be *extremely* indebted to me."

Her gaze remains on my face for long moments. "I'm not sure about that. But we do have to buy a different diaper bag if you're going to carry it. It's unseemly for the head of a dozen huge companies to be wandering around with llamas on his shoulder."

I can't help but laugh. "I am happy to carry your llamas. But we can stop at a baby shop first. We can outfit Rebel like a true Parisian child."

Her whole face lights up. "Parisian baby store. That sounds so perfect. Let's do it!" Apparently baby purchases fall outside of personal debt.

She fairly glows as we continue down the streets. We enter another giant roundabout, and she squeals as usual as the driver maneuvers his way into the circle and back out. "I'll never get used to that!"

We arrive at the line of shops I had in mind. As expected, the traffic here is low, and there are no souvenir stands. The clientele is mostly local, and extraordinarily well dressed.

Havannah observes all this as well. She peers out the

window as she moves the sling across her shoulders. "I'm glad I changed. That cotton sundress wouldn't have cut it here."

She turns to the bucket seat, where Rebel is starting to wake up now that the lulling movement of the car has stopped. "Come on, baby boy. Let's see what we can find for you."

The midmorning sunshine has begun to break through the gloom as we wander the sidewalk and peer into shop windows. Havannah keeps one hand on the baby for support, but with the other, she takes mine.

As I close my fingers over hers, an unfamiliar calm takes over. I've certainly never walked the Paris streets with a baby in tow.

The elegant shoppers glance from me to Havannah, then to her baby with soft smiles. We are the picture of family bliss.

A space in my chest opens and expands. I never thought an outing such as this would create so much pleasure.

"Oh," Havannah breathes, pausing by a shop window. It's the baby store, and a beautifully designed window display shows off an entire suite of charming outfits, shoes, and coordinated accessories. "Let's go," she says.

I hurry ahead of her and open the door. The store is two stories tall, most of it wide-open space. A young woman approaches, her khaki skirt and blue blouse perfectly coordinated with the store's color palette. "*Bonjour*," she says. "Who do we have here?"

"*Bonjour*," Havannah replies, her voice uncertain. "This is Rebel."

"What a beautiful baby. So little. Two months?" The shopkeeper's English is heavily accented with French.

"Almost seven weeks," Havannah says.

The woman claps her hands. "*C'est gentil!* We have so many things. Are you looking for anything in particular?"

Havannah shakes her head. "It's all so beautiful."

"Look around. I will be here for any questions."

Only after this entire conversation is complete does the woman consider me. "You must be Dad."

Havannah and I exchange a glance. "I'm here to carry everything," I say easily.

The shopkeeper giggles. "Very well. We will give all the bags to you."

Havannah circles the store. Everything she pauses on, everything she touches, I give a nod to the shopkeeper. She confers with another woman, who follows discreetly behind and covertly picks up all of the items in Havannah's wake.

"Look at this," Havannah says, lifting a blue overall set with a handsome button-down shirt beneath. It includes a tiny bow tie. "This would be perfect for the wedding."

"Definitely," I say.

"We have some shoes to go with that," the woman says, leading Havannah over to a shelf full of the tiniest footwear.

They review the choices, and I move close to the

woman who is collecting items for the bigger purchase. "Send everything to Le Meurice hotel," I tell her. She nods.

Havannah returns with a pair of tiny brown loafers. "Aren't they precious?"

"Absolutely."

Havannah moves on to the accessories. "What about this bag?" She holds up a diaper bag similar in size to the one she currently has. But this one is simple brown leather, and the pockets and flaps are functional, yet discreetly placed.

"Love it."

The shopkeeper steps forward. "Would you like me to repack your bag here?"

"Oh," Havannah says. "Well, sure. I guess that would save us some time."

I pass the llama bag to the woman. "Thank you."

"Keep looking around," the shopkeeper says.

Havannah runs her hands along the front of a baby sleeper. "So soft, but he has so many."

I stroll up to Havannah. "Are you going to pick a few things in larger sizes so he has Paris outfits as he grows?"

She glances around. "Maybe one. I can't believe this sleeper has a set of matching pacifiers."

The shopkeeper opens the package. "And look, they attach with a fastener that matches as well." She clips the pacifier to a special snap already built into the sleeper.

"I love it." Havannah glances up at me. "Should we get one anyway?"

"Get three sizes," I say to her. "That way you keep that feature for longer."

The shopkeeper nods and pulls three sets plus the package of pacifiers.

"I think that's quite enough," Havannah says. "We've done some damage."

The shopkeeper tilts her head. "Done some *damage?*"

"It's an expression," Havannah says. "We've bought a lot. Damage to our bank account." She realizes she's said *our*, and bites her lip, glancing up at me with a shrug.

I pass a credit card to the shopkeeper while the other repacks the bag. "You might want to supervise that so you know where everything is," I suggest to Havannah.

She moves down to the end of the counter, which makes it easier for me to pay for the additional packages without her knowing.

"We will get these sent over straight away," the shopkeeper says. "Do you want the old diaper bag in your car?"

I shake my head. "Send it with the other things."

Havannah has the woman tuck the sleeper plus a pacifier into the new diaper bag as a backup outfit. When we walk back outside, she takes a breath in. "That was very fun. Thank you so much for the gifts."

"We will have the best-dressed baby at the wedding," I say.

I extend my elbow, and she takes it.

"Where next?" she asks.

"How is Rebel doing?"

She shifts the fabric of the sling. "Out like a light."

"Very good. I think if the baby gets a new outfit for the wedding, so should Mom."

"Oh, I couldn't."

I give her a wink. "I bet you can."

She smiles up at me, her eyes bright with excitement.

"Okay. Maybe one little thing."

13

HAVANNAH

Donovan thinks he's pulled one over on me, but I saw the pile of baby things collected in my wake at the store. As we settle in the limo so I can nurse Rebel before hitting the next shop, I consider whether I should accept any more gifts.

He's taking a call at the far side, facing the window to give me privacy as I struggle with Rebel. The baby is so *over* the sling, so I've decided to lie down on the long bench and nurse him beside me.

So basically I have a soggy boob splayed out over the leather. Thank goodness for the darkly tinted windows.

I watch Donovan talk. His voice maintains a steady, unfazed quality. But sometimes his hands clench into fists, and I can tell he's working at keeping his cool.

He must not have trimmed his beard today, because he keeps passing his palm over it as if it's unfamiliar terrain.

I wonder what it would be like to run my thumb across that rough cheek. He hasn't approached me in any way since the kiss in my apartment before we left Colorado.

I'm good at reading men. Really good. I know he's interested.

But he's not making a move. He must be taking into consideration that our situation is complicated.

And he's right. The baby would be enough, but we also live thousands of miles apart. And the lifestyle differences are outrageous.

He begins to tap his foot, the next level of his irritation. Tiny notes of impatience tinge more of his words. He turns away from the window, and I drop my gaze so he won't know I've been staring. Rebel has fallen asleep, his jaw slack.

Oh no, sweet boy. You have to take your entire meal right now.

I roll over, facing the back of the seat so I can switch him to the other side. I'm concentrating on getting him latched again when I realize the phone conversation has stopped.

I glance over my shoulder. Donovan lies back on the seat, his arm thrown over his forehead.

"Tough call?" I ask.

I like that we can have these casual conversations about his work and feel like something other than two near-strangers on this unexpected trip together.

"Not my favorite client," he says.

"Who is your favorite?"

He doesn't answer right away, so I focus back on the baby. Still not well latched. He doesn't like this side as well, never has. As we tussle, I try to keep the conversation going. "Hard to decide?"

"I'm thinking. I guess there's a delineation between who I like as humans, and which companies are my best investments."

"They're never the same?"

"Rarely. But there's this toy company in Zürich I like a lot. Almost a century old. The people are great."

"Why did they need you?"

"It was more like I needed them. I was trying to make inroads in a market, and owning this toy company got me access to other places."

"So you bought them just to use them?"

"It was a win-win. They needed an influx of cash to launch more innovative lines, preferably without a heavy hand telling them what to do. And I needed clout."

"There's no need for clout in the family deli business," I say.

"I think you did run into some trouble when Anthony first showed up on the Boulder scene with his deli."

That was true. The rivalry is what led to the whole debacle between him and Magnolia. "But that worked out well," I say. "They're getting married."

"Society's oldest style of merger."

"Aren't *you* jaded?" I tease.

"I'm not, really. Phone calls like that can take the jollies out of anybody."

The leather beneath him squeaks, so I look over. He sits up and slides down the seat until he's across from me on the other side.

"What would be fun for you?" I ask. "Going frock shopping can't possibly be your idea of a good time."

His grin sets me at ease. "It will be if you're the one wearing the frocks."

In old Havannah land, this would be my moment to make an insanely sexy double entendre about taking *off* the frocks.

But I'm not the same person I was before those two lines appeared on my pregnancy test. I'm not even sure these cranky parts work the same way they used to. I've heard the stories.

More than once, as an insensitive, ignorant college girl, I cracked a joke with my clubbing girlfriends about the loosening up of our nether regions after childbirth.

I regret that.

Rebel falls off the boob again. I push on it. It's pretty slack. He's had enough.

I tuck myself back into my nursing bra and wiggle around until I'm sitting up. I throw a burp cloth over my shoulder and lift Rebel to pat his back. When no burp comes out, I jiggle him, pounding harder.

"That doesn't hurt him?" Donovan asks.

"Nope. He likes it. I'm relieved he's not an over-achiever on spitting up. Some babies are volcanoes."

When Donovan scrunches his face, I regret providing him that image. But taking care of a baby isn't exactly sexy.

Rebel erupts in a burp that would make a sixty-year-old sailor proud.

Case in point.

And then, of course, because I said he wouldn't, a long stream of white goo oozes out of his mouth. It catches in the strands of my hair that have fallen out of my updo. Great.

"Uh oh," Donovan says. "How can I help?"

I carefully wipe Rebel down with the burp cloth, feeling embarrassed. "Maybe hold him a second so I can get this out of my hair before we shop any more?"

Donovan takes the baby. "Should I watch for more spewing action?"

I quickly grab a fresh burp cloth and tuck it under Rebel's chin. "Sure. Could be all the car movement."

I search around for the wipes and use one to clean the spit-up out of the loose strands. I use the dampness of the wipe to help me tuck the errant piece back into the updo. If this isn't a mom thing to do, I don't know what is.

"Well done," Donovan says. "Should we shop? Hang out in the car longer? Take a respite at the hotel?"

I lift Rebel to stare into his eyes. "You done, little man?" I can't even look at Donovan. I'm such a mess. "Let me change his diaper, and I think we'll be good. He should be content for a while."

Donovan doesn't comment on what's happened, simply passes the diaper bag over to me. "I had my assistant advise me on the best shops to try. I wanted to make sure we didn't spin our wheels, since we don't know how long Rebel will last."

I open the changing pad and lay Rebel down. "Now you're thinking like a dad."

Once he's clean and dry, I settle him back in his sling, and Donovan shoulders the new diaper bag.

The sun came out fully while we were in the limo. I

lower my sunglasses and check my hair in the shiny window. All good. Spit-up disaster averted.

Donovan takes my arm and leads me down the Parisian street, now starting to bustle with activity. I take everything in. There are many old ladies with unmissable hair, poufed out or slicked down, some dyed within an inch of their lives, others left white. But they are all dressed like runway models, stiletto heels and all.

They look a hell of a lot better than I do. I'm twenty-seven and barely able to squish my foot into a wedge heel after one baby.

They're superheroes.

Some walk tiny, well-manicured dogs. Others carry their pets in clever purses that fit beneath their elbows. But most of them have canine companions. Some stereotypes are true.

Younger women walk by with ease and confidence. Men are dressed in skinny pants and shirts tailored specifically for their shoulders and waists. No socks to be seen, and lots of mankles.

There's no off-the-rack here. And definitely no leisurewear. Even at the nicest downtown boardwalk in Boulder, half the women wear yoga pants and running shoes with memory foam. Surely this isn't everyday Paris.

I lean into Donovan. "Is there a fashion show near here today?"

He grins. "Pretty different, huh?"

"Like going from Walmart to Louis Vuitton."

"An astute assessment."

I thought I'd dressed the part, but even so, eyes take

me in and skitter away like I'm an abomination. They see right through my store-bought dress and practical shoes.

I have no swagger with a baby strapped to my chest, but I do drop one shoulder and try to lead with my hips as I hold every gaze that meets mine. I won't be intimidated.

Donovan stops us in front of a pair of solid gold doors.

Gold doors. What does that mean?

"What is this place?"

"La Fleur D'or. My assistant was able to secure an appointment." He pulls the door open.

I expect racks of dresses and a snooty vibe.

But I see none of that.

Instead, a circular gold reception desk is manned by a beautifully dressed twenty-something with a gracious smile. "*Bonjour*," she says. "Welcome."

I glance around. The desk fronts a curtained space filled with statues, paintings, and coordinated flower arrangements. It looks more like an art gallery than a dress shop. I want to ask Donovan if we're lost, but then the young woman says, "Mr. McDonald, Miss Boudreaux, let me call up your personal shopper today. Her name is Olivia."

She presses a button on her gold desk. "Can I interest you in a glass of champagne, or wine, or a light snack?"

Donovan turns to me. "Are you drinking?"

Today I am. I can pump and dump. "Champagne, please. And perhaps some cheese?"

The woman nods. "Of course."

The heavy red velvet drapes part to the left of the gold desk. A lovely mid-thirties woman in a smart Swiss dotted dress and perilous heels emerges.

"Mr. McDonald, Miss Boudreaux. We're so delighted to assist you today. This way."

We follow her through the gap in the drapery. On the other side is a long room. A gold brocade sofa and two armchairs surround a low table immediately to our left. In front of us is a small elevated stage, only as big around as a coffee table, before a trio of connected mirrors.

The setup reminds me of the high-end wedding boutique where a friend of mine from college tried on dresses before determining a gown from there would cost as much as the catering bill.

Olivia turns to us. "Please have a seat. We will begin showing our late summer collection. I understand this is for a wedding in the country, no?"

"At a castle," I add. I don't want her to get the idea we are headed to a farm.

Olivia smiles with a nod. "Of course. The American family. Pickles, no?" I listen for a hint of disdain, but if she has an opinion about us, she hides it well.

"That's right," I say.

"Cheri will model the first outfit. She is very similar to your height and body style. Anything you would like to try on, let us know."

Donovan and I settle on the sofa. I adjust Rebel against my chest. He's awake. I think he's going to fuss, but Donovan digs the pacifier out of the diaper bag and passes it over. He's a quick learner.

A young man emerges from the back with a tray holding a bottle of champagne and two bottles of water. He wouldn't be old enough to drink in the States, but he opens the champagne bottle with practiced ease and pours two glasses.

Olivia stands to the right of the small stage. "Our first gown is a taffeta brocade by Angelino Blanchet."

A tall blond woman emerges from the back. Her hair is shorter than mine, but she's my height, and not willowy, as I would've once envisioned my body style on someone else.

She has a chest to her, and a hint of belly. Nailed it, postpartum. The dress is pale peach, floaty, and completely backless. Right. Like I can put these leaky boobs in a dress without a bra. I want to shout, "Next!" but I sip my champagne instead.

"What will the weather be like?" Donovan asks. "Warm like today?"

Olivia is prepared for this. "On Saturday, it will be thirty degrees Celsius, or eighty-seven in Fahrenheit, as I believe you are accustomed." This time I *do* detect a faint note of derision in Olivia's voice.

Maybe I'm looking too hard for it.

When I don't indicate my interest, Olivia waves the woman on.

Another blond woman enters. Her hair is longer, and she has less tummy than me, but it's another close approximation. How do they do that? I guess that's why you need an appointment. Donovan must have sent pictures.

"This is an Alana Lemieux," Olivia says.

I sit up. The sapphire dress is a showstopper with a plunging neckline and fitted bodice. Could I pull this off? Pre-Rebel me would have worn it without hesitation. The model steps onto the small stage and turns.

"Maybe," I say to Olivia. "I'd have to see how it fits."

She nods.

The young man returns with another tray. It's filled with cheese, bits of bread, and grapes.

This is the life.

By the time I look up again, the first model has returned, this time in an off-white satin dress with a square neckline, short sleeves, and a hemline just below the knee. It looks like something an older woman would wear to a second wedding.

"No," I say definitively.

We go through ten more dresses, and I choose three.

"Are you ready to try them on?" Olivia asks.

I glance down at Rebel. The looking was easy. The next part might not be.

"I'll take the baby," Donovan says. "If he puts up a fuss I can't handle, we'll send for you."

Oh boy. I pass Rebel, sling and all, over to Donovan. "I'll be quick." I remember the bed disaster on the plane. "Don't change him if he needs it. I'll do it."

"Understood."

I fairly race to follow Olivia to another red-curtained space. The three dresses hang on bright gold hooks.

"I'll help you," Olivia says. "I sense time is of the essence." She unzips the back of my sheath as I kick off my sandals.

My intention is to try on my favorite, and if it works, go with it. The sapphire one is definitely first.

I slide it over my head, inhaling the scent of expensive fabric. It's heavenly.

But when Olivia fastens the back, I know it won't work. My boobs are in the wrong spot. They need to be smaller and higher. Besides, what if Rebel needs to nurse? It's so fitted, I'd have to practically take it off. I shake my head.

The second one, a pale gold empire waist with beaded accents, fits nicely, but the sequins cut into my arms. I can't imagine trying to hold Rebel with these sharp circles all over me. "No."

I start to wonder if anything is going to work.

I turn to the last one. It's not something I would normally choose. It's emerald green and flutters with airy scarves that create an asymmetrical hem.

I step in, and Olivia slides it up. It skims my body, not tight, not loose. The scarves tease my knees. The color makes my hair almost glow gold.

I realize the dress overlaps in the front, creating a plunging neckline, but one I can also move aside. I can nurse in this! The fitted waist makes me look like I have one.

"I like it," I say.

"Let's accessorize," she says.

The young man enters again, pushing a small trolley lined with bright green shoes.

There are stilettos, one with a gold heel, a pair of open-toed sandals, a modest pump, and barely-there clear shoes with diamond and emerald accents that seem to float.

"Those," I say immediately, pointing to the last pair. They are probably impractically high, but I've never seen anything like them and have to try them on.

The young man pulls up a chair and gestures for me to sit. He kneels in front of me and slips the first shoe on my bare foot like I'm Cinderella.

Oh, they're good.

When I stand, I find I can walk in them fine, and my confident stride has returned. The gems wink on my feet, a band of rhinestones encircling my ankle.

I love them.

"Yes, these," I say.

"Very good." Olivia nods. She approves, finally.

The young man reappears to pass a tray of jewelry to Olivia.

"And the *pièce de résistance*." She lifts a necklace made of white gold lined with diamonds. At its center is a perfect triangle of emerald.

When she fastens it around my neck, the angle of the necklace perfectly nestles against my skin to accentuate the line of the dress. It's breathlessly beautiful. I can't help but press my hand to the cool line of gems.

"Gorgeous," Olivia says. "We have an entire set with a matching bracelet, statement ring, and earrings."

"I don't know," I say, not even imagining what they might cost.

Olivia's expression doesn't waver. "Let's present the look to Mr. McDonald."

She leads me back into the main room. Donovan is now standing, jiggling Rebel against his chest. My heart squeezes.

"He got a little fussy, but not too much."

I almost rush across the room to take him, but then I imagine spit-up all over this pricey dress. Donovan does seem to have the situation under control.

Olivia takes my hand and leads me up the stairs to the stage.

I turn to Donovan. He seems to forget about the baby, his hand stilling on Rebel's back.

He takes in every inch of me, pausing on the deep cut of my cleavage and how the dress fits across my hips.

"Turn around," he says.

I have to swallow, as I make a slow circle, watching him in the mirrors. His eyes never leave my body, and he swallows deeply, his Adam's apple bobbing.

"You like it?" I ask.

"You're breathtaking."

I press my hand to the necklace nervously. "Of course we don't need the jewels."

"Of course we do," he says. He turns to Olivia. "Shouldn't there be more? Earrings? A bracelet?"

She nods. "A full set."

"Please wrap up the full set."

She dips her head. "I'll package up the dress."

"You okay with him?" I ask.

He nods. "We're already planning a golf vacation in Monterey."

I shake my head. "I'll be right back. Thank you."

Olivia follows me through the curtain. "A man willing to hold a baby while you shop," she says as we return the dress to a hanger, but I detect no sarcasm there. "Lucky you."

I have to agree. Lucky me.

14

DONOVAN

I have to hand it to Havannah: she's got stamina.

We've shopped, taken a quick guided tour of the Louvre, gone up the Eiffel Tower, and stopped by Notre Dame and the Sacré Coeur. All in one day.

She and the baby have crashed on the bed in her room. I stand in the doorway for long moments, making sure they are all right, before quietly ordering a feast of Parisian dishes to be delivered to the suite.

It's been a good day. I haven't had the opportunity to show Paris to a newcomer before. It's refreshing to see the city through someone else's eyes. Today it was no longer simply a flash of buildings between limo rides to various boardrooms. It was itself, a city as old as time, as beautiful as the woman I got to share it with today.

My phone buzzes with a text from my personal concierge about the arrival of the food. I didn't want room service waking Havannah unnecessarily by banging on the door.

I hurry across the suite and carefully let the delivery

inside, wincing at the squeak of the trolley wheels as he moves it next to the dining table.

I give the man a nod. "I'll handle it from here." Can't have him banging plates and metal containers.

When he's gone, I move to the wet bar and pour a few swallows of scotch. My thoughts turn to the conversation on the phone earlier that day. I'm being pushed out of a deal, and my competitive streak has been engaged. I want to consult with Dell, but he's in the air.

Thankfully, Havannah and Rebel have been a happy distraction. I can almost forget the entire messy business when they're around. I can see why Dell has rearranged his priorities.

Maybe it's time to change mine.

I swirl the amber liquid in the glass. Dell is twelve years older than me, and I don't question for a moment where I'd be if he hadn't led the way. But he might not expect me to settle down yet. He's barely done it himself.

How long will I travel like this? Five years? Ten?

A quiet voice says, "You seem lost in thought."

I glance over and spot Havannah in the doorway. She's changed out of the dress she wore all day and into a loose sundress. The thin straps on her bare shoulders mean she can't be wearing a bra. My groin tightens.

Her hair is down, cascading in spun gold along her arms. She's barefoot, and her steps are a mere whisper across the carpet.

"Rebel down?"

She nods. "Should be the long stretch." My fingers twitch on the glass. Her gaze falls on the liquid. "Got a sip of that for me?"

"I can fetch you a glass."

She shakes her head. "I can't have that much. Just a taste."

She picks up my glass and tilts it, exposing her long, beautiful neck. I want to press my lips to it, but draw in a slow breath instead.

"Delicious." She sets the glass in front of me. "Can't afford to dump any more milk." Her hands move to her breasts, full and round beneath the cotton, and despite the fact she's referring to feeding her child and intending to only reference that part of her body as a tool, my mouth goes dry.

Down, boy.

"Did you get a chance to pump?" I have no idea what this entails, only that she unpacked a small machine from her bag and asked if I had a converter to fit the plug.

"I did. I should drink some water, refill the girls. I'd like to pump some more tonight to make sure I have what I need for the train."

My gaze slides to her sundress again. "Happy to get you some water."

Stepping behind the bar is a good call. I need to chill my thoughts. Her needs are practical. Mine most definitely are not.

"You ordered food?" She lifts one of the silver domes and inhales. "Oh, it smells so good."

"Take a look through it. Pick out what you like."

"Is any of it yours?"

"I'll choose whatever you don't."

She eagerly sorts through the various dishes, making me smile. There is a surprise in there.

She finds the chilled platter and lifts the lid. "Donovan McDonald, did you order stinky cheese?"

I can't help but laugh. "When in France…" I set the crystal glass of water in front of her.

Her lips pinch. "You better Google it first. I'm not going to eat that if it makes my milk smell like goats."

I unlock my phone and pass it to her, trying to hold back an unexpectedly gut-busting laugh.

She takes it and rushes to the other side of the room. "Aha! I have the phone of Donovan McDonald! I could control the world with this thing!" She holds it in the air like it's a great prize.

"You might indeed," I say. She's a wonder, standing in the beautiful room like a goddess, the lightweight dress lit from behind, revealing her silhouette beneath. I want to seduce her, ravish her, but I'm out of my element here. A new mother. Under my care. I can't make any moves. It's not appropriate.

I'll have to bide my time.

She laughs and sits on the sofa, her long legs stretching along the cushion. "Okay, let me see." She taps and scrolls while I shift all the plates to the table. "Asparagus can make breast milk taste bad. So can garlic. Spicy foods, too." She keeps searching. "However, it's good to get flavors into the breast milk." She glances up. "Prepares the kids for a family's diet. Doesn't hurt anything."

"So Rebel can look like a little Parisian and be ready to eat like one, too."

Havannah saunters back to the table and sets the phone down in front of me. "All right. I'll try it." She slides into the chair and picks up a piece of cheese. "This is going to be our joke forever, isn't it?"

"Among so many things," I say.

"Indeed." She sniffs the square. "So bad." Then she takes a tiny nibble. Her eyebrows shoot up. "Oh! This is good! It doesn't taste anything like it smells!"

I sip the scotch, savoring both its flavor and the fact that Havannah's mouth has been on my glass. I'm having to actively control myself.

She eats several pieces of cheese, then slides one of the plates closer to her. "How about we share everything?"

"I'm game."

She unfurls a cloth napkin and drags it across her lap.

We eat in companionable silence for a few minutes, the quiet occasionally broken when she asks the name of a dish, or exclaims with delight or uncertainty.

Eventually, we stack all the dishes back on the trolley, and Havannah kicks back, bare feet propped on an empty chair. She leans her head back, letting her golden hair spill behind her. I pour another scotch, taking her in.

I'm unused to these platonic encounters, especially here in a hotel room. I wonder if I should suggest a movie, or some way to pass the time, but Havannah says, "It's great to sit here and *be*, isn't it?"

"It is." She's right. I have no meetings, no one expecting to hear from me after today. It's time we've cleared for the wedding and surrounding events. I'm pleased I'll get to spend it with her.

She stares at the ceiling. "So what's the plan?"

"A leisurely breakfast, take the limo to the train—"

"No," she interrupts, dropping her feet to the floor and sitting up to watch my face. "I mean for us." Her blue eyes hold my gaze.

"I don't think there's a plan. You wanted to come. I found a way to make that happen."

She plants her elbow on the table and props her chin in her hand. Her attention is strictly focused on my face. "And then you buy me clothing and jewelry. With no ulterior motive."

I can't quite hold back the quirk in my smile. "I believe we discussed indebtedness before."

Her gaze shifts to the ceiling, but most certainly not due to nerves. She's in full control of herself. My groin shifts. I have no idea what this woman might do next.

"I should tell you something about me," she says, her eyes moving back to me, her long lashes emphasizing the blue. "You may have gotten the idea I'm a damsel in distress, or that I'm desperate."

I sit up. "I assure you I think neither thing of you."

She holds up a hand. "Okay, good."

"I hold you in great esteem. You put Rebel first. You're a model mother."

She shakes her head. "We'll see about that. But I think a woman with a newborn tends to evoke protective feelings."

I'm not quite sure what she's getting at. "You can't

argue that life with a baby is more challenging than without."

"Certainly. But I get the sense you're playing the role of the knight. I'm not looking to be rescued."

This stops me. Maybe I was walking along that path. I sip my scotch, not sure how to respond.

"You didn't know the Havannah I was before you met me. Before I was pregnant. And to be honest, Rebel has slowed me down, but I feel the same way inside as I did before he came along."

"And what is that?" Havannah has struck me as business-savvy and sharp with her observations. She's funny and quick-witted, always willing to crack a joke. I can picture her on the day of the deli's opening, dancing a jig, wobbling her belly back and forth.

"I'm wild. Absolutely wild. I can't seem to get enough crazy."

I set down the crystal glass with a thunk. "In what way?"

She bites her lip and closes her eyes, drumming her fingertips on the table. "You know what, never mind. I'm going to go pump so I can have another drink of that."

She disappears into the other room.

Well, damn.

This night is going to take a lot more scotch.

15

———

HAVANNAH

Oh, that man doesn't get it.

I check on Rebel, then lock myself in the bathroom with my pump. The plastic pieces are set out on a towel, totally out of sync with the gold and marble splendor surrounding them.

I sit on the padded vanity chair near an inset section of the counter. I face the mirror and slide the thin straps off my shoulders, lowering the sundress.

I was risking it out there, braless, which means without nursing pads either. I could have easily started leaking. That would have been a nice bodily fluid addition to my dinner history with Donovan.

But I didn't. In fact, the boobs are getting more reliable on that score, tending to function as expected as long as I don't go too long without a feeding or a pump. We're off schedule today, for sure, with all the travel, but that's meant extra feedings, not fewer.

I assemble the pump parts, screwing the bottles on.

Thank goodness I received the double pump with the heavy-duty motor as a gift. It can deflate these girls in less than ten minutes.

I regret sitting in front of the mirror, though, watching my blue-veined breasts press into the clear plastic shields. Is this sexy?

Maybe, if you're a loving couple with a long history, and this period of your life is precious and sweet with a newborn adding to your family. Love multiplied.

But outside this room is a very powerful and wealthy man, by all accounts used to the most perfect specimens, either by nature or the knife, and I doubt he's ever seen a veiny, deflated boob in his life.

What was I thinking? Me out there talking about getting crazy, like he would pull me into his lap, and we'd hook up faster than the contestants of *Love Island*.

Which is totally what I want right now. Paris zips through my veins, the most romantic city in the world, the backdrop of many of my favorite movies.

And here I am getting about as much action as the Mona Lisa, only there isn't any security rope keeping Donovan away. Just my situation.

I close my eyes to shut off the view of the pump squirting milk through the long plastic tubing. I guess those are *my* security ropes.

But old Havannah, the one who got me into this mess to begin with, is starting to make unexpected appearances. I squeeze my thighs together, trying not to picture all the wild gyrations I could be doing with Donovan.

My parts healed fine, and at the six-week checkup, I was given the all-clear for sex, plus I got a birth control shot like I intended to a year ago when everything went south.

Donovan was on my mind at that doctor visit, of course, and I imagined all sorts of wild things. And now he is right outside this bedroom!

There's a second bedroom to the suite. We could go there and not disturb Rebel crashed out in his car seat in this one. I could make Donovan do all the things I've been thinking about since we met two months ago.

The pump groans. It's pumping dry.

I shut it off and press my finger between my skin and the plastic cones to break the seal. Now my boobs aren't just veiny, they are red from the suction, deflated as a three-day-old balloon, and my nipples could poke someone's eye out.

I can't go out there like this.

I rinse everything off, taking my time. Maybe if I'm too long going back out, Donovan will have retired to his room and this whole idea can remain a fantasy. If I go for it and get rejected, this trip will fall apart.

I slide the sundress straps back on my shoulders. The stretchy top looks better post-pumping. I guess I'm fit for being seen. Besides, the fridge is under the bar. I can't keep the milk cold in here.

I screw on the bottle lids and survey the loot. That will get us through part of the day. If I feed him normally at two a.m., then feed and pump in the morning, I'll have enough to supplement the public parts of tomorrow. I won't have a limo to hide in on this leg of the journey.

I tiptoe through the bedroom. Rebel is still out. When I arrive back in the living area, Donovan remains seated at the table. More of his shirt is unbuttoned, and his hair is mussed where he's probably been running his hands through it. He sets his phone down when he sees me.

"You okay?" I ask. "Bad business email?"

"It's almost close of business in New York," he says.

I circle the bar and tug open the small fridge. "Problems crop up?"

"Nah. My assistant isn't going to forward anything non-emergency at this point."

"Has she been your assistant long?"

"*He* has been with me for three years. One of my roommates from undergrad. Smarter than me. Our positions should probably be reversed."

I slide back into the chair I occupied earlier. "Somehow I doubt that."

Donovan turns the empty glass on the table. "Imposter syndrome runs all the way to the top."

"I'm not familiar with it."

"The idea or the feeling?"

"The feeling. Imposter syndrome is for people who are successful and have doubts. I work in a family deli franchise that started thirty years before I was born. I can't feel like an imposter over something I was more or less born into."

"Well, be glad."

He won't look at me, so I soften my tone. "I don't

buy you'd feel it for a minute. You're at the top of the food chain."

"Based on my brother's success."

I sit back in the chair. This is a Donovan I haven't seen before. "You think you couldn't have made it on your own?"

"Not like this. It's a lot to be in the shadow of a titan like Dell."

"I get it. Magnolia is the brains of our family."

"You've got plenty yourself."

"No, I have *style*. If something frustrates me for more than ten seconds, I'm apt to say *forget it*."

He nods, continuing to turn the glass in circles between his hands.

I want to touch him, but I hold myself back. We're finally getting to know each other. "I think feeling the way you do about your brother is a sign of being strong. The people who don't question their success are often either clueless to their weaknesses or raging egomaniacs."

"I've been called that."

"People at the top are easy to aim at."

He shakes his head. "I'm sure there will be some potshots at the wedding."

"Really? It's a social occasion! It should be fun!"

"There will be people there. Powerful people."

"Like *The Godfather*? Will there be back-room meetings?" I put on my best Marlon Brando voice. "You come to my castle on the day of my daughter's wedding."

He laughs. "Now, see, you're good for me. I got myself in a bit of a spiral, and you pulled me right out."

Now I can touch him. I lean forward, putting my fingers over his to stop the movement of the glass. His hands are warm and strong, and this connection sends a thousand sparks through my body. "The one thing I've always been good at is showing someone a great time."

His eyebrows lift and his gaze meets mine, but then slides to the open door of my bedroom, where Rebel sleeps.

Right.

He wants the damsel in distress, the poor, unwed mother who needs a pretty dress to the ball.

I pull back. "I'm not looking for a fairy godfather," I say, anger replacing the sparks I felt a moment ago.

His mouth opens, then his eyebrows cinch together. "Are we still talking about that?"

"You got me a dress. You're taking me to the ball."

"What does that—"

"I don't even know what I am to you. What is it? Do you think I'm looking for my next man to trap with a baby? Because it worked so well last time?"

"Havannah! I don't think any such thing."

I register his confusion, but I can't back down. "Maybe I do have imposter syndrome after all," I say. "Because I feel like an imposter in this fancy hotel, buying jewelry at shops where you need an appointment, and sitting at the table with someone like you!"

He reaches across the table this time, grasping my hand. "Havannah. Hey. Listen. I want you here. We're new to each other. I admit I wanted to be the hero. But mainly, I want you to be here."

"Then why do you treat me like I'm made of crystal?" I pick up his empty glass. "At least this you'll allow close to you."

His jaw tightens. "Havannah, I've been working overtime—"

"I know! You have a lot to do. Big meetings. Huge deals. Businesses to buy."

"No! Listen. Hey! I've been working overtime to keep my damn hands off you! It's a full-time job to walk the streets of Paris without dragging you to some alley and fucking you senseless. And in the limo? I had to sit as far from you as possible or we'd never have made a single stop!"

Oh.

He easily shifts from one chair to the other so he sits beside me. "You've just had a baby! I have to set all this aside while you recover from that."

"Shut up," I say. "Just shut up."

He rakes his fingers through his hair. "Shit. Sorry. I'm here talking absolute trash to you and cussing one room over from your baby."

"Donovan! Shut up! Jesus! Shut up and kiss my fucking mouth, you fucking idiot."

He stares at me a moment. "That's the hottest thing you've ever said to me."

"I have so much more where that came from."

He drags me to him, and the kiss starts where the last one ended, hot and fiery, an ocean away but as if it never stopped. As if, in our minds, the kiss continued through all the travel and the shops and the museums, waiting to keep going.

His mouth is hot on mine, his beard rough on my chin. There's no gentle easing into it, but a wild frenzy of lips and tongue. He slides his hand beneath the fall of my hair and clasps the back of my neck, pulling me in so tightly that I slide off my chair and land on his knee.

Donovan lifts his leg so my body eases down his thigh, pure fire between my legs as my dress rides up. When I land against his chest, straddling his leg, I feel exactly how much he's waited for this moment.

I pull back for a ragged breath, threading my fingers through his unruly hair. "Donovan."

I don't get a chance to say anything else before he's back, crushing my mouth against his. One of my straps slides off my shoulders, and his hand is instantly there, dragging the top down.

Then he moves, kissing along my neck, my collarbone, the slope of a breast.

I can't even feel self-conscious about anything. He's everywhere, hands moving, mouth kissing. He cups my bottom and shifts me to straddle him completely.

He's hard against me through our clothes. I drape my arms over his shoulders, slipping up and down. I've missed this oh so much. I'm lightheaded, lost, more in a moment than I have been in a year.

He drags the other strap down, and I'm fully revealed to him. He knows what *not* to do, slipping his tongue around my nipple but not engaging in a way that might make a real mess of things, even as empty as I am.

His hands slide up my thighs, thumbs flirting with the lace edge of my panties. I suck in a breath, cradling his head to my chest. Everything splinters into shards of white-hot need. I'm desperate for him, to feel him in me. I want it *now*.

"I'm on the shot," I whisper. "No more Rebels forthcoming."

"Would you like a condom? Shouldn't be necessary, but I'm happy to."

I shake my head and rock against his hardness, already feeling my swollen body parts waking up, tightening. Oh, I'm ready for this. I hear a funny quiet sound as his head nuzzles my neck and a finger slides into the silkiness beneath my panties.

I'm going to come from finger banging, no doubt about it. I clutch him, moving with his motion. As he adds another finger, there it is again. That sound.

This time we both pause.

And the noise connects with our understanding.

Rebel is awake.

I drop my head to Donovan's shoulder. His hand is still on me, waiting. Our heartbeats collide like two toddlers banging on soup pots.

And the keening cry rises from the other room.

"He's up," I say, biting my lip as I slide off Donovan's lap. "He's off schedule." Donovan shifts his hands to my waist and helps me stand. I quickly pull my dress back up and smooth the skirt down. "I have a feeling he'll be up a while."

And shoot, I just pumped. Unless he only needs a nightcap, I might have to warm a bottle.

The cry comes again. I run the back of my hand across Donovan's cheek. "To be continued?"

He nods. "To be continued."

He holds his hand against mine for a moment, until Rebel's cry comes again. I pull away and pad across the carpet to my room and the baby who needs me.

16

DONOVAN

I wait a while to see if Havannah will re-emerge after tending to the baby, but after about an hour, I peek through the open doorway and the two of them are fast asleep on the bed.

To be honest, more just happened than I expected with a new mother. All my life, I've been slammed with memes, cartoons, and jokes about life with a newborn. The fact that Havannah is even interested is a wonder to me.

When I wake up the next morning, I hear her singing. I slide on a pair of sweatpants and head out into the living room. She's slipping a bottle into the fridge, Rebel on her shoulder.

She wears tiny blue shorts and a matching top. Her hair is tied in a messy knot and she smiles over at me. She turns so I can see Rebel. His slate eyes are open and taking in the room.

"How's that boy this morning?" I ask.

He shoves a fist toward his mouth, misses, and bonks

himself on the nose. He's not fazed by it, though, just blinks a few times and tries again.

"He's about to get his bath," Havannah says. "Better now while I have the perfect-sized sink." She glances at my bare chest and low-slung pants. "How are you?"

"Good. Should I order some breakfast? We have a couple of hours before we head out to catch the train."

"Definitely. I could eat a mule."

She makes me laugh. "Not a horse?"

Havannah spins again, and I catch a glimpse of her impish smile. "My dad said I was so stubborn I must eat mules."

I may be starting to see that streak in her. "I'll inquire as to how the chef will prepare the mule meat, then. With eggs and toast, perhaps?"

Her huge grin is my reward for playing along. "And that jam from yesterday. I love jam on my mule steak."

I head to the telephone to place an order while she half walks, half dances the baby across the room.

My throat tightens. It's magic, watching her move, the baby content on her bare shoulder, her long legs moving to a beat only she knows.

Our night got cut short, and I'm feeling the pinch of that. But this morning has that same glow, the same contentment of waking with a beautiful woman in your space.

She disappears, and I open the menu in my lap to get one of pretty much everything. I want to make sure that smile stays on her face.

The train ride is smooth and uneventful. When we arrive in the country, Dell and Arianna have sent their car and driver because a wedding of this size means every motorized vehicle for a hundred miles has already been taken.

Havannah can't take her eyes off the charming scenery, rolling meadows and farms lined with low stone walls. Rebel snoozes easily in his car seat. I begin to wonder if we shouldn't make our first tryst in a car to avoid interruption.

She looks like something out of a Disney movie, her golden hair pinned in loose curls, the pale pink dress simple and wholesome. "Is that the castle?" she asks.

I duck down to see what she's looking at. "That's a different one. I think we have a half-hour before we reach ours."

"This is so wild." Her big blue eyes take it all in. "There's so many flowers and fields! It's so open!"

She reaches across the car seat to squeeze my hand. I lift hers to my lips. I've never been so smitten with a woman in a relationship that has been so chaste. Although last night wouldn't have been, had we been given another ten minutes.

But tonight will be impossible. The castle has thirty suites in eight wings, sorted by family. I will be in a section with Dell, Arianna, and Grace. Havannah and Rebel will be off near the Pickles, since Havannah's sister is engaged into the family.

Dell arrived at the castle last night and warned me the place was a labyrinth. The Pickles were a million miles away on the other side of the château through a maze of hallways, stairwells, and twisty paths. He tried to find them last night to offer congratulations and failed to make it. An escort was required to navigate one end to the other.

Dell's last comment on the matter was "You might be better off sneaking into the garden to meet."

He's killed my notion of winding my way through the castle at midnight to slip into Havannah's bed. That plan was contingent on her sister slipping off to Anthony's bed, since Havannah and her sister share a room.

The garden might be the ticket. We'll have the benefit of grandparents to watch over Rebel. And that's a big, big plus, given the difficulty we've had so far in finding time alone.

When the castle appears on the horizon, then the car turns down a bright white drive to head toward it, Havannah gasps. "It's straight out of a fairytale! It can't be real. It's like a painted backdrop or something."

I see her point. The place is stunning. The walls are as white as clean sheets and the turrets and towers are a grayish-blue. With the bright sky as a backdrop, it indeed looks like a Cinderella story come to life.

"I'm totally going to drop a shoe on a staircase," Havannah says. "I mean, I'm literally compelled."

"I'll be happy to scoop it up."

But she's not even listening to me. She finds the controls for the sunroof and manages to get it open. In seconds, she's kicked off her shoes and is standing on the leather seat to poke through, only the bottom half of her visible from inside the car.

I hear a loud "whoop," and the driver turns to look.

He is not amused that Havannah is hanging out the top. I can't help but laugh. Once she's comfortable in a situation, it's clear this woman does what she wants.

As we crunch along the drive and enter the circle to the front entrance, she ducks back inside. The top immediately closes, the driver expressing his opinion.

Havannah doesn't even notice. "Look at these pictures I got!" She shows me her phone. She's taken something like fifty of them. "I could start a whole fairy-tale Instagram from this visit."

"Make a matching dessert for your deli and light up the menu," I say.

"That's brilliant. I'm totally going to do that. It can be in honor of the new in-laws." She leans over and presses a kiss to my cheek. "This is the best day ever!"

When we arrive, two men approach the car, wearing gray and white uniforms that are vaguely military, somewhat butler-esque, but match the venue in style and color.

One opens the door. "Mademoiselle, please watch your step."

He takes her hand, and she stands up as if in a dream. "It's so different from Paris," she says.

"The country air, milady," the man says. "Shall I take your bit of baggage from the seat?"

She laughs. "That bit of baggage is my son Rebel."

"Oh!" The man chortles. "Then I shall take extra precautions."

I tug the car seat from the base and scoot it toward the door. "I can carry him," I say.

"I've got it," Havannah says, ducking down to pull

him out. "I think we're about to go separate ways. Magnolia said she's in the wing with the wedding party."

I jump out. "How about I come with you? I'd like to say hello to the Pickles anyway before I settle in." I turn to the porters. "Can you make sure my luggage ends up with the Brants? I'll escort Havannah."

I shoulder the diaper bag, and we start up the steps. "Here's my StairMaster workout," Havannah says.

I think she's nervous. She watches her feet.

"Sure you don't want me to carry him?"

She passes the bucket seat over. "Maybe I do. I'm not making a very elegant entrance."

"You look beautiful. Like you belong."

She touches her hair self-consciously. "I'm not so sure about that. Regardless, I'm here."

Two more uniformed men open the immense doors, towering over us at least twenty feet high. You could drive a truck through the entrance.

"Ooh," Havannah breathes.

We enter the great hall, and the mere size of it is mind-blowing. I've been all over the world, and I've never seen anything like it.

The ceiling soars two, maybe three stories high. Chandeliers dip down on long chains, their fixtures made quite convincingly to look like candles.

Everything is white, gold, or blue. The fireplace takes up a huge wall on the far side. Sprinkled in front of it, almost as if they are doll furniture in comparison, are clusters of stuffed chairs, sofas, and side tables.

Ornate archways lead off in six directions, and a set

of stairs wide enough for a car curves up to a landing on either side.

We pause, not sure where to go next.

A white-haired woman in a vivid green suit hustles forward. "Hello, and welcome to the wedding weekend for Max Pickle and Camryn Schultz. Let's get you situated."

Behind us, two of the uniformed men wait with our baggage, easily sorted between my brown leather set and Havannah's eclectic mix of hot-pink suitcases and colored duffels.

"This is Havannah Boudreaux," I say. "I'm going to walk her to her suite before settling in mine with Dell Brant."

"Very good," the woman says, flicking on an iPad tucked into an embroidered pouch. "You must be Donovan McDonald."

"The one and only," Havannah says, then bites her lip.

I hate that she feels outclassed. I can sense her anxiety. I shift both the diaper bag and Rebel's bucket to one side, so I can wrap an arm around her waist.

The woman smiles at us. "Sienna?" she calls.

A young woman in simple gray pants and a white shirt emerges from one of the halls.

"Please take Mademoiselle Boudreaux and Monsieur McDonald to the Diamond wing, and then you may show Monsieur McDonald to his suite in the Rose wing."

"This way," Sienna says. "Would you like someone to carry the baby?"

"We've got him," Havannah says.

We follow her through one of the arches. The long hallway is made of stone and lined with painted portraits of aristocrats from many eras. Every few feet is a narrow table filled with fresh flowers between tall wooden doors.

"I'm dead," Havannah says. "That's the only explanation. I'm dead and I'm walking the halls of heaven."

Sienna smiles back at her. "It feels that way sometimes."

"What's it like to work here?" Havannah asks. "Do you pinch yourself every day?"

"It is a beautiful place to call your office," Sienna says.

"Are you in hospitality? Hotel management? How do you end up working someplace like this?"

"Many of us are tourism students," Sienna says.

"Ooh. I haven't heard of that. I don't think we have that in the States." Havannah glances at me. "Do we?"

"There are a few," I say. "I met someone doing recreation and tourism at A&M in Texas. I think it tends to roll into hotel management for us."

We come to a fork, and Sienna takes us down another long hall, this one with portraits of fruit.

"I feel like I should be leaving a trail of breadcrumbs," Havannah says. "Did it take you a long time to learn your way around?"

"The halls are arranged around themes," Sienna says. "You learn to navigate the fruit hall, the hall of old men, the flower hall, etc."

Rebel lets out a cry, and I rock the bucket seat back

and forth. "Almost there, little man," I say, although I have no idea if it's true. We have passed a hundred doors already, it seems.

"One more turn. The largest wing is Diamond and Lace," Sienna says. "It helps to remember it, since you associate it with weddings."

Here the walls are bright white, and lacy curtains adorned with sparkling rhinestones soften the rough stone. The hallway suddenly opens into a circle. "We're in a turret," she says. "The bride and groom will be at the top. Havannah, you're this way."

We climb a short set of stairs until we come to a landing. A large oak door stands partially open.

A woman inside cries, "Havannah! Magnolia told us you were coming! I can't believe it!" It's Malina, Havannah's mother.

She hurries to the door, well dressed for early afternoon in an ivory silk dress and pearls. Everyone must be preparing for the rehearsal dinner tonight. "Where's that grandbaby?"

I lift the bucket seat, and Malina peers in, her eyes bright beneath a swirl of dark gold hair. "There's my sweet Rebel!"

John Paul appears behind her. "We're grateful you could bring Havannah along. It will be a great family getaway." He reaches out and takes the baby bucket from me. "Havannah, you're bunking with your sister." His eyes meet mine as if to add, *And you're not coming.*

I pass the diaper bag to Havannah. "I was seeing Havannah here before heading to my wing." I lean in. "I'll text you later."

She nods, and I can't miss the glance that passes between her parents. No telling what they're thinking.

The hall feels quiet when they've gone inside their suite. Sienna turns to me. "Would you like to check to see if the Pickles are upstairs before we head to your wing?"

"Sure," I say. Since Magnolia didn't turn up, she's probably upstairs with the brothers.

We head up the stairs, this stretch a bit longer, before coming to the next landing. This door is also open.

"Knock, knock!" Sienna calls.

I glance inside. My brother is there, seated in a chair opposite a striped satin sofa that holds Alma, the great matriarch of the Pickle family and grandmother to the three brothers, as well as the two girl cousins, Greta and Sunny. Greta hangs on to Caden, who keeps trying to wiggle out of her grasp.

"I thought you'd end up over here," Dell says, standing to shake my hand. "Sherman and the brothers are about to come down. There's a last-minute fitting of the tuxes, and Magnolia, Nova, and the bride are having their hair done for the rehearsal."

"Good bonding time for the three of them," Alma says, her silvery hair a perfect puff atop her tiny frame. "Three Pickle brothers and three Pickle brides." She claps her hands together. "Now just Sunny here left."

Sunny frowns. She hates to be reminded that she's the last single of the Pickle clan.

"How was the train?" Dell asks.

"Good." I turn back to Sienna. "Dell can get me to our wing later. Thank you."

She nods. "Have a lovely stay."

"She's cute," Sunny says. "She had her eye on you."

Dell laughs. "Donovan has his hands full, I think."

"Oh, really?" She glances at her sister. I'm sure I'll be the big topic of conversation later.

"I hear you brought Havannah Boudreaux in your private jet," Alma says, her tiny gray eyes twinkling. "And you learned to change a diaper."

I turn a beady glare to my brother. "Someone's been speaking out of turn."

Dell laughs. "You're the one who called me in the middle of the night worried about—"

"Nope. That's enough." I hold up a hand. "So what's the plan for the rest of the day?"

We run through the schedule and chat until footsteps on the stairs alert us to the new arrivals. Jason, Max, and Anthony all arrive at the same time, decked out in custom suits and coordinating ties.

Max tugs on his. "I had no idea Camryn was going to go full Disney princess on me," he says. "For someone who never wears anything but spandex, she sure did turn on a dime for the wedding."

Jason claps him on the back. "Get ready for all the changes that are about to be afoot."

Anthony leans forward. He's only been engaged to Magnolia for a couple of months. "Like what?"

The men laugh, including Dell, and I wonder what the hell is so funny. Anthony and I exchange a look, then shrug. We're both the youngest brothers, so we know all about getting punked by the elders.

The women come down next, packing the room.

They smell of gardenias and hair spray, and all of them look like magazine models. Magnolia sidles up to me. "So, how was the plane ride with my sister?" The smile in her voice tells me she knows about the diaper predicament too.

"Just fine, thank you." I shake my head and turn to Camryn. "You're already glowing. Thank you for inviting me."

Dell moves beside me. We both sense it's time to let the family have their moment. He kisses Camryn's hand. "Stunning, Cam. Sure you want to shackle yourself to that piece of meat?" He tilts his head toward Max.

"Quite sure," she says, moving to stand beside him. "He's put up with this whole wedding ordeal."

"It is a production," Max says, kissing her head, then making a face when he realizes he's gotten a mouthful of hair products. "It's really something, though. No one's going to forget it."

Dell and I shake everyone's hands and head back to the stairwell. It continues up, where the other Pickles must be staying. We go down instead, and pass Havannah's door, but it's closed this time.

"Prepare for the hike back," Dell says. "At least we don't have to do it in three-inch heels."

"There should be golf carts or something," I say.

We pass through the lacy hall, then arrive at a fork of fruit and forest.

"This way," Dell says, turning to the forest.

"Fruit is the way to the great hall," I say. "Lace, fruit, old men."

"I didn't go through the main room," he says.

We walk for fifteen minutes solid, pausing at forks several times, before admitting defeat. Dell calls Arianna, who uses the room phone to call the castle staff, who sends Sienna to find us.

She has an admirably straight face as she arrives in the hall full of paintings of dogs. "You almost made it," she says. "You should have done lace, forest, meadow, roses. You made a wrong turn at meadow into dog."

Dell shakes his head. "You need a GPS for this place."

Sienna nods. "We hear that a lot."

"So how do you get outside?" I ask. "Like to the gardens?"

Dell shoots me a knowing smirk.

"When you get to the junction of roses and meadow, choose the tulips. All flower halls lead outdoors."

"Good tip."

We arrive at a long hall. "This is your wing," Sienna says. "Dell and Arianna are first. Donovan, your door is second."

"Who else is on this wing?" I ask.

"I'd have to check for names," she says. "But this hall houses close friends of the family."

"Makes sense," Dell says. "Thank you."

She nods and heads back through the rose hall.

I take a moment to say hello to Arianna and swing Grace in a circle, then I move onto my room. It's smaller than I'm used to, but beautifully appointed with a tall canopy bed in dark wood, gilt chairs, and a towering window that looks out on the gardens. It's the ground floor, and I wonder if it might be simpler to crawl outside through the window.

But I text Havannah the names of the hallways between our wings, and we agree to meet in the gardens after the dinner.

I can't wait.

17

HAVANNAH

Magnolia and Anthony pop in a couple of hours after I settle Rebel with my parents.

"It's almost time, then?" Dad asks.

"Half an hour," Anthony says. He smiles at Magnolia.

My sister is transformed. Her hair is spun into an intricate arrangement of curls. She's wearing a pale blue silk dress I bought in undergrad. It slides along her body like an ocean wave.

I press my hand to my belly. Time for some control-top action.

Mom leaves her seat, Rebel on her shoulder. "Magnolia, what a beauty you are. Your big day will be next!" She cups Magnolia's chin.

"It's the stylists. This team is amazing," Magnolia says. "Even with all the talk shows, I didn't have someone like this!"

Including me. I did her hair and makeup for much of her tour. I arrange my skirt around my calves, feeling very much the wallflower. This is not my usual mode whatsoever. Having Rebel has changed me in every way possible. I'm not sure how to get my mojo back, although it occasionally makes brief appearances, like last night.

I need to change clothes, fix my face, and up my hair game before the rehearsal dinner. But Mom passes Rebel back to me. "Anthony, sit," she says. "I'd love a little time with you before the festivities take you away."

She and Dad engage in a lively talk about the deli business. I stand up. "I guess it's you and me," I say to the baby.

I head to the bathroom attached to our room. Magnolia's bed is piled with clothes, as if she struggled with what to wear. What of *mine* to wear.

I flip on the light and turn to the mirror. "Bitterness doesn't look good on you," I tell myself. Rebel burps on my shoulder in agreement.

The yellow walls of the bathroom reflect color onto my skin that makes me look sickly. I shake my head at myself. "You're not giving up."

I head back to my suitcase, rummaging through it with one hand to find my cosmetic bag. I set up a small folding mirror on a table by the window. I need natural light. I line up the foundation, blush, and eye makeup.

"Now, how about you?" I say to Rebel, shifting him to the crook of my arm. He seems content. I can try.

The bucket seat is out in the other room, so I lay him on the middle of the bed, popping a pacifier in. "I need five minutes, okay?"

By the time I've sat down, the pacifier has fallen out,

but there's no crying, so I move fast, working with the brushes and sponges to turn my light daytime look into a glam evening face to match Magnolia. No doubt the others will be just as made up.

As I deepen my eye shadow, I glance at Rebel. He's happily waving his arms, watching the slow turn of the ceiling fan. Love those things. The best babysitter ever.

Now the dress. I swiftly unload the suitcase, looking to see what isn't creased. Not much. I should have rolled everything up in tissue paper.

But it had all happened so fast. Donovan's unexpected arrival. The hurried packing.

There's one dress with enough Lycra to prevent it from wrinkling. It's possibly too bright, a red so vivid it could stop traffic. The top is fitted but stretches to accommodate my ever-changing boobs, and right where my belly pooch would show, it flares into a full skirt.

I quickly toss the pink sundress and pull on the red one. Unfortunately, the straps of the oversized nursing bra show on the neckline. I pull it back off. I have to make it work.

It has been hours since I've nursed or pumped. Gah. I can't risk not wearing nursing pads. I might leak, and the dress would show the circles like a painted sign.

I press my hand to my chest. Yeah, pretty full. And I have to do my hair.

I run back to the mirror. My hair has been twisted tight all day. The look is too casual to leave, but if I let it down, it will probably fall into loose curls.

It'll have to do.

I dump the suitcase on the floor and lie down next to

Rebel. "I'm counting on you, baby boy," I say. "Get enough out of me that I can wear a normal bra. K?"

He kicks his legs. I drag him close and lean in. While he's latched, I pull pins out of my hair.

I'm a multitasking machine.

The voices in the other room assure me that they are all occupied. This is madness. Why did I think this trip would be some easy dream? I have a baby. Mom and Dad may be here, but the buck stops with me.

My hair falls in a pile of curls on the pillow. So far, so good. I compare one boob to the other. All is well.

I pull Rebel off, and he gives a startled cry of protest.

"Hold on, baby. There's more." I move back to the chair and shift him to the other side. Now I can hold him with my right arm and use my left to work on my hair.

I did plan this ahead, since I'm left-handed.

I finger-comb the curls. They're uneven. I walk, Rebel attached, back to my bag to find my hair products. I'm determined to make this work. I used to dazzle. I need to dazzle tonight.

I sit down, hold the can between my thighs, and push on the nozzle in hopes the mousse will land in my hand.

But I can't judge the pressure from this angle, and the mousse shoots out, landing all over my thighs and Rebel's arm.

I yelp. Seriously! I shove the can on the table and look around for something to clean up this mess. There's nothing but lace curtains, a pen with a long feather, and textured writing paper.

It'll have to do.

I snatch up a piece of the paper and attempt to slide it along my legs to scoop up the pile of white hair mousse. It mostly works, enough that I can stand up and head to the bathroom.

I wet a soft white washcloth, scrub my legs, and wipe the mousse off Rebel's arm. He's asleep. Thank God. I pull him away and rest him on the bed, praying he'll stay down when I let go.

He shifts, his jaw pumping as if he's on the boob. But he doesn't wake.

I race back to the table, snatch up the mousse, and run to the bathroom. I'm about to put in the mousse when I think—dress first.

I snatch it back up, realize I still have the fat-strap nursing bra on, and rip it off again.

I dig for something daintier, swap it out, and shove nursing pads in the cups just in case.

Now the dress.

And back to the bathroom.

My heart hammers like I'm running a sprint. I think I am. A chair scrapes in the next room, and I sense people are moving.

Shoot!

I squirt mousse into my palm and take a breath. I have to get this right the first time.

I work it through, teasing the front curl into a big wave like a 1940s starlet. Then I squeeze it down, forming the curls into long, lush waves. I brush and brush until it shines.

Magnolia peeks through the door. "Getting ready?"

"I'm frantically finishing!"

She leans over the baby. "He's out like a light. What are you going to do with him?"

I have no idea. Donovan mentioned a nanny, but that's for the wedding. "Carry him with me, I guess?"

Mom steps in. "You can't eat at a formal dinner holding a baby!"

I close my eyes a moment. She's probably right. He might fuss and wreck the fairytale dinner.

My hairbrush falls off the narrow ledge over the sink with a clatter. I bite my lip to hold back my tears. Stupid hormones.

Magnolia speaks up. "It will be fine, Mom. Besides, we have time. Remember, the rehearsal will take forty-five minutes."

My shoulders drop about a mile. "I thought Dad said half an hour?"

"Until the rehearsal," Mags says. "That's when Anthony has to report to the garden. The rest of us have plenty of time."

I stare into my own eyes. Forty-five more minutes. And I killed myself nursing while mousse-ing.

"What's on the table?" Mom asks. "It looks like whipped cream on paper."

All I can do is laugh. And when I start, it takes over, making my ungirdled belly jiggle. I press my hand in, but I'm lost, bent over the sink. I can't stop.

Mom comes to the doorway. "Havannah, are you all right?"

I hold up a hand. "Fine. Just…" I can't stop laughing.

Magnolia picks up Rebel. "Mom, how about we take shifts? Havannah can start off with Rebel for the salad course. Then you take him for the soup, and I'll take him during the entree."

"But Anthony's your date!" Mom argues.

"Then Dad takes him for the entree." Magnolia's face is set. She's always willing to stand up directly to our parents. I've always just snuck around them.

"All right," Mom says. "If you think that's best."

"Let Havannah have some time," Magnolia says. "She can't possibly get herself ready while also watching him."

Except I was!

But I'm so relieved. "Thanks, Mags," I whisper.

She gives me a wink. "You watch. Everyone is going to want a chance to hold the baby. You have a bottle?"

"I do. I'll run some hot water to warm it right before we go."

Magnolia nods, and I realize how strong she's become, how competent and reliable.

I'm grateful. I return to the bathroom to set my hair.

Baby or not, I'm going to enjoy myself.

18

DONOVAN

The dinner is lavish, as expected. A ballroom has been transformed into a lush dining space, walls lined with silk, and an explosion of flowers in every corner.

It's mostly family, with the Pickle and the Boudreaux families taking up much of the U-shaped table.

Dell, Arianna, and I are at the end of the Schultz side, which is light on attendees representing Camryn. Her parents sit to her right, but I heard her brother refused the trip. There's one little old lady who is likely a grandmother. Next to her, it's three women who must be bridesmaids, one with a boyfriend. Then us.

Havannah sits directly opposite me on the side with the Pickles. She has Rebel on her shoulder, and our eyes frequently meet across the room. She's stunning, like a movie star with long golden waves of hair and a siren-red dress. I can't take my eyes off her.

Arianna leans over. "Should we see if Diya can fetch

the baby? I got it all arranged for tomorrow, but I didn't even think about tonight."

"If he fusses, I'll walk them over to our wing," I say.

She nods and returns to her salad.

But the Boudreaux clan has a plan, and as the second course comes out, Malina takes her grandbaby so Havannah can quickly eat.

I don't see how anyone functions without a full-time nanny. But then, my own brother scaled back his career significantly to work around Grace.

Of course, Grace is his. Rebel will never be mine.

I ponder this predicament for the thousandth time as we move through to the main course. Havannah and I barely know each other compared to couples like Dell and Arianna, or Magnolia and Anthony.

But I've spent more time with Havannah than any of the women in recent memory. My relationships, if you can call them that, generally involve a couple of charity events, a few evenings out, then a prolonged time apart due to my travel that seems to end things.

Nobody has gotten clingy or dramatic about the beginnings or ends. I've only circled back once—Felicia O'Connor. And that was because she ended up in a boardroom with me about a year after our initial meeting, so we went through it a second time.

I almost flew back to New York for a party she threw. A birthday or celebration of some sort. But I got stuck in Germany. She expected me to come, and when I failed to show, another dalliance fizzled into oblivion.

But Havannah… I've flown to Boulder twice—once

from Italy—just to see her. I'm up to six canceled or delayed meetings on her behalf.

Clearly, this is different.

She catches me watching her and gives a wave. I like the view from here. I can see her well and spot her interactions with her mother. But I also get a tasty glimpse of her long legs below the table. Her red shoes are killing me.

I wonder if she'll get away later.

And if she'll be in that dress.

I can already feel her in my arms, her hair spilling down her back as I peel that red dress down her body like I did the sundress last night.

I shift in my chair. *Cool your jets, Donovan. You're about to make a spectacle at a rehearsal dinner.*

Sherman Pickle stands for a toast, followed by several others. The dessert moves in, then out, and I tap my fingers on my leg impatiently. How long is this affair going to go on?

Despite my attempts to redirect my thoughts, every glance at Havannah fills me with lurid visions. Kissing her skin. Revealing her body in the moonlight. Could I carry her back to my room? Would she be missed?

Of course she would. The baby. The feedings.

I blow out a long gust of air, causing Dell and Arianna to turn. I wave their concern away.

Arianna leans in. "It *is* long."

At last, chairs scrape back and the family stands. Thank God.

The moment people start to move, I head straight for Havannah and stand opposite her at the long table.

"Fancy seeing you here," she says, setting her napkin beside her plate.

"Donovan," Malina says. "We can't thank you enough for getting Havannah here. It's made this event all the more special."

"Of course. Glad we found a way to make it work." I keep my gaze on Havannah, who grins up at me.

Her parents share a glance. John Paul pats Rebel's back. He has baby duty at the moment. "Will she be going back to Colorado with you?" he asks.

"Yes," I say. "I'll work out a schedule with Dell. He'll probably go back before we do."

Havannah's eyebrows lift at that. We didn't discuss an end date. Only getting here.

But suddenly, I can't imagine taking her back to Boulder while I'm in New York, or whatever far-flung place. I want her with me. We've made it work so far, with feedings and naps in car rides.

"How long will you two stay in France?" her mother asks, concern on her face.

"Not long," Havannah says. "There's only so much travel you can do with a baby."

Malina glances at Rebel, sleeping soundly on his grandfather's shoulder. "He's awfully little."

"It's been fine," Havannah says. "I've nursed him in the car between sightseeing. He's slept well. Hardly fussy at all."

Havannah subtly pushes her chair back. She's done with this line of talk. I don't blame her.

When Havannah stands, Malina asks, "Should we take the baby back to the room? I saw you had bottles."

"Yes, there's several in the tiny fridge," Havannah says. "I planned to run hot water over them to warm them."

Magnolia leans over from where she sits on the other side of their dad. "Get while the gettin's good."

"I thought we could walk in the gardens," I say.

Havannah doesn't have to be asked twice. She hops up and scoots around the end of the table. "Mom, Dad, text me if you run into a problem!"

We dash out of the hall and into the great room with its towering fireplace. A few guests sit on the scattered sofas. I recognize some of them, but we quickly cross and head into the peony hall.

"Where are we going?" Havannah asks, her heels clicking on the parquet wood floor.

"Flowers lead to the garden," I say, gesturing to the paintings.

"Ohh, I saw it from the window," Havannah says. "It's quite an elaborate labyrinth of hedges and rosebushes."

"That's what I'm counting on."

The sun is beginning to set when we finally locate an exterior door and push outside.

It's warm, and the scent of roses is heavy. Ahead of us is a line of tall, perfectly trimmed hedges that create the effect of walls. The pathways are made of flat white stones filled in with sparkling quartz. Off in the distance, rolling hills fill the countryside.

"The light," Havannah says. "I never thought sunlight could have such a different color in another part of the world."

"It's more golden here. I've noticed it too." I don't want to talk about light. I want to kiss her. But a few other people wander the garden paths, and it's only dusk.

Havannah pauses at a row of ornate clay pots, each filled with a rosebush of a different color. Pink. Red. White. Yellow. She cups a blossom and breathes it in. "So magical." She smiles up at me.

I take her hand. She squeezes my fingers, and we continue walking.

"It's so strange not having my little chaperone attached to me," she says.

"Or in the bucket seat."

"He's quite the cock-blocker, isn't he?"

God, she makes me laugh. "He is. Maybe he senses the competition—not that I'm anything compared to him."

Havannah sighs. "It's different, of course. He needs me. I apparently need you."

Not as much as I currently need her. "We enjoy each other's company."

"You're helpful. My parents are over the moon that I'm here."

"Glad it worked out."

We turn into the labyrinth. Unlike the halls inside the castle, we have no system of themed paintings here. Just a long wall of tall hedges blocking the view, occasionally broken by a bench or a pot of roses.

"We could get lost in here forever," she says, looking up.

"We should have brought bread to crumble."

She pauses, looking back. "How will we find our way back?"

"There haven't been any forks," I say. "So you simply have to return the way you came."

"Oh, I see." She continues walking. "It's not like a maze, where you could get stuck."

"Correct. When you turn off the main path, you simply stay in your section until you return. It might even circle back."

"Hmm. Maybe I was liking the idea of getting lost in here with you."

We turn another corner. There is no one on our path. I pull her into my arms. "Perhaps that was my nefarious plan all along."

Finally, we're here. Alone. I slide my hand beneath her hair and pull her to me.

She tastes of sweet cream and coffee from the dinner. I nibble along her lips, her back arching to press into me. The heat of last night's interruption flares back.

I slide my hands along her body, feeling every inch of her. The length of her spine, that sweet, round ass, the curve of her hips. My hand cups a soft, round breast.

She breaks the kiss. "Careful. It's been hours since I nursed."

I can feel the difference between now and last night. So taut and firm. I run my fingers gently over the fullness.

I reclaim her mouth, sliding a hand down to her leg, lifting her by the back of the knee so we connect fully. I grind against her, and she clasps me tightly to increase the pressure.

Our mouths part, Havannah's head falling back. "I need something very quick, before anything stops us."

"Here?"

She pulls back, lowering her leg, and takes my hand. It's almost full dark. The half-moon has begun to take over with its pale luminous light.

She pulls me farther along the path. We come to a flat bench, huge pots of roses on either end. We circle it to the back side, and she pushes me to sit on the bench, close to the wall of the hedge.

Then she bends, lifting her skirt. After a moment, pale blue panties slip down her calves and she steps out of them. "I don't have a pocket," she says.

I take them and stuff them into one of mine. "You sure about this?"

"Totally. We can have a long, leisurely go at it some other time." She reaches down for my pants. "I mean, I guess I should ask if you're consenting?"

I shut her up with a kiss. My hands slide up her thighs to her bared skin, smooth and soft. I jerk her close. She laughs softly, fumbling with the buttons to my suit pants. With a soft zip, I'm freed and she pushes the fabric out of the way.

My hands continue to touch every soft part of her, fingers slipping between her thighs and up inside her. She sucks in a breath, gripping my shoulders. "Yesss," she whispers, close to my ear.

Her chest is at my face, and I bury myself against the silk dress. She's so slick and ready. My thumb finds the tiny, swollen nub of her clit. I start to work it, and she clutches me, a whimper escaping. "It's been so long," she says.

I learn her, the things that make her legs shake and the cries come. When I sense she's barely containing herself, I pull her leg over the bench.

She straddles me, and as she lowers down, the warmth of her body surrounds me. I pull her other leg around, still working that clit, now tightly against me.

Her arms snake around my neck. I use my free hand to lift her body, then bring her back down.

It doesn't take much, only a few strokes in, before her body begins to shudder from her hips to her arms. "Donovan!" she cries, dropping her face to my shoulder and biting me through my suit jacket.

I slam her down on me with more force, taking it deeper. As she quivers around me, I release my control and empty into her. All my tension releases. It's taken so long to get here. The trip to fetch her, the uncertainty if she would come. The plane, the diaper incident, the long day shopping. The night we were interrupted.

It all falls away, and my body is less clenched than it has been in days. Months. Maybe as long as I can remember. How tightly have I held myself, taking on this role in my brother's company? Having to prove myself, day in and day out?

My whole life seems to unravel with her on my lap, her body surrounding part of mine. She's the other half of me, the missing part of the equation that has long needed solving. I hold onto her with wonder, thinking maybe I've just figured everything out.

The night cools around us, and Havannah rests her cheek on my shoulder, her face nestled into my neck. I hold her close, making sure the full skirt of her dress covers us, two lovers in an embrace in the gardens.

But no one comes. The evening settles into a quiet so complete that we could be in the middle of nowhere. And nothing, not work or family or the pressure of regular life, can reach us here.

19

HAVANNAH

Whoa. Last night was something.

My mind might be on Donovan, but our schedules don't align at all today. The men are meeting at the on-site alehouse tucked into a copse of trees on the northern border of the property. They're riding out there via horse-drawn wagon. No lie.

The sweet nanny Diya, who traveled with Dell and Arianna, comes midmorning to fetch Rebel. She's lovely, and young Grace, who's expecting a sibling of her own soon, is delighted to play big sister to Rebel.

We ladies have a bride's luncheon in a large gazebo at the far end of the hedge. When we're escorted through the gardens, I cast glances at the entrance to the section where Donovan and I had our tryst.

The gazebo lunch is in full sight of the preparations for the wedding so Camryn can keep an eye on it. Her idea, apparently. The day is bright and sunshiny. The castle gleams like a movie set in the background.

The men get more than a little drunk, evidenced by the number of texts the ladies receive.

Camryn holds up her phone. "Max sent me a bunch of texts I can't decipher and three heart emojis."

Everyone laughs. I keep my cell screen tilted under the table, the sound off. Donovan texts, *I wish you were here*, three times in a row, each with a different variation of *her, hear, here*. Yeah, the boys are drinking.

While our events end at the same time, the men spend the afternoon sleeping off the booze while the rest of us take turns with nail technicians, hairdressers, and makeup artists.

I'm surprised to discover that even with my late arrival, one has been set aside for me. Diya returns a hungry baby to me, and I get a pedicure while nursing him.

With the lavish attention, the nanny, and the excitement of the upcoming wedding, I feel more like my old self than since even before Rebel was born. Truth be told, that era when I went on a hookup spree was not my best.

But my life is completely turned around. I'm in France at a fairytale wedding. My nails are getting painted a gemlike green to match a dress purchased by a powerful, wealthy businessman who brought me here on a private plane. Who's helped me with my newborn baby and was even present at his birth.

And who banged the hell out me in an enchanted garden out behind a castle.

Who's life am I living?

I shift Rebel to wake him up so he can feed on the

other side. I need to pump to ensure I have enough bottles prepared for the wedding and reception. Even so, if I need to escape, I'm sure the evening will go long and I can return after nursing.

There will be dancing. I close my eyes for a moment and think about moving across a ballroom in Donovan's arms. It's been a perfect few days.

Still, I know this dream will end. The wedding will soon be over, and I will fly back to the United States, and Donovan will continue his jet-set business ways. But in this moment, my life is more perfect than it has ever been. I just have to hold on with both hands.

The tech sits back and begins to pack her things. She's done. I wiggle my toes. They sparkle like the emeralds on the jewelry Donovan bought for me.

"It's perfect," I tell the lady. "Thank you."

"Enjoy your night," she says.

Rebel has fallen asleep on the boob again. I pull him off and walk him over to the bed. He's so tiny there, nestled among the burp cloths and changing pad, totally out of sync with the gold satin bedspread and beaded draperies.

He's already filling out, more chubby-cheeked on this trip. Everyone says the early months are so fleeting. I believe it. I undress him, marveling over his plump belly and chubby thighs. He wakes, gives me a milk-drunk look, and falls asleep again.

I change his diaper and slide on the fancy outfit Donovan bought in Paris. The children will come down for the family photographs. The Pickles asked for all of the Boudreaux clan to be included as we prepare for my sister's marriage to Anthony. It's a lot, a dramatic expansion of our family.

Magnolia enters our room in her T-shirt and sweatpants. She had her nails done yesterday, and she got an early slot for one of the hairdressers. Her hair is braided into an intricate half updo that crowns an explosion of long blond curls. It's breathtaking.

"Turn around," I tell her. "Let me see that better."

Magnolia touches the coil lightly. "I hope I can find someone as good as her when it's my turn."

"You're stunning. What should I do?"

"You want up or down?" Magnolia sits on the bed and squeezes Rebel's tiny foot. After some fussiness about being dressed, he's out cold again.

I step to the bathroom and peer into the mirror at my windblown hair. It's a mess from the outdoor luncheon. I should probably shower and start over. "Up, I think. But those curls you got. Wow."

"What are you wearing?" she asks.

"Donovan bought me a dress in Paris. It's emerald green." I head to the closet to pull out the zippered bag.

"He bought you a dress?"

"He did." I unzip the bag and hang the dress on a hook of the closet door.

"I love it. It will set off your hair."

"There's more." I head to the desk. One of the drawers is outfitted with a digital lock where you can program the combination. I drop the ornate cover that hides the modern addition and punch in the code.

When I turn with the box and open it, Magnolia draws in a breath. "Are those real?"

I nod. "I didn't want to accept them. But—"

"Then why did you?"

I suddenly remember that Anthony Pickle tried to buy jewelry for Magnolia early in their relationship, and she turned him down.

"It was hard to say no. You think I did the wrong thing?" Ugh. Guilt washes over me. Old Havannah wouldn't have given a thought to her baby sister's opinion. But after this last year, I've tried to straighten my moral compass.

Magnolia brushes a hand across Rebel's forehead, smoothing a frown line that has crossed his expression in his sleep. "Your situation is very different." She reaches out to hold the box of jewelry. "So it seems this is going to work out? You weren't sure before."

"At least while we're here. As soon as we get back home, he has to return to his life."

Magnolia's gaze meets mine "Have you two…"

"Bumped uglies?"

I hesitate. Normally I don't keep many things from Magnolia. She's always known about Rebel, and she came with me on the doctor visits before I managed to summon the courage to tell our parents.

But I'm smarting from that hint of judgment I sense in her about the jewelry.

"Hopefully tonight," I say. And that is not a lie. "I've got the nanny and the wedding, plus Donovan has a room to himself." I glance meaningfully around the room as if to prove nothing could've happened since I've been here. I'm not about to confess about our rose garden moment.

Magnolia is unconvinced. "But you were at the hotel with him. And on that plane."

"With the baby. Who inconveniently seems to cry any time Donovan and I get hot and heavy."

This makes her laugh. "I bet. You seem happy."

"I am. Don't worry, Mags. I know I'm in a dream state. It can't last. I'll have a good time for a few days, and pick up a few goodies along the way." I take the box and close the lid. "Then I'll continue my life as a young single mother in a Colorado town, working at a family restaurant."

Rebel stirs, and Magnolia places her hand on his belly. "You know, that sounds exactly like the plot of a Hallmark movie."

It's true. Watching those movies is one of our favorite pastimes. "It does, doesn't it? But they don't usually have billionaires in them. It's always a baker or a handyman."

Magnolia scrunches her face, thinking. "You're right. But I do remember *Pretty Woman.*"

This makes me snort-giggle. "I'm not a prostitute, Mags."

Her cheeks go bright red. "I didn't mean that."

"You sure?" I tease. "You were asking me about bumping uglies."

"Those were your words." She pretends to cover Rebel's ears. "What I mean is the overworked busi-nessman who needs to slow down and smell the roses."

For a moment, I pause, remembering the rose garden and wondering if she knows more than she's letting on. But I see nothing accusatory in her face. "I'm not expecting a Cinderella story. I'm fine with a few days here and there when he's in town. I'm not going to do much else in my current predicament."

Mags heads to the desk and touches the jewelry box. "Don't sell yourself short. There could be some nice man in Boulder ready to step in."

"Right. We'll be spending all our hours getting the new deli up to speed, and what I don't use up there, I'll spend with the baby." Rebel fusses again, so I pick him up and put him on my shoulder. He immediately lets out a big burp.

A light knock makes me turn to the door.

Diya pokes her head in. "Ooh, look at your hair, Magnolia!"

Magnolia touches it. "Havannah is up next."

"I should take this little wonder, then," Diya says, holding out her arms for the baby. "Did he get a good feeding in?"

"He did." I pass the baby to her and tuck his things back in the diaper bag.

Grace bounces into the room. "I'll take the bag!"

"What a big helper you are," I say, handing it to her.

"I have to! I'm going to be a big sister!" Her eyes shine as she looks up at Rebel. "I hope I get a brother like baby Rebel!"

"Me too," I say.

"I'll text you if we need you," Diya says. "I'll be mindful of the ceremony."

"I'm going to pump once more. Should I send it to you?"

"Leave it here. I can send someone after it. I have

two bottles in my fridge." She waves. "Have a nice time, Mama!" she says, turning Rebel to me. He's asleep again on her shoulder.

"Jump in the shower, lady," Mags says. "We're going to have to head up to the bridal wing to get your hair and makeup done soon. Time to make our transformations."

I hurry to the bathroom.

I'm living the most delicious dream.

20

DONOVAN

I knock on the door to Havannah's suite about a half-hour before the ceremony.

John Paul opens the door. "Donovan," he says, and there's a harsher note there than usual. Has something changed?

He steps aside to let me into the sitting room. Malina sits on a sofa, tucking Kleenex into a purse. "I always cry at weddings," she says. "Does your mother?"

I picture my mom at the last Alabama wedding we attended, stuffing chicken wings from the buffet in a plastic bag and trying to decide whether or not to actually leave the gift, and say, "Sometimes."

"Oh, I'm the worst." She shoves another tissue into the bag.

John Paul remains standing. "I expect the girls to come out any moment. They looked ready the last time I saw them."

"They had some jewelry to put on," Malina says. Her gaze shifts from me to her husband and back again.

My instincts are good when reading a room. I've been discussed. Might as well clear the air.

"I've enjoyed my time with Havannah immensely," I say, my traitorous brain instantly shifting to last night's moment in the rose garden.

John Paul stands a bit taller. "It does seem you've become a regular in her life, being at the birth and all."

"The timing is off, but—"

"Has she told you who the father is?" he bellows.

"John Paul!" Malina says, clutching her bag.

"It's all right," I tell her. I turn to John Paul. His face is a blustery red, and he's formidable in his charcoal suit. I meet his eye. "Havannah's history before I met her is her own. I am only interested in the time we can find to spend together, given her new deli and the addition to the family."

His eyes narrow. "So she hasn't told you either."

"It's no interest of mine."

"You know I have to be concerned for her."

I hold his gaze. "She's an adult."

"With a newborn. I will not have some rich, entitled man thinking he can use her however he likes!"

"John Paul!" Malina leaps from the sofa. "Don't scare him off."

John Paul keeps a menacing eye on me. "If he can be scared, let him be scared."

"I can't be scared," I assure him.

One of the bedroom doors flies open, and Havannah stumbles out, trying to buckle her shoe. "Dad, who in the world are you yelling at?" Then she sees me and drops her leg, the end of the shoe strap sticking out. "Donovan! Dad, what did you say to him?"

"It's fine," her mother says. "Your father is expressing his concern about this delicate time of your life."

I would never dare to call Havannah *delicate*, but I know when to keep my mouth shut.

"Delicate!" Havannah says. "Good grief, Mom! Give me some credit here."

Malina grips her purse with both hands. She glances up at John Paul with a look that telegraphs, *What do we do?*

I shut them out and focus on Havannah. If I thought she was stunning last night, today I'm knocked backward. The green dress skims along her body, leading to long legs and those killer shoes. Her cute toes match today.

And her hair. Last night she had elegant waves, but today, it's swept up into an intricate weave of braids and curls, falling into a cascade over one shoulder. Tiny white flowers with vivid green leaves are tucked over her ear. The jeweled necklace sparkles at the dip in the dress, and the earrings swing over her shoulders.

I steel my jaw to control my response to her.

She seems reluctant to bend down and finish fastening her shoe, so I walk up to her, take her hand, and kiss the back of it. "You are a vision," I say.

She smiles, and I drop to my knee, take her slender ankle in my hand to poke the buckle into the hole of the strap, and tuck it through the loop.

She steadies herself with a hand on my shoulder.

When I stand, she takes my hand. "Mom, Dad, we're heading out. See you at the reception."

Behind us, Magnolia says, "I'll find you later."

Havannah nods at her. I lead her to the hall and down the flight of stairs.

"What was that?" she asks when we're moved far enough from the door.

"He's only worried."

She halts. "What did he say?"

"It seems he thought you might have told me about Rebel's paternity. If he thought I was a weak link in an information pipeline, he most definitely thought wrong."

She starts walking again. "I'm sorry about that."

"It's fine. I told him that your history before me is yours to tell."

"So he thinks you know?"

I squeeze her fingers. "He decided that I didn't."

She lets out a long sigh. "I'm not sure what I'll do about that. It seems as though it's going to become a bigger deal over time."

Another couple we've seen around the castle, dressed for the wedding, enters the hall from another branch. We slow down to let them get ahead.

"You intend to keep it a secret?" I ask.

"Rebel will ask eventually."

"Did you make a notation on the birth certificate? That's public record."

She bites her lip. "I did something terrible on that."

"Oh?"

"I wrote 'Edward Cullen.'"

"The sparkly vampire?"

"Yeah."

Another couple closes in from behind, and we pause by a flower arrangement to let them pass. "That will take some legal maneuvering to remove," I say.

"Not as much as you think. Since dear Edward wasn't there to sign the affidavit of paternity, he won't go on the official birth certificate. I only wrote something on the form to get the evil nurse off my back."

"I remember her."

"She stuck around like I was the only thing getting her through the pearly gates one day."

We arrive at the back door of the gardens. A string quartet plays outside, set up beneath a small white canopy with blue flags flying.

"So it begins," I say.

We walk along the white path, following the other guests headed to the wedding site. As the music fades behind us, another band becomes audible. This time it's a brass trio, playing a livelier tune.

Their bright music gets us all the way to the large gazebo at the end of the path. Here we walk across an expanse of green to the rows of white chairs set up in front of a large white stage dressed in white roses.

On one side, a larger arrangement of musicians plays lilting classical music—Chopin, I believe.

Everything faces the castle, and the silvery-blue accents of the castle exactly match the flags flying over the stage, as well as the ribbons and accent flowers.

They have this down.

A uniformed usher in gray and blue holds out his arm to Havannah. "The bride and groom consider all the guests to be part of their circle, so you may choose either side," he says.

"On the left, then," Havannah says.

I follow them to a row partway up. Havannah crosses to the last seat, and I take my place beside her.

"I want an easy getaway in case the nanny needs me," she says.

"Good call."

We've arrived ahead of the masses, and the seats quickly fill in around us. We spot Magnolia, John Paul, and Malina, who slide into the second row on the other side.

"I'm glad I get to sit with you," Havannah says. "Did you want to find Dell? We're about to be surrounded."

"We can find them at the reception."

"I didn't think about the dinner. I assume they will have stuck me with my family instead of you." She purses her lips into an adorable pout.

"There's no set seating. There will be a half-dozen cuisine choices to take to any table."

She grins. "I love that!"

I squeeze her hand.

The musicians stop playing, and a hush falls over the guests. A new, lively march begins, and Max climbs the steps to the stage, followed by Anthony, his eldest brother Jason, and their father Sherman. They stand in almost identical poses, hands clasped behind their backs, as the first bridesmaid appears from the back.

There's a murmur because this woman is extraordinary. I remember her from last night. Six feet tall, easy, and her muscles make me feel like I should go hit the gym before bed. Her dark skin gleams in the early evening light. Her stride is confident, like a model's.

Havannah leans in. "Two of Camryn's bridesmaids are bodybuilders," she says. "Aren't they amazing?"

The second one arrives. She's not as tall as the first one, but perfectly tan. When she passes, her back looks like it should be on an ad for protein supplements.

"Impressive," I whisper.

Havannah slugs my arm playfully.

"If you're into that," I add.

The maid of honor arrives, delicate and petite. She also sports a killer tan. Behind her, the littlest Pickle child Caden walks solemnly with a white satin pillow, concentrating hard.

Havannah leans close. "I heard Jason slid on the floor of the hospital when Greta was in labor with him, thinking he'd need to catch the baby."

I nod. "Dell told me about it. It's part of the family lore."

We chuckle quietly at the boy, who is so intent on watching the pillow that he veers off course and runs into one of the chairs. The guest pats his head and points to the stage.

Once Caden has made it to the front, a ripple of laughter begins at the back of the crowd. It moves forward, and Havannah and I glance at each other, wondering if some cute flower girl is making a spectacle.

But then we spot her. Granny Alma, the elderly

grandmother of the Pickle clan, grasps a handful of petals and dumps them on the ground.

"It's a flower granny." Havannah giggles. "I've heard some brides are doing that!"

One of the male guests on the row opposite us claps his hand over his mouth to suppress his laughter. Alma pauses to give him a cold stare. Then she snatches another fistful of petals and chucks them in his face.

The entire crowd bursts out laughing.

"She showed him," I say.

Alma spreads more petals on the stairs and throws a good number at the feet of the three brothers, who hold their smirks in line. Then she settles on the front row by the cousins.

The music changes, and a woman holding a red book comes on stage and motions for everyone to stand.

Because we're at the far end of the row, it takes a moment to spot the bride. Even in the stacked platforms Max said Camryn was going to wear, she's tiny.

We don't get a good look until she starts up the steps to the stage. Her train is miles long, flowing down the silver-lined stairs even when she's at the top. Her hair is piled on top of her head, the lace veil falling down her back.

"She walked alone," Havannah whispers. "Look. Her parents are in the seats."

Max mentioned that, too. Camryn didn't expect her parents to come, but they didn't pass up an all-expenses-paid trip to France. They aren't close, and her brother didn't bother. Camryn decided her father wasn't worthy of the honor of giving her away. She wanted to move into the next part of her life on her own.

But she turns to Max, and the happy expressions on both of their faces, and the way Sherman Pickle steps forward to kiss her forehead, tells us she is in good hands. Her true family has found her.

Havannah and I clasp our hands tightly as the ceremony moves forward. They repeat the standard vows, standing close together.

The backdrop is spectacular, and I can see the stars in Havannah's eyes as Max kisses his bride and fireworks pop as the sun sets behind the castle.

She loves a good fairytale.

If she wants one of her own, I'm the man for the job.

21

HAVANNAH

I can't get over how amazing everything is.

The ceremony was short, but the reception ought to have an entire TV series scripted about it, because I can't stop looking and gasping.

There are swans in a small lake surrounded with flowers. Three music stages are set far apart. One is classical, one swing dancing, and one has a singer covering pop songs.

After the photos are done and Diya has taken Rebel back to her room, Donovan and I wander the gardens. We can have anything we might want to eat. There's the Italian station, the French buffet, the Asian cuisine, steaks, lobster, an entire table devoted to cheese, and, of course, a deli cart with Pickle specialties.

And the fountains. A champagne one. A chocolate one. A wine one. Two with fondue.

Donovan and I move from one place to the next, sampling everything until I'm afraid I'll have to be cut out of the dress.

He knows how to dance everything, of course. He shows me a waltz at the main stage, then we spin to a jazz number with the swing band. After trading dances with Magnolia and Anthony, we wander back to the singer's stage and press tightly together as she belts out a classic rock ballad.

When my milk feels ready to explode out of my chest and the dress is painfully tight, I excuse myself, leaving Donovan with Dell and Arianna, to go visit Rebel.

Grace has gone to bed, and Diya sits in the dim light of their room, rocking Rebel on her shoulder. "Good timing," she says. "He was hungry a bit ago, but I settled him."

"I'll feed him."

"I can let you into Donovan's room."

We head into the hall, and she punches the code to enter. It's dark and smells of him in that woodsy linen way I've come to recognize.

"I'll be next door when you're done," Diya says, and quietly closes the door.

I drop the top of the dress and lie on the bed, Rebel beside me. My hair will be a bit mussed, but that's okay. It's night, and only the food stations are lit well enough for anyone to see clearly.

Rebel latches easily, wrapping his tiny hand around my finger. I sigh and think over the evening. It's been like a dream. I can't believe I almost missed it entirely.

Donovan has been a perfect date, charming and attentive. I feel like I've known him forever. When I close my eyes, I see his face.

I glance around his room. It's neat, his suits carefully spaced in the closet. Only a few bits, a watch and charger and a key chain, sit on his dresser.

I breathe in all the lovely smells. The castle, Donovan's aftershave, and the sweet scent of the baby. It's a perfect moment, and I wish I could stay right here, have Donovan come in, and I can almost pretend we're a family.

Rebel pops off his latch with an unhappy cry. He's hungry. I flip over and attach him to the other side. Just a few minutes and I can return to the party.

I want to dance more, hold Donovan close. Mostly, I never want the night to end.

"Another waltz, another slow dance. And maybe one more serving of chocolate-dipped strawberries," I tell Rebel.

I hear a soft click and turn. It's Donovan, standing in the doorway. "Your wish is my command."

"Oh!"

"Diya let me know you were in here. And I see I have a beautiful woman in my bed."

"And a newborn."

"And a cool and clever little tyke." He kneels by the bed and strokes Rebel's head. "Looks like he's getting a good meal in."

"The milk has to taste so wild after all the different meals I've had," I say. "But he's into it."

I watch him watch the baby, the tiny jaw working. A happy glow spreads through my belly. So this is what it could be like. But would it? Our time is so short.

I almost ask him how long we'll stay in France,

when he has to get back. But I don't. I want the dream to seem endless. To know when it will be over is to already acknowledge it will end. And I don't want to.

Donovan's gaze lifts to meet mine. "I think he's nodded off."

I glance down. Rebel has let go, completely zonked.

"I'll let Diya burp him in case he decides he needs to experiment in explosive spit-up."

As soon as the words are out, I want to retract them. *So sexy, Havannah.*

"You want me to take him?"

"Sure. I have to tidy up a bit."

Donovan lifts Rebel to his chest. The baby expels a big burp, and I hold my breath, sure he's going to wreck Donovan's suit.

But nothing comes out. Donovan heads into the hall to return him to Diya while I race to Donovan's small bathroom. I flip on the light.

Oh my. Smudged eyeliner. A crease on my cheek. My dress is askew. The necklace has shifted.

I quickly repair what I can and press my hand to my cheek. Even with all the flaws, though, I see a light in my face that hasn't been there in a while. With the craziness of the last year, my bad patch, the resulting man-fest, then the pregnancy, I haven't felt like myself in a long, long time.

But I'm coming back. I see it. I almost forgot what it looks like to be confident and content, not worried or strung out all the time.

Donovan comes up behind me and wraps his arms

around my waist. "Hey, beautiful. You ready for those dances?"

I watch his face in the mirror. "Maybe."

"Or?"

"Maybe we can dance right here."

He grins, his lips near my ear. I settle against him, my body relaxing.

"Right here is good," he says.

"Unless you were thinking about cake."

"Why would anyone want cake when they have you to devour?"

A small shudder ripples through me.

He walks us to the bedroom, and his hands skim my body, up the sides of my waist, cupping both breasts at once. A long sigh escapes me. He shifts the fall of curls to press his lips to my neck.

Another shiver.

This is nothing like the kiss before we left, or the interrupted moment at the hotel. And so much more relaxed than the encounter in the garden.

We have time. Quiet. Privacy.

The room is dim from the nursing session. The only suggestion of the wedding is a faraway hint of music from the closest band.

Donovan's fingers find my collarbone, sliding across my skin. My chin lifts, giving him space, turning myself over to him.

The zipper of my dress slides down, exposing my back to the cool air. He slides the fabric off one shoulder, moving his gentle kisses to the newly exposed parts of me.

The bra strap goes with it, one side, then the other.

The bodice falls, and he unhooks the bra, tugging it away to land on the floor. His hands are gentle, fingertips brushing lightly across my nipples, cupping me carefully.

I lean into him, his strong chest pressed to my back. We stay there a moment, his hands warm on me, relishing the stillness, the silence. Then he releases me a moment to shrug out of his suit jacket, tossing it to the foot of the bed.

This is happening. Finally, we're here, taking our time.

He turns me around and lifts my chin. His mouth claims mine, his hands on my body, holding me against him, squeezing my waist.

My arms go around his neck, then slide to the front to loosen his tie. I remember that first dinner when I tied his into my hair. I have it tucked in a drawer at home.

The silk slides through his collar with a quiet hiss. I toss it onto his suit jacket.

Each button on his shirt is another tiny thrill. I'm undressing this perfect, charismatic man. When I reach the bottom, I find his wrist and bring it around front to unfasten the cuff link, one, then the other. I palm the bits of gold while he kisses me then shrugs out of his shirt.

Beneath, his undershirt is silky cotton, like the very best sheets. I want to pet it, but he steps back for a moment, tugging the back of the neck and pulling it over his head.

I take the moment to drop the cuff links on the table

by the bed. I can't easily slip out of my shoes due to the straps, so I leave them, shimmying sideways until the dress falls into a heap.

I step out of it, trying not to think about my belly as I stand in the moonlight from the window, wearing only panties and the clear heels.

Donovan steps out of his dress shoes, but I come forward to unbuckle his belt. I have no idea what nights we might have ahead of us, so I will treat each one like the last.

The leather slides fluidly through the loops. A small button opens the waistband, and another hiss of a zipper lets him free, pressing against the soft cotton boxers.

He shifts, and the pants fall. He steps aside, leaving behind both the pants and his socks.

With my shoes on and his off, our height differential is less. I can almost look into his eyes.

"I want to kiss everything," he whispers against my jaw.

"Yes." My nipples tighten, and I wonder for a fearful second if it will cause my milk to drop. But it doesn't. Thank goodness I just nursed.

He releases me and turns to the bed, drawing down the covers. I shift the fall of my hair behind my shoulder.

He turns back to me, his hand cradling my neck, a thumb caressing the hollow of my throat. "You're perfect," he says.

My first urge is to argue with him. My belly. My

stretch marks. But I'm not allowed to speak when his mouth crashes into mine.

Everything bursts into heat at once. The fire licks through my belly, between my legs, in every place he touches.

My mouth is scorched, my skin aflame where his hand grasps one breast and the other reaches behind to press me against him.

I want those boxers gone, I want to feel him, so I grasp the elastic and tug them down.

He springs against my belly, hot and throbbing. The need courses through me, as fast and intense as last night.

But Donovan has no intention of hurrying.

His mouth moves along my body, down my jaw to my neck, between my breasts. He pulls me against him, and suddenly my feet aren't on the ground. He's lifted me and laid me on the cool sheets.

He leans over me, hands on either side of my body. We only touch where his mouth leaves warm trails.

He kisses down my belly, his tongue dipping into my navel. Then he continues his journey, hands on the waist of my panties, sliding them down.

I lift up, and he drags them down, his lips inching along my thigh, down my knee and to my shins.

He pauses to unbuckle the straps of my shoes. They hit the floor with one thunk, then another.

Then the panties come down my ankles in a whisper and are gone.

He shifts his mouth to the other leg, making his way back up.

I could set off fire alarms with the raging heat of my need for him. I press my hands into the pillow, gripping it as he slides inside my thigh, then finds his destination.

He spreads me wide and dives in, thumb circling my nub, breathing hot against everything tender and desperate for him.

I want to hold out, let him take his time, but I spiral quickly, the ache moving into a pulse.

"Oh, Donovan," I cry, tightening against his mouth. The heat becomes a flash across my body, and petals from the flowers in my hair flutter across the pillow as I arch my back.

I can scarcely breathe, every muscle clenching, the pleasure surging through each part of me.

Every fear flies away, every worry, each moment of feeling insignificant or broken. I relax back against the bed, my eyes closed, the night air cool on my skin.

Donovan kisses my thighs, my hip, working his way along my abdomen. I drop my legs to the bed, reaching up to receive him.

He nuzzles into my neck, his beard tickling my shoulder. He lets me have this moment, the happiness shining in me, pure and happy.

I think that maybe I glow.

22

DONOVAN

avannah stays still a moment, eyes open, staring up as if captivated by the ceiling. Occasionally, a tremor goes through her and she presses her hand to her ribs as if to steady herself.

"You okay?" I ask, my face pressed in that delicious space between her shoulder and her throat.

She nods. Flower petals cascade from her hair with every movement. She reaches up to touch them. "I don't think my stylist expected the likes of you."

I smile against her skin. "Perhaps not. I will be happy to wake up to Havannah's garden in my bed."

"Mmm."

After a moment, I graze my fingers down her ribs, across her hip, and along her thigh. Her breathing speeds up again.

I lift my chin, my lips finding her cheek. I make my way to her mouth and capture it, biting her lower lip.

She laughs and bites back, but I shift to avoid her.

"Hey!" She turns on her side, her teeth connecting with my shoulder.

"You bite!" I say.

"You bit first!"

I roll on top of her, trapping her body beneath mine. "I bite hard," I warn her.

"Try me."

My cock swells hard and heavy, pressed against her belly. I lean down and trap the skin of her neck between my teeth.

"That's nothing," she says, and lifts her head, clamping her jaw on my bicep. Her teeth are sharp.

"Now we're talking," I say.

"Are we?" She knocks me sideways. I could easily maintain my position, but I let her roll us around. Then she's on top of me, sitting low on my belly, her knees on either side of my chest.

She's a goddess, the gold curls falling over one shoulder, the tips of her breasts barely a shadow in the moonlight. I want a painting of her, exactly like this, the golden hair, the gleaming skin.

She shakes her head, and more petals fall, cascading on my chest. My throat tightens. I don't want this feeling to ever go away. It's so much more than what I usually feel about a woman.

I grasp her hips, holding her tight against me. She leans down, nipping down the center of my chest, making her way down. She lets out a laugh, then bites me hard right above my belly.

"That's right," I say.

Her eyes flash in the low light as she looks up at me. She lowers her head again, this time continuing down.

When her mouth covers the head of my cock, I groan. God. This woman.

She works it, cupping me with her hands. Then she moves down, her hair tickling my thighs, and by God if she doesn't nip my balls.

I lurch up. "Jesus!"

"You like that?" She's all temptress, sliding along my skin, her breasts skimming my chest as she returns to my mouth, her lips soft and warm.

"You'll pay for that," I say.

"Will I?" She laughs against my cheek. "I don't believe you, mister gentleman."

"Not tonight."

I lift her, knocking her knees apart. And when she comes down, it's straight onto me, my cock slamming inside her.

"Oh my God," she cries, her body shuddering around me.

I clutch her ass, driving her up and down.

Her hair falls everywhere, the rest of the flowers fluttering over the bed. I'm relentless, brutal, holding her so tightly that she couldn't escape if she wanted to.

Her eyes are closed, her chin high. "Donovan, Donovan, Donovan." On and on, like a song we both hope will never end.

I bring my thumb around to press into her clit, and she jerks sharply against me. "Yes, yes, yes, again, again."

I work the nub, feeling her thighs tremble.

I have to smile at her unrelenting "God, God, God, God."

This time I feel the squeeze of her orgasm from the inside. I intend to hold out, but somehow, she's contracted around me in a way I can't resist.

All the energy in my body flows in one direction, and then I've let loose inside her, our pulses working against each other, then shifting into the same slow rhythm until they go quiet and still.

She collapses on my chest. She seems so small suddenly, fragile and light.

I turn to my side and tuck her into me, smoothing her hair from her face. "You okay?"

She nods against my chest. "Amazing."

But I feel something wet on my skin. "Hey." I lift her chin.

Her eyes glisten, just visible in the low light. "Sorry. I don't mean to cry. I'm not sure what it is."

I pull her up to my shoulder to rest her head against me. "It's all right."

She nods, letting out a sniffle. "I'm so emotional."

"It's a wedding. Everyone gets that way."

"You're right. I'm sure that's part of it." She draws in a shaky breath, then lets it out. "This feels like stolen time. A break from everything. I don't want it to end."

"Me neither."

I draw her close so our bodies are flush against each other, then reach down to draw up the sheet.

She cries a while longer, and I'm not sure what to do. There's a lot going on in her life. The travel. The baby. John Paul has been all over me since I showed up with his daughter, so likely he's talking to her about me too.

"Is your family okay with all this? You being here? With me?" I ask.

She shrugs. "I don't know. I'm the hot mess of the family, you know. I always was. The wild child. The disobedient one. The underachiever. I told them once I'd never settle for life in their dark, old deli."

"Ouch."

"I know."

"But you seem to love it now."

"I do. I grew up. I guess. I mean, look at me. What choice did I have anyway? Single mother. Raising a baby alone." She pauses to sniffle.

I reach past her to the tissue box on the bedside table and tug one out. "You're making it look flawless," I tell her, touching the tissue to her cheek.

She takes it from me and dabs beneath her eyes. "I'm good at faking it."

"Hmm. Should I be worried?"

She laughs and shoves at my chest. "Oh you. How do you always make me feel better?"

"I feel the same way about you."

She goes still. "Really?"

"Of course. You talked me down at the hotel."

"I can't believe someone like you would ever doubt yourself."

"We all do. Every single one."

She wipes her face again. "This weekend was the first time in my whole life I've felt I could live up to my potential."

"And what is that potential? What does Havannah Boudreaux dream of?"

She relaxes against my arm. "You know, I'm not even sure anymore. I resisted the family business all my life, but I'm happy with our new restaurant. We got the idea in a blind panic because suddenly I needed to be supported. But it's worked out so far."

"I think it's going to be a smashing success. All those new dishes Magnolia and Anthony dreamed up during their television tour were very clever."

She turns her face up to mine. "They do bring in a lot of money online. But that feels like theirs, you know? I didn't have any part in that."

"So what would you like to contribute?"

"I honestly don't know."

I squeeze her shoulders. "That's fine. And I do know what you mean. I was rudderless until Dell took me in hand and gave me a direction. Sometimes a path chooses you."

"A path chooses you. Huh."

She gets quiet, so I let her marinate on that one for a bit.

Finally, she says, "Do you think Rebel was part of that? I didn't plan to have a baby anytime soon, much less on my own."

I have no idea what to say to that. I choose my words carefully. It's an intimate conversation. "I'm not sure how all that came about, but I do know he's very loved and surrounded with support, so whatever's next for you, you two get to take it on together."

She closes her eyes, and I assume that's the end of it. I brush flower petals out of her hair while she lies there.

Then she speaks again. "His dad is in jail for beating his wife."

Her words knock the air out of me, but my time in boardrooms has enabled me to hold back reactions and maintain composure no matter what is said at the table.

"That's a lot."

"Only Magnolia knows."

"I assumed so, the way your father was pressing me for information."

She turns her face into my neck. "It's so horrible."

I picture some faceless man raising a hand to Havannah, and I can no longer keep my cool. "Did he ever hurt you? I will kill that motherf—"

"No," she says quickly. "I barely knew him. I met him on a dating app. We were only together one night. He probably doesn't remember my name. I only figured out his based on some clues he gave me. And I found his arrest notification online."

I force my breathing down. "So he was fine with you?"

"He was fine. I had no idea he was married. She was pregnant too."

"Shit."

"I know. That's why he got such a long sentence for hitting her."

"Is she and the baby all right?"

"I don't know. They don't live in Boulder. He was in town playing a gig."

"A musician."

"The cliché. I know."

"It's okay. They're charismatic. That's why it's a cliché."

"Well, he's in for two years, I think."

I pull her in tight. "He doesn't deserve to know about Rebel."

"I don't think so either. But what about when Rebel asks? And there's all these DNA tests."

"I think you should get help figuring these answers out."

"With who?"

"A therapist. An expert. Don't leave it to chance. Know what to do."

My shoulder gets wet again. "I'll try."

The tears trickle down my arm. "Hey," I say. "I'm here. Let's not think too far ahead. Remember, we're in France. In a castle. And nothing can touch us here."

She slowly relaxes again. "We are," she says finally. "This night will never end."

"It will never end." I run my fingers along the side of her head.

But of course it must. We lie together for another hour, occasionally hearing a jovial wedding guest talk in the hallway as they find their way back to their rooms.

Then we get up and dress again, Havannah repairing her hair and plucking out the rest of the flowers.

We collect Rebel from Diya and I walk Havannah back to her suite.

A few wedding guests have gathered in the great

room and we wave at them as we pass. It seems the festivities have wound down.

When we arrive at Havannah's door, she stops me. "I'm going to go in alone, if that's all right."

"Of course."

She stands on tiptoes, and I lean down to press a soft kiss on her lips.

"I'll see you for breakfast?" I ask. "I can arrange something for you and the baby out in the garden."

"That sounds nice," she says. "Thank you."

I lift her hand to my lips. "I vow to always give you the next thing to look forward to."

"You've done a valiant job so far." Her eyes shine as she gazes up at me.

I release her. "Until tomorrow."

Then I head along the long hallways, passing a random guest here and there. I'm not of a mind to go to bed yet, so I wander out amongst the roses where the staff is breaking down the awnings and the servers are clearing the tables.

The night is quiet, the silence deep. I walk to clear my head, to think about my future, and to figure out a way forward.

I know exactly what I want. Just not how to get there.

23

HAVANNAH

The next morning Grace and Diya show up early because Grace has "missed" Rebel. I send them along with the diaper bag and the bottle, realizing I suddenly have time free.

While I pump, I text Donovan and we agree to meet in the gazebo in half an hour. I race through a shower, choosing a pretty sundress and leaving my hair long and straight down my back.

I discover a few errant petals in my green dress and carefully press them between two pages of the hotel's luxurious stationary to keep. By the time there's a knock at the door of the suite, I'm ready to go.

Mom and Dad sit on the sofa, sipping coffee. They've ordered a tray of French pastries. Magnolia is long gone. I'm not totally sure she ever came in last night, which is amusing given our parents share the suite.

"Is Magnolia up?" Mom asks, confirming they are clueless. It's super funny, because of course we're both adult women and Magnolia is engaged. But parents are parents.

I choose not to answer and redirect instead. "I'm heading to breakfast with Donovan. Rebel is with Diya and Grace."

"Diya is such a sweet lady," Mom says. "Perhaps we can find some help for you in Boulder."

Dad lets out a *harrumph*. I already know his opinion about women raising babies, which I've shut down more than once. Besides, it's hard to be a stay-at-home mom when you're also the breadwinner.

I ignore it and open the door.

Donovan looks like he's about to enter a photoshoot in a short-sleeved ice blue Polo and slim gray pants. His hair is more unruly than usual, an errant curl falling on his forehead. A zip goes through me as he extends his elbow for me to take. He's *mine*.

We follow the flower halls to the back door.

"We're learning our way around," Donovan says. "It's like home."

"Do individual people ever live in castles nowadays?"

"A few," he says. "But it's not *Downton Abbey*. Nobody has sharecroppers to lord over."

"It has to be wildly expensive to keep a place like this up."

We make it outside to the morning sunshine. A pair of gardeners in blue and gray coveralls snip at the rose-bushes, removing dead blooms. They give us a quick nod as we pass.

"I imagine it is," Donovan says.

We wander along the main path, then turn into the maze of hedges. My heart speeds up at the sight of the tall, leafy walls. "In here?" I ask.

"There are four hidden gazebos in the maze," he says. "My brother told me about them after spotting them from the Pickle tower." He turns back to the castle and points to the huge, round turret where the family suites are located. Mine is on the bottom tier.

"You should go up there before you go," he says. "It's quite the view."

We turn another corner, and there it is—a small white structure with a gray pointed roof. Three steps lead up to a half-circle of cushioned bench. A white table set with a dove-gray cloth holds two place settings, several domed dishes, and a pot of coffee.

I slide onto one of the cushions. Behind us, a bird quickly flees the scene, displaced. "Sorry," I call to it.

A few voices in the distance let us know there are others in the gardens, but the primary sounds are of birds.

We open the domes to find crusty bread, jams, cheese, fruit, and poached eggs. Donovan pours coffee in our cups, and I breathe in the smell. A breeze races along the tops of the walls, making the leaves rustle. Our bird returns to a branch a few feet away, cocking his head as if to ask, "Can I join you?"

"Is bread safe to feed him?" I ask Donovan. "I seem to remember reading something saying it was bad."

"It is," he says. "A bit of fruit is better." He picks up an apple and quickly slices a few random bits onto his plate.

I pick one up and toss it into the grass beyond the gazebo. The bird looks at it for a moment, then back to us.

"He doesn't want it!" I say.

"He's making sure it's safe," Donovan says.

The bird flits closer to the treat, moving along the branches, his head swiveling back and forth, ever watchful.

"I guess we should stay very still," I say.

"Until he gets it."

In one quick swoop, the bird dives down to the bit of apple, snatches it with his beak, and flies away.

"He got it!" This moment elates me beyond what I'd expect. I spread jam on a slice of bread. "What a beautiful scene."

"I couldn't agree more." Donovan watches me while he says it, and I scrunch my face at him, feeling self-conscious. I only had time for the barest of makeup jobs, and my hair is practically wash and go.

But he squeezes my thigh and sips his coffee.

I bite the bread, swooning at the jam. This whole week has been one beautiful experience after another. "When is everyone leaving?" I ask.

"Dell and Arianna fly out later tonight. The Pickles are staying two more nights, although Max and Cam leave this morning for their honeymoon in Rome."

Rome. France. It's all so far from Boulder and my experience. But I am here, breakfasting on the grounds of a castle.

"What about you?" I watch him over the rim of my mug.

"Dell will have the plane today, and it will take another day and a half to make it back. I have until Wednesday free, then I'd have to shift my workload to extend any further."

"What part of the world needs you on Thursday?"

"New York. Home."

"So you'll fly back Wednesday? Or early to prepare?" His schedule is my schedule, since he's my ride.

His thumb makes lazy circles on my knee. "I think we can stay in France until Wednesday, don't you?"

"My parents leave tonight, but I don't need them," I say. "And I wasn't exactly helping at the deli."

He squeezes my leg and lets go, adding a poached egg to his plate. "Then it's settled. Should we see if we can stay here tonight? We'll need a different room, since both our suites are emptying. Or return to Paris?"

All the options are delicious. "I would love to see something new. Do you have a favorite place?"

"There are some beautiful sights along the French Riviera. We could base out of Saint-Tropez easily and see abbeys and find secluded places to boat or splash around."

My vision swims. I could never have even imagined such a vacation. "It's Sunday. So we have four days?"

He nods. "Four days. Or more, if I push aside some work."

I want him to. I want him to never return. For us never to go back.

"I say let's go."

"Absolutely. I'll make some calls after breakfast."

The decision made, we return to the food with new fervor. Our bird friend comes back, and we name him Mack after the sound he makes, demanding more apple.

We linger as long as possible, until Diya texts that the baby is hungry, and Mom texts saying they are packing the room. And Dell texts Donovan asking when he'll want the plane and where so he can prep the pilot.

And the real world invades again.

24

DONOVAN

I don't miss the look in Havannah's father's eye when I arrive to collect her and the baby with a porter for her bags.

But he says nothing, stepping aside as she makes sure everything is packed, then hugs her mom and sister and sends her dad a warning look I believe means, "Don't say a word."

Then we're driving through the countryside, the baby between us in the back seat. And loading another train, then getting in another car.

But the time we arrive at a hotel suite in Saint-Tropez, Havannah is drooping. We had a late night and a lot of travel, and Rebel's been upset about all the change.

When the bellboy leaves our bags, I send Havannah straight to the oval tub for a long bath while I hang out with Rebel. Today he will only settle if he's swaddled in a soft blanket with a pacifier, on your shoulder, while you walk. He's had enough of car seats and straps.

So I do, pulling aside the floor-to-ceiling curtains so I can look out on the port, the boats lighting up the docks along the coastline. Far out in the water, ocean liners blink with red lights, and beyond that, the darkening sky melts with the water.

Rebel falls asleep, but I know better than to put him down. When I hear Havannah splashing as if she'll leave the bath quickly, I move to the door. "Take your time. He's asleep."

I catch her standing near the edge of the sunken tub, water dripping down her body. Her hands are on her head, trying to tuck strands back into the knot of golden hair that slips to one side.

She immediately sinks back down, seeming shy, but the clear water of the oversized tub hides nothing, the image of her beautiful skin undulating in the shift of its surface.

I sit on the edge and turn on the jets.

Havannah lets out an "Oh!" and shifts to the side. "There's one down low!"

"Some people like to avail themselves of that," I tell her with a wink. "He's sleeping. Take your time."

Her mouth falls open, but her eyes cast back down to the water. Rebel shifts on my shoulder, so I stand back up before he can fuss.

I pause by the door and turn the knob to lower the lights. When I glance at her before closing the door, she's pressing her hand to the bottom jet. I hold my smile until I'm back out in the living room.

Since we'll be here a few days, I call down to the concierge asking how we can procure a baby swing or some other similar device. Within an hour, a young woman in a gray uniform has arrived with a strange oval seat with a toy hanging over it.

I let her in, and she asks where to place it. I suggest near the end of the sofa, and she snakes the power cord to an outlet.

"There's an LCD screen here," she says. "It controls the speed and motions of the chair." She pushes on it, and the cushioned oval begins to gyrate in smooth circles. "You'll have to experiment with what he likes, but I'll set it up in the most common configuration. It feels like a car ride."

"Oh, that's good."

She smiles. "It usually is." She holds out her arms. "I'll show you how to strap him in."

Rebel stirs, his pacifier falling out. He opens his mouth as if to yell, but the woman draws him into her arms. "Quiet, little one," she says.

She slides him into the seat, but before he can cry out, she quickly pushes on the screen, starting the motion. His eyes fly open. He's startled to feel such a thing. The machine shifts ever so slightly to the left and right, as if a car is maneuvering on the road.

His eyes close, then his mouth goes slack.

"Where has this thing been all my life?" I ask.

She smiles. "They are a wonder."

"Thank you so much," I say.

She stands. "My pleasure. We do have a nanny service should you need it. All vetted and with wonderful references."

I know Havannah will never do that, but I thank the woman again.

By the time Havannah has come out in a thick cotton robe, towel-drying her hair, I have a glass of wine and a small plate of cheese and bread for her.

"You got a Mamaroo!"

"I called around."

She kneels in front of it. "They're so expensive!"

"I think I rented it, but I'm happy to buy you one."

"I have a swing at home." She runs her hands along the side. "This is a pricey thing."

"Anything for Rebel."

"Hard to travel with it." She bumps the toys atop the device. "If it proves invaluable, I'll get one stateside."

"So how was your bath?"

"Good." Her cheeks go pink.

Aha. My groin tightens at the thought of her in the jet stream. "Mmm hmm." I lift her to standing.

She wraps her arms around my neck. "You have good ideas."

"I have plenty more."

"I bet." Her eyes brighten with amusement.

I lower my head to press a kiss on her soft mouth. All of her is warm from the bath, the hair at her nape still damp.

She molds her body to mine. The heat of her penetrates my clothes. I can't resist her, not in any form, any state of dress.

I tease the robe away from her neck, moving my lips along her skin. She's mine, her head falling back. We're back in the heat of last night in the castle. The two of us, we work.

I untie the front of the robe, the long sash falling away. I reveal her inch by inch, shoulders, arms, and heavy, luscious breasts. I'm beginning to learn all their states, full and round, soft and pliant.

The robe catches on her elbows, then slips to the floor. It's delicious, Havannah naked in this living room, the bay stretching beyond the windows.

My fingers stroke her skin, releasing the light scent of soap like spring air. I've become familiar with the curve of her hip, the indention of her belly button. My hand slides down, parting her thighs. I lift one of her legs to rest her foot on the sofa.

My touch moves inside, making her gasp and clutch my shoulders. I watch her face, her eyes closed, cheeks rosy from the bath. I curl my finger up, remembering everything from last night, and she sucks in a breath. "Donovan, yes."

I work her body, her muscles warming up, a leg quivering. When her grip is wildly tight, her breathing broken and ragged, I whip her around, pushing her over the back of the pillowed sofa.

I've released my pants in an instant, slipping inside her from behind. She grasps the sofa, pressing back against me. I hold her hips, rocking her body into mine with quick, rapid jerks.

She whimpers, moving us even faster. Her hair tumbles from its precarious knot, the long gold strands falling over the cushions.

"Donovan," she says. "Make it hard. Make it so hard."

I am nothing but obedient on matters like these. We crash into each other, my muscles warming up. Our bodies find their rhythm, the intensity of the friction growing as she tightens around me.

I reach around, finding her swollen clit and working it in a hard, merciless tug.

Havannah cries out, then presses her arm to her mouth to avoid waking the baby. She begins to shudder, jerking, pulsing in my arms. I push even harder, faster, frantic, the world dissolving into only her body and mine, slamming into each other like waves on a beach.

Then my own release comes, sudden, intense. I lean over her, my mouth on her shoulder. It's like a storm, flashing like lighting, crashing in the aftermath with thunder.

I sink my teeth lightly into her skin, and the bite renews the tremors in her body. She fails to stifle her cry. "Oh my God!"

I hold her tight in my hand, the quivering muscles fluttering against my palm. She buries her face into the cushion, bent in half. She shivers for long moments, her breathing fast, until at least her upper body relaxes in one big sigh.

For a moment, I think she might be crying again, but then she laughs. "We woke him."

I glance over at the baby swing. Rebel's eyes are open, staring up at the light in the ceiling as if he has to avert his gaze.

I press a kiss to Havannah's shoulder. "He was kind enough to let us finish."

"Poor kid is going to get scarred." She turns around in my arms. "I'm really into sex, and an exhibitionist to boot." She aims a thumb at the open windows. "I know it's a bay and no one can see us, but it's so *hot*."

She turns in circles as she heads for the window, and I'm at half-mast just watching her. *Fuck*. She's something.

She leans her back against the window. "The glass is cold," she says, then cups her own nipples, watching them pucker.

Forget half-mast. I'm recycling like a seventeen-year-old boy.

I glance back down at the baby. His eyes are closed. He must have woken up to the sound, then settled again.

I press Havannah into the window, my body tight against her. "You want it here? Where some dirty sailor is watching from his boat with a telescope?"

Her head falls back on the window. "I was hoping to hide my kinks until you knew I was a nice girl."

"Fuck the nice girl," I growl.

"Please do."

I reach behind her for the latch to the window. It glides open, the salty sea air entering on the breeze. Her hair flutters along her shoulders, teasing her nipples.

"On the balcony," I say.

Her eyelids flutter. "Yes, sir."

I leave the glass door open an inch so we can hear Rebel if he wakes. The wind whips Havannah's hair. We're on the top floor on the corner of the hotel jutting over the bay. Beneath us are a hundred yachts and catamarans, a few people walking along the docks, small and indistinct.

We look down, the moon reflecting on the water, and I draw Havannah close to me. "This is sexy as hell," she says. "I'm stupidly wet being out here like this."

"Good."

I draw her to me and kiss her, collecting her hair in my fist. I pull down, drawing her chin up and forcing her back, so her breasts are an easy feast.

I lick my way around them, watching them tighten and pucker in the cool air. I press my hand inside her again, pushing her legs apart.

"They're all watching you, Havannah," I say against her skin. "Wishing they were me."

Her body pulses against my hand. She wasn't lying about the exhibitionist thrill in her.

I release her hair, scoop her in my arms, and deposit her on the cushioned chaise near the rail. I kiss all along her body, lifting each leg, making my way down her thigh and spreading her wide. "Show them all of you, Havannah."

She moans. "You have no idea how hot this makes me."

But I do. I press my hand to her again. She's practically throbbing.

I drop a knee to the cushion and pull her legs up, bracing her body as I lift her to me. "I won't hide an inch of your luscious skin while I fuck you this time. Let them see."

In truth, there isn't a single person who can see us,

but Havannah is rapt with the whole idea. I imagine the clubs I could take her to if she wants this fantasy for real. But for now, I plunge into her, resting her ankles on my shoulders.

She holds on to the sides of the lounger.

"Arch your back, baby," I say. "Give them a good view."

She does as I say, already trembling. I pump into her, ready to go forever this time. I squeeze her ass, working her in and out, occasionally reaching up to cup a breast.

"Fuck, Donovan, shit!" She tightens around me, her body contracting then releasing. Her long groan goes on and on, her face tight.

I lift her, easily reversing our positions so she's on top of me.

"Show them what you've got," I say.

She rocks on top of me, lifting her hair away. Her skin gleams in the moonlight, and she's so into it, all of it. She's a wonder.

She undulates, her eyes closed. Then she releases her hair, cupping herself, working her hips.

"I love it," I say. "Next time I'll record it."

She sucks in, her eyes wide. "Will you do the finish like the movies?"

I know what she wants. "Anything you want."

She pulls her hair back. "Tell me when."

She rocks against me, and I picture what she's after, the pressure growing. "Now," I tell her, and she slides off me, down my thighs.

I unleash on her, across her breasts, sliding down her dewy skin.

She looks down, shuddering, and I slide a hand inside her.

"Fuck," she says, leaning over me, her body convulsing the moment I find her clit. "Fuck, fuck, fuck." She grinds against me, her arms starting to shake as she holds herself over my body.

At least she collapses on top of me, her hair spilling over us. Her face is planted on my chest. "Jesus, Donovan. You've been such a gentleman. Where did *this* come from?"

I can't help but laugh. I collect her hair and slide it away from her face. "Even a gentleman knows when to turn into a rogue."

We lie together in the night air, the night settling into quiet, until the only sound we hear is the crash of waves against the dock and the faint wafting of a slow song coming from a boat below.

We're in paradise.

25

HAVANNAH

Donovan and I walk the beach the next morning, Rebel snug in his sling. The hope that my life will be the dream I once envisioned roars back. That vision has been gone too long, ever since my meltdown a year ago, the ensuing dick-fest, and getting pregnant.

Then finding out about the father.

Dark days.

Despite everything, here I am in one of the most glamorous cities in the world, home to celebrities and designers and glitterati. We've already spotted two actresses and the aging Giorgio Armani, who calls Saint-Tropez home much of each summer.

The breeze whips at my sheer skirt, drying my suit from our quick dip a bit ago. Rebel wasn't having it, not the bright sun or the cold water. He only likes the sling.

Donovan holds my hand, his hair a wreck of sand and ocean water, curling over his ears. He's perfect.

"Do you have a boat?" I ask him as we approach another series of docks.

"I don't, actually," he says. "Should I make that a future purchase?" He grins at me, and I melt even more than I already have over the past few days.

"I guess it isn't a useful purchase in Manhattan."

He adjusts the diaper bag on his shoulder. He hasn't complained about it one bit. "I could dock it somewhere. I don't usually spend much time at the beach."

The area gets busy, more commercial and crowded. We turn around to head back to the secluded area we've been walking.

Donovan pauses and stoops to pick up a shell. "Nice one," he says, holding it out to me.

It's a perfect conch, long and smooth, white with rows of brown dots. "Pretty," I say. I tuck it in one of the outer pockets of the bag.

We resume walking. "It's a great day," he says. "There's a service where you can have a picnic delivered on the beach if you like."

I glance down at the baby. He's stirring. He might be gritty. "We should probably get him in a bath and air conditioning for the hottest part of the day."

"Room service it is." Donovan's fingers find my hand, and we take our time retracing our steps.

We've made it about halfway back when his phone buzzes. He's been ignoring it for days, but this morning he spent a couple of hours talking while I fed the baby, pumped, and packed for the day.

He pulls out his phone and frowns. "I'm going to have to take this," he says.

"Sure." I let go of his hand.

His voice is clipped and curt when he answers. "Donovan."

We keep walking while he listens. I peep in at Rebel, who shifts back and forth, a little fussy. "Almost home," I whisper to him, then realize what I've said. *Home.* Right. Home is a cheap apartment I share with my sister back in Boulder. Not a luxury suite on the French Riviera.

When Donovan speaks again, it's the toughest I've ever heard him sound. "That is not the deal, Baker. We have already been through legal with this." His jaw is set tight. "We're way past the stage for that."

Rebel shifts again, his eyes open. I lean down to peek, but my movement gives him a blast of sun. He squeezes his eyes tight, and the pacifier pops out. His first cry is a short bleat of displeasure, but there will be more.

I lean over so my hat shades him and tug the sling around so his tender skin isn't exposed. "Shh, shh, baby."

Donovan stops in his tracks. "Baker, we're not doing this. Brant Industries will pull out."

I pause, glancing back at him. He's miles away, staring up at the towering hotel buildings.

"I'm not. No— We—" He's obviously getting interrupted.

He notices me and motions for us to start walking again. I'm relieved, because I haven't paid near enough attention, and I have no idea which of these massive structures is ours.

His steps become long, trudging movements through the sand. "Baker, this isn't just about you. There's Devenough and Schmidt. The Mercers. The board is not going to be on your side."

I hurry to keep up with him. Rebel fusses in protest, and I hug him carefully to my chest to keep him from getting tossed from side to side.

Donovan stops again. "Saint-Tropez," he says, and I realize he's talking about us, right now. Then, "Tomorrow."

I wait beside him. He glances over at me, his face hard. "Fine. Tonight. Set it up."

Does he mean he has to be somewhere tonight? My belly quakes.

He jams his finger on his phone and resumes walking. "I'm sorry."

"Everything okay?" I fail to keep the shake out of my voice.

"We're going to have to drive to Milan in a few hours. Let's get the baby good and settled so we can make the trip."

I'm relieved I'm not being ditched in Saint-Tropez. "What's happening?"

"A three-hundred-million-dollar deal is about to collapse over one greedy director on the board." He presses his hand to my back to turn me up toward a back gate to a lavish pool area behind one of the hotels. I realize with a sigh that it is ours.

"What are you going to do?"

"Get to Milan." He digs out his key card and passes it over the gate lock so we can enter the resort. "I was afraid this might happen."

"Can you save the deal?"

"Maybe."

His face is tight as we walk the sidewalk around the pools and under the veranda. It's blissful relief to be out of the sun.

We're quiet as we take the elevator up to the room. Donovan punches messages madly on his phone. Our idyllic getaway is coming to a close, I can feel it.

When we're in the room, Donovan immediately sets up his laptop. Rebel continues to fuss, so I take him to the bedroom to strip him down. I'm a hot mess too, so I settle on a cool bath with him in my arms, the water low enough that I can nurse him while we both rinse away the grit.

I think Donovan will come talk to me before we're done, but despite my lingering in the water until we're both chilly, then dressing myself and the baby and putting him into the seat, Donovan remains at his computer.

I return to pump and prepare for the journey. There's a ton of sand collected in the crevices of the bag. I'm feeling sentimental, so I dry out one of Rebel's spare bottles and scoop the sand into it, dropping the shell inside a well. It's my own piece of Saint-Tropez to take home.

I pack all of the baby's things and set the bags in the living room. "Should I pack our bags as well?"

He glances up. "Let me shower quickly. I'm sorry I suddenly dropped you. You're probably starving."

"I can order some food."

He nods. "You do that." He closes the computer. "I've got everything arranged."

That doesn't sound good. "What's arranged?"

"Your flight back. I'm going to be stuck in Milan for days."

My belly quakes again. "I'm flying back alone?"

"No. I got hold of Sunny. She's at the castle. She's going to grab a train to Milan and fly back with you. The plane's on its way."

"Oh. Arianna and Grace are already back?" I don't know Sunny that well.

"Yes, they landed in New York yesterday." He finally notices my distress and crosses the room. "Havannah, I'm so sorry this is ending so abruptly. I knew it was a risk after things started to fall through last week. But I wanted to do it. I thought it would hold off."

He lifts my chin with his finger. "I'll swing through Boulder when I get back to the States. Will that be okay?"

I have trouble swallowing, but I nod. Tears are welling up and I have to fight them down. "It's been great."

"It has." He leans forward to press a gentle kiss on my mouth. He smells of salty air. His beard is gritty. He must feel it, because he pulls back and laughs. "Even my kisses have gotten salty."

"Go shower. I'll get food."

He nods and heads to the bedroom.

I check on Rebel, who snoozes in the fancy chair. Then I pick up the room service menu. Time to end the fantasy and get back to reality.

26

DONOVAN

The ride to Milan is long and quiet. I can sense Havannah's disappointment in her quiet fortitude, the way she whispers to the baby but doesn't often speak to me.

When we arrive at the hotel, I check us in quickly and text Sunny. She needs to arrive before I have to be at the meeting.

I change into my suit, angry at the late-afternoon time slot. This couldn't have waited until tomorrow? At least I could have soothed Havannah, brought us down slowly with one last tender night. As it is, I'm not sure when I'll get back to her.

I should have been more forceful with Baker. But this situation is a clusterfuck. If I fail here, six more holdings will fall like dominoes. This deal is the first link in a chain.

I stare in the mirror as I yank on the tie. This is utter bullshit.

Havannah comes up behind me. "Let me." I turn to

her, my anger dropping a notch as she calmly makes the knot. She slides her hands along my shoulders. "I love this suit," she says. "You're going to set it all right."

I draw her to me. "This is the last thing I want to be doing."

"I know."

We stand there a long moment, until my phone buzzes. It's Sunny. We've barely made it.

"I'll come down with you." I have to go anyway. I shrug on my suit coat.

Havannah moves the baby from his car seat to the sling. The porter knocks on the door, thankfully right on time. I pull my last two bags off the cart so he can take all of Havannah's things right back down.

"Text me the moment you land," I say when we're safely in the elevator. "Sunny is hilarious. You got to meet her, right?"

"I did." She nods. "And Bianca will be with us, right?"

"Absolutely," I assure her. "You will go straight to the municipal airport in Boulder. Sunny will return to New York after."

"You sure? I'm okay with just Bianca."

"Sunny doesn't mind."

The doors slide open. I step out, pulling on Havannah's hand. God, I hate this rush. I spot Sunny on a sofa in the lobby, her dark hair tied into a knot on her head. She stands when she sees us, her long skirt falling to her ankles. "Donovan! Havannah!" She waves merrily.

I pause with Havannah and turn her to face me. "I will talk to you the moment you land, okay?"

She nods. I kiss her again, trying to push away the sounds of the lobby, the proximity of Sunny and the porter, and the urgent need to get to the meeting.

But all these things intrude, and I pull away wishing I could say goodbye to her in some more intimate way.

"Knock 'em dead," Havannah says. "See you on the other side."

"I had my car wait," Sunny says. "It's outside."

Then they are off, their chatter fading into the noise of the lobby, the porter trailing behind them.

I check my watch and hurry to the side door, where the car that brought us here will be waiting for me.

Only when I'm in the back seat, zooming through the Italian traffic crisscrossed with mopeds, do I pick up my phone and start to make a real plan to salvage this business deal. I have half an hour to get there, and I must put Havannah from my mind.

It's back to the real world.

27

HAVANNAH

Everything's a whirl after leaving the hotel. The driver doesn't understand how to get to the private airfield, and neither Sunny nor I speak any Italian—not that we could have explained. It's new to both of us.

After an hour of circling, Simon, the pilot, has to meet us in one of the terminal parking lots to show him where to go. He has to file a new amended flight plan, but at least we get to load onto the plane.

Bianca is there and ready for us. "What an ordeal!" she says, reaching for the baby.

I'm more than relieved to give him over, as my stress has caused him to go into a cranky crying jag. I'm not feeling great, moody over the sudden ending to my vacation, hot from a sunburn, and weary of traveling now that the high of being with Donovan has crashed into a low.

Bianca gets the baby settled and suggests I pump so she can make some strong margaritas to get us through.

I agree completely and hide in the quiet darkness of the back bedroom, filling bottles Bianca can use to help me out as we fly back over the ocean.

I'm suddenly exhausted and nod off several times while the cones suck the milk out of me. Then it's done, and the bottles are in the fridge and the pump parts rinsed. Sunny holds out a colored glass with a tiny straw and I'm back in paradise.

Starr pops out of the cockpit. "We got the all-clear!" She gives me a wave. "You got some sun, Mama!"

I nod and hold my drink aloft.

The baby is well enough asleep that Bianca is able to strap him into his car seat. Sunny and I buckle into the leather chairs I sat in with Donovan at the beginning of the first trip, and finally, we're taxiing down the runway toward home.

Sunny sips her drink and gestures toward Rebel. "He's adorable. I remember when my nephew Caden was that age. So precious."

"He was the cutest ring bearer," I say. "And how fun your grandmother got to be a flower granny."

"Right! When Max told me they were doing that, I about smashed my bananas. But she was great." Sunny tucks a strand of hair behind her ear. Her messy bun has gotten loose during our rushing around. She's beautiful in a bright, fun-loving way, like some of my college girl-friends. We're probably about the same age.

"Smashed your bananas?" I've never heard that expression.

Sunny laughs. "I'm the queen of remixed

metaphors. I'll try to tone it down. Don't want to drive you up the canary."

Now I have to laugh. Donovan was right. She's a hoot. "Do you get this skill from your family?"

"Not the Pickle side," she says. "Dad stayed a Packwood. It was Sherman who had to change everyone's names."

"It's funny, though," I say.

"It is."

I realize we're airborne, and Rebel has slept through it again. Must be the rumble of the engine. I sink back into the chair. "Well, that was a wild rush."

"I hear you. I was about to head to the train station for the commercial flight when Donovan called." She runs her hands along the supple arm of the chair. "But you want me to ride in your private jet instead? Don't mind if I do."

I guess she *is* getting a nice ride. I set aside my guilt. "I'm glad you're here."

"Me too." She takes a long pull of the drink. "This is the life."

We're quiet a moment. Rebel squeaks in his sleep.

"That was the most adorable thing," she says. "I think my ovaries just howled at the moon."

I accidentally snort my sip of margarita and lean forward to sputter through my laugh.

Sunny smacks my back. "Your booze have a bone in it?"

I hold up my hand. "You're too funny. It's going to kill me."

"I'll dial it down."

I press my hand to my chest, cough-laughing for a moment until I manage to pull myself together. "Not on my account."

"Don't want to wake the baby."

Now that's true.

"How long have you known Donovan?" Sunny asks.

"He came in June with Dell to give me and my sister lessons on owning a business."

"That's right. You own a deli too. Tasty Pepper, right?"

"My grandparents started that one. Magnolia and I opened the Tasty Mango."

Now it's her turn to snort-laugh. "Tasty? Mango? Was that the milk boobs talking?"

Now we're both dissolving into laughter again.

I can barely talk. "I…think…Bianca…made these drinks strong."

Sunny ponders the dregs of her glass. "I think you're right." She sucks on the straw until it makes a terrible slurping noise. She brings on her best Thor voice. "Another!"

And we're off and giggling again. I realize my glass is also empty. Bianca bustles into the room and sweeps away the empties, leaving two cups of water. "I've got some lightweights on board," she says. "How about you both hydrate before round two?"

Sunny nods. "You're way more smartical than me."

We sip our waters, the laughter finally ebbing. The plane levels out, and Starr comes out to tell us we can walk around if we like.

Sunny moves next to the baby, sweeping her hand

across his head. "Such a sweetie. I guess things didn't work out with his dad?"

There is it. "No," I say. "They didn't."

She nods. "I haven't dated anyone in forever."

"How come?"

Sunny shrugs. "Nobody worth it."

"I went on a bad run up until Donovan myself."

"Including this one's dad, I take it."

I nod and sip my water. I'm feeling sober.

She returns to the seat. "So you got pregnant about a year ago. You talk to this guy?"

I shake my head. "He was more of a one-night deal."

"Oh." She picks up her cup, frowns at the water, and sets it down again. "Greta and Jude had words at their first sonogram."

"Really?"

"Oh, they gave the due date for Caden. Then the doctor said he was conceived on such and such date. But Jude had been on a trip that week."

My face suddenly goes hot. "What?"

"Yeah. Jude's a tender guy and Greta's a card. He wasn't accusing her of anything, but he got all bent out of shape."

"What happened? Were they wrong?"

"Oh sure. Turns out when they give you those dates, it's based on how long your cycle is. It can be, like, a week off."

"A week?" My voice is barely a squeak. Why didn't my doctor say this? Probably because I didn't mention it was important. I was so terrified at every visit.

"Sure. If you have a long cycle, you have to scoot forward a few days because you got pregnant later than you think. If you have a short one, you scoot the date back. Mother Nature likes to keep us on our bunions."

I ignore the joke, dead sober. My cycles are always long. It's been the bane of my adult life, waiting for my period during iffy months, although it's often nice for them to be farther apart. Because of this, Magnolia and I have never synced up like many roommates do. She's a strict twenty-eight-dayer.

I don't remember the dates anymore, but I do remember it seemed like Jesse was the only one in range. But if I have to add ten days for a thirty-eight-day cycle, then it could have been one of the other two.

The light dawns. Maybe Rebel's father isn't the home-wrecking psychopath after all.

I glance over at Sunny, but she's crashed, her head on her shoulder. I unbuckle and pace the small room, thinking.

Who were the others? Did I write their names down? Surely. The trail was cold, but I think I knew at the time. I was so sure it was Jesse that I didn't pursue the others.

I remember the app where I met them. They might still be on it. I snatch my phone out of the diaper bag sitting next to Rebel. I power it up, then realize I'm in the air so it can't connect. This will have to wait.

But when I get to Boulder, it's time to reassess my situation completely.

28

DONOVAN

It's four in the morning Milan time when I get the text from Havannah that they have landed in Boulder.

I've only been back to the hotel an hour. The meetings ran all night. It's late evening in New York, and I've been on the phone with Dell, trying to figure out how to salvage this deal. I tell him I'll call him back in a minute.

Havannah sounds tired. "Hey," she says, and the tone is so familiar that my chest pangs with missing her. We've been together every hour for almost a week. I feel her absence.

"You have a ride home?" I ask.

"We haven't unloaded yet. I'll call a car or something. It's no big deal."

I hate that it's not easy for me to arrange things for her. She's no longer in my world.

"Did the meetings go okay?" she asks.

"Long."

"God, it has to be almost morning there. You must be tired."

I stand by the window, staring out onto the quiet streets of Milan. "I'm all right. But you, it's a long flight. How was Sunny?"

"Hilarious. I love her."

"Everyone does. Did the baby manage okay?"

"Bianca took care of him mostly. She plied us with terribly strong margaritas to steal all the turns holding him."

I pull the sliding door and step onto the balcony. The air is heavy with humidity. "She never gives me strong margaritas."

"Perhaps you should pop a child from your nether regions, and she'll show you the same favor."

The rumble of my laugh is a nice feeling after a long and terrible night. I wish I could have kept her here, but the talks will resume in a few hours, and I would have had zero time to spend with her and no end in sight.

"I miss you," I say, even though it seems too familiar, too tender. I want her to know.

"I miss you too," she says. "The whole trip already seems like a dream."

"I feel the same."

We're quiet a moment, then she says, "Oh! I think we're unloading! I need to call a car. Please let me know how things go. I'll probably end up sleeping for a week."

"I will." I don't want to let go of her. I suspect that once real life fully intrudes for her, something will be lost, the tie between us loosening until it eventually falls away. "Talk to you soon, Havannah."

"Bye, Donovan."

I lean over the rail of the balcony. The hotel is in the bright Porta Nuova business district. From my room, I can see the tall, mirrored towers of the modern architecture as well as the orange-roofed historic buildings that fill out the city.

I long for the beach, the water lapping the shore, and Havannah's hand in mine. The room seems so empty, although I can turn to the window and see where she stood, Rebel in the sling on her chest. I wish we'd spent more time here, had more memories in this place together.

It's another hotel room in a long string of them, trailing behind me from my past and stretching out ahead.

I remember I'm supposed to call Dell back, and punch his name in my contact list. He skips the hellos and goes straight to the point. "I spoke with Fontaine, and we're going to intervene with the bank. They won't have a loan, and that will seal the position."

Damn. I hadn't even thought of going for their funding. That's why Dell is the experienced one.

"So we have a next move," I say.

"We do. You can take it from here. I'm grateful for your quick movement on this. I know you had to sacrifice a great deal."

He's aware of Havannah and Saint-Tropez. "I did."

"There will come a time when it won't be worth it. But I'm glad it's not yet."

"Not yet." But it's coming, I think. The day is coming.

"I need to go. Arianna's struggling with Grace, and she's exhausted. We all are."

"I'll let you know if there are any other complications. I think vacations are worse than work."

"Probably so."

I click off the phone. Dell will have another baby soon, and if their lives are anything like what I experienced with Havannah the last five days, he's going to be even more tied up with home life than he is now.

That means more travel for me. More meetings.

More empty hotels.

I step back inside the room and slide the door closed. If silence has a sound, it's the roar in your ears when you're underwater. There isn't anything to hear, exactly, but the pressure is there, strong and unrelenting.

I'm feeling the pull of it in the quiet of the room. I tug my tie loose and sink onto the sofa. Maybe it's easier traveling alone, but it's definitely not better.

But this is my life. It's what I chose.

I don't know how to un-choose it.

29

HAVANNAH

Mom and Dad figure that if I can haul Rebel all over Europe, I can certainly drag him to work. So I'm expected to take over some of the responsibilities at the delis.

Dad keeps a suspicious eye on me whenever he's near. I already know what he thinks about my wildness with men. So of course he's concerned that I took off for France with Donovan. I even left them behind to head to the beach.

Does he think I'll get myself knocked up a second time?

I'm not even sure what sort of relationship I can have with Donovan. As the week wears on, we practically devolve right into the place we were before the trip, random texts and the rare phone call when our schedules align. It's almost as if the magical week never happened.

I avoid thinking about Rebel's father, but unfortunately, at the two-month checkup, the subject comes up again. When I return the clipboard of questions, the receptionist mentions there is no father on file. "Can we get his name for the records?" she asks.

"There is no father!" I say, exasperated. It's hot and the sling is making me sweat, and Rebel already seems to know something dreadful is coming. It must be the smell of the place. He got a shot last time, and there are several today. It's going to be a doozy.

The woman drops her gaze to the desk. "I see."

"I'm a big ol' trollop," I say. "Could be one of six."

Okay, so maybe I'm exaggerating a bit. But the woman shuts up at that and awkwardly shuffles papers around. "The nurse will call for you when it's your turn."

I adjust Rebel and lug his car seat to the row of chairs. He's coming out of the sling. I can't take it another minute.

I tug him out, and a few errant grains of sand spill from the inner folds onto my lap.

Once he's down, fussing and fighting his pacifier, I brush the sand into my palm. Saint-Tropez. I remember the night out on the balcony and shiver. Dang. That's a memory.

Rebel kicks his legs, and I lean down to press my hand on his belly. "We could use that Mamaroo, couldn't we?" I say.

He sucks mightily on the pacifier, and I figure maybe he's hungry. Or at least wants food as a comfort. I can always use a snack when I'm stressed. I pull out one of the bottles I've filled. It's cool, but hopefully he'll take it.

The moment he spots it, the pacifier falls out of his mouth.

"Hey!" I say. "You're learning!"

I hold the bottle for him, kicking the front of the car seat up so he's at a good angle. I'd pull him out, but I'm exhausted and hot. He seems to be doing all right.

I catch the receptionist staring at me. I'm sure she's judging me on all counts. "Oh, you won't believe this one patient of ours," she'll tell her friends at her book club where they never actually read anything but use the excuse to drink wine and gossip. "She has six possible fathers and can't even be bothered to hold her baby while she feeds it."

My self-shaming works well enough that I bend down to pick Rebel up, except I realize he's fallen asleep, bottle in his mouth. I pull it away slowly, and he stays down.

Fine. I cap the bottle. Perhaps I ought to at least look at those other two guys in my hookup app. Now that Rebel's features are filling out, maybe I can spot some resemblance in their eyebrows or nose.

The nurse calls someone who's been here longer than me, and three others look hopeful they are going soon. It's going to be a while. I tug out my phone. Might as well make use of the time.

I know I told Magnolia I used Blendr to find men to date. But even as wild as that app can be, it's nothing compared to what I used. The whole point is to have a random hookup and not bother with names.

Which, in hindsight, was dumb as all get-out. I

mean, if there's a baby daddy in the end, you have to know who they are.

I shift in my seat and tilt my phone to ensure nobody can see my screen. This app would certainly give the receptionist something to talk about.

I click on the app.

Welcome back, BlondieGoesDown.

Yeah, I know. Classy. Sometimes you want to be sure it's understood that you're a *sure thing*.

I've got hundreds of matches piled up. The app was working in the background while I was busily percolating a human.

I swipe them all away and go into my history. There's CheetahGuitar, which is Jesse, the violent psychopath who wound up in jail. Talk about a near-miss there.

I can barely remember him, a smile over tacos, the sexy rock-n-roll hair, and the messy back seat. He was the first of three in that ten-day period. Hot as hell, too.

And probably not it, now that I know how the sonograms determine conception dates.

The next guy was MarcoPoloYou. Mark, actually. I vaguely remember him. We went to a hotel proper. He was a weirdo I never would have dated in normal circumstances.

And the last was BriGuy92. Brian.

Either one of those could be the candidate. Brian might be the most likely, but Mark's sperm could have been sitting and waiting.

I glance down at Rebel, holding the phone next to

him. There's nothing to compare. The fuzzy phone images are too flat, too different.

The receptionist is watching, so I pretend I'm taking a picture of my sleeping angel.

But what now? I guess I can ask to meet them. I have no way to cross-reference them like I did Jesse, since their profiles have nothing that will help me, like playing guitar in a band. Mark likes snow skiing and blow jobs, which I knew.

And Brian is a gamer nerd and computer programmer, but that doesn't get me very far either.

Since I've already had a successful hookup with both, the app has marked us as official matches. I'm able to message each of them directly. So why not? I send a message to each, asking to see them for something important.

Mark pings me in minutes, asking if I need his dick in my mouth again. I say, *Sure.* We agree on a time and a very public place. I don't know what he's going to think when I show up with a baby, but he's probably not going to like it.

This is about to get wild.

Magnolia insists on coming with me to meet Mark. She's worried about me and the baby. Honestly, it's a good call, so I take her up on it.

We sit at a hole-in-the-wall coffee shop, off in a nook that is about as private as we can get in a public place.

We're tucked behind the counter holding the sugar and honey and the bin for empties.

Magnolia is more nervous than me, tapping her foot and turning her coffee cup in endless circles. Rebel is awake, staring up at the toys hanging from the handle of his car seat.

"Chill out," I tell her. "Mark is harmless. A sex-crazed dick, but harmless."

"I don't know how you're so calm," she says. "This is worse than those soap operas Mom used to watch."

I shrug. "I met him before."

"You did more than that."

I sigh. "Mags, I'm not here to be preached at." I want to add I'm not in hookup mode anymore, but probably my behavior with Donovan in Europe means my wild streak is alive and well.

Thinking about him makes me long to use my phone to flip through some of the pictures of our week together, but right now is probably not the time.

The door flings open, and there he is, Mark himself.

He's shorter than I remember, and a bit paunchier. Though I guess I am, too. It's been a year.

"Hey, babe," he says, hurrying over. "What, there's two of you? Blond sisters? Hey, hey, hey, it's my lucky day." He frowns when he spots Rebel. "What's with the kid?"

I kick out a chair. "Have a seat," I say. "And hold on to your balls."

Mags shoots me a look, but I know how to handle guys like Mark.

He sits, a lot less sure of himself. "What gives, Peaches?"

"I'm not sure if math is your strong suit," I say, "but this baby is almost exactly two months old, which puts his conception date during the week I met you at the Summit Inn."

He stumbles to his feet, making his chair skid back with an ear-piercing screech. "Oh, no. Nobody's trapping ol' Marco Polo."

I roll my eyes. "You're not the only candidate, my friend." I tug a mailer pouch from the diaper bag and push it across the table. "Stick this DNA test in the mail, and we'll rule you out."

He stares at it like it's a dead possum on the road. "What do I have to do?"

"It's just a cheek swab. Super easy."

"What if I don't do it?"

"Then I play process of elimination, and if you're the one left standing, I come after you with a court order." I have no idea how that works, but I'm good at bluffing.

He looks from the pouch to me to the baby then to me like we're at a tennis match gone berserk. "You don't even know who I am. If I run, you'll never find me."

"Better be quick. I'm ready to photograph your license plate."

"Ha!" Mark says. "Ha! Ha! I took an Uber! Ha!" He runs out of the place so fast that the other customers look up.

"That went well," Mags says. "You really knew how to handle him."

I open the app. I've barely screenshot his information when it disappears. The page shifts to a screen that reads, *Member no longer available.*

Whether he blocked me or deleted himself off the app, I won't be finding him that way again.

"He wasn't going to be a keeper anyway." I jiggle the toys over Rebel's head. "A bad dad is worse than no dad."

"But you could have hit him up for child support."

"And had to endure visitation for my trouble. If I want him, I'm sure a lawyer can make the app spit out his info. Plus there's the Uber data he so kindly informed me about."

Magnolia tweaks Rebel's tiny foot. "I guess this is about finding a good one. Otherwise you're no worse off than you were before."

"Exactly," I say. "I'm doing my due diligence before giving up for good."

"When are you meeting the other one?" Magnolia asks.

"Not sure. He said he's out of town for his job."

"Maybe Rebel and I should stay home for that one."

I nod. This meeting showed me how wild these interactions could go. I should have known. Finding out there's potentially a kid in your life is a huge shock to the system. The guys coming out of a hookup app aren't likely great candidates for adjusting to domestic bliss.

But I have to give it a shot.

I'm determined to have a lengthier call with Havannah than I've managed so far this past week. The time zones, the meetings, the wine-and-dines have all added up to little time for anything.

But things are working out. The business in Milan should wrap up in a day or two, and I can head stateside again.

We finally catch a break on Friday afternoon, which is early morning for her. She's somewhat breathless but agrees to FaceTime so I can see her.

Her hair is up in a ponytail, loose tendrils all around her pinked-up face.

"What's got you all hot and heavy?" I ask her.

"Tried…to…run…with the stroller," she says. "Ugh. I'm so out of shape!"

"Back at it, then?"

She flops on the sofa, the image a blur for a second, then I see her against the floral cushions. "I'm determined to fit in my old dresses."

"We can shop for new ones," I say. "You're perfect." She sticks out her tongue, and I laugh at the sheer silliness. "Where's that baby?"

She turns the phone to a black stroller, where Rebel is sacked out. "He took a nap while I nearly died of heatstroke."

There's that dramatic flair I enjoy.

She turns the phone back to herself and flings an arm over her forehead. "How is Italy?"

"I think I'll be able to return to the good ol' US of A on Tuesday."

She moves her arm to peer at the screen in surprise. "Really?"

"Absolutely."

"But you'll be behind on your work in New York, I bet." She bites her lip, probably trying to control her expectations. I get it. My lifestyle is a lot, and I did have to abandon her in Milan.

"Not so much. I have a few meetings, then I'm hitting the road."

"Flying over any mountainous regions?" She can't hide the hope in her expression.

"I'm thinking a night in Boulder will make it onto the agenda."

She pops up from the sofa, blurring her feed again. "Are you serious?"

I laugh. She's so excited. It's such a refreshing thing to see after the jaded and closed-off society women I've run with for the last few years.

"It's my hope. I'm going to do my level best to get there. Tell me where you've always wanted to stay and I will make it happen."

"Ooh." She walks around her apartment, her hair askew. "There's a fancy hotel here with a spa."

"Consider it done. Any packages to book?"

"Not sure. I'll have to worry about Rebel. And mainly I want to see you."

"I can have them come to the room."

Her eyes get big. "Then *yes*. All the things. All. The Things." She falls back on the sofa. "Dating a bazillion-aire has its perks."

"And its downsides."

"If you didn't have a plane, I wouldn't see you at all," she says.

"Quite possibly true." I head to the balcony. "Take a look at Milan." She sits up, peering into the camera. I turn my phone and slowly pan it over the view. "Where history meets the modern era," I say.

"It's lovely. I got to see some of it as we drove to the airport."

"Hopefully one day we can return."

She casts her gaze off to the side, as if she's thinking.

"Everything okay, Havannah?"

"Oh, gosh. Well…"

So something *is* up. I thought I heard it in her voice. There are a thousand things it could be, all legitimately aimed at me, since I jettisoned her with no notice.

"Are you upset about Milan?" I ask.

Her eyes pop back to the screen. "No! Oh, no. It's nothing to do with you."

"Is your dad still mad about us seeing each other?"

She grins. "Probably." Then she sobers. "No, this is about Rebel's dad."

"The one in jail?"

"Actually…" She bites her lip again. "Oh, this will sound bad."

I re-enter the suite to escape the heat and settle on an armchair, leaning forward so I can concentrate on her. "Did he get out? Are you in danger?"

"No! I mean, not that I know of. I doubt it." She focuses on the ceiling. "I'm thinking he's not the father after all."

"Oh?" I try to take this in. Havannah mentioned in France that he was a one-night stand. If he's not the one, there must have been others.

"I got a little wild there for a while." She shifts the phone, and the view is only of her ceiling. "So this is another guy."

I keep my voice level as I ask, "What made you realize it could be someone else?"

She turns the camera back to her. Her face is flushed again. "I learned some things—from Sunny—about conception dates. Turns out mine was about ten days later than I thought."

Ten days. So she had a couple of rendezvous. That doesn't seem too crazy. "Who is this other guy?"

"His name is Brian. I'm going to meet with him this afternoon. See if he'll do a DNA test."

I picture Havannah being accosted by some strange man while holding Rebel, and my concern rises. "Is he safe? What do you know about him?"

She shrugs. "He was all right the night I met him. A bit nerdy. He's a computer programmer. Nothing wild."

"Where are you meeting?"

"A coffee shop. Very public."

"Are you bringing Rebel?"

"Oh, no. Magnolia is watching him. I'll try to bring it up gently."

I realize I'm clutching the armrest with an iron grip. I force myself to release it. "What will happen if he's the one?"

"I don't know. I haven't thought that far ahead."

"If you need a lawyer, or any legal help, I can give you some options."

"I know. That's great. I feel like, I don't know, maybe I should handle this on my own." She gives me a small smile. "I'm a big girl."

"I know. I worry. What time is the meeting? Can I talk to you after?"

"Not until six. It will be, like, two or three in the morning there."

"I don't care. I'll wait up."

"Okay, Donovan. I'll let you know how it goes."

She changes the subject after that, and we talk about the castle again, and how she's looked into the tourism programs that might be like the ones in Europe. "Just for fun," she says. "I was curious. I already have a degree in hospitality."

"You want a castle, eh?"

"I guess that's something you could drum up in a day."

"It does seem there are some for sale." I click on a

few keys, bringing up castles in France and the U.K. "I see about ten in my price range."

"You have a price range?"

"Not really." And it's true—I could procure any of them. Not that they'd be a good investment.

She laughs. "Is there anything you can't do?"

"Hold you in my arms."

She sighs. "True. We're pretty far apart."

"Soon, though. I'll move heaven and earth to get there."

"That will be perfect." She closes her eyes. "Until then, I'll just have to picture you on a balcony."

"Now that's a good memory."

"And imagine reliving it all over again."

"We will."

We sit in silence for a while, both of us thinking about the future moments we'll have together.

And I try to push her meeting with this Brian guy out of my mind.

31

HAVANNAH

I figure the other coffee shop is bad luck, and Magnolia agrees, as it's the same place where she first learned her feud with Anthony had gone viral, and not in a good way.

So I pick a Starbucks for its bright interior and commercial familiarity. I can't imagine anything going epically wrong in a Starbucks.

When I arrive, Brian is already there. I remember him a little better than the others, mostly because we went to a nice dinner and had an actual conversation before getting down to the matter we'd joined the app for.

He stands up and heads over to me, his expression rather serious. "Hello, Havannah. You said it was important we see each other."

"Let me get a latte first," I say, and I notice that even though Brian was certainly a gentleman the first time, he doesn't offer to head to the counter with me or buy me a coffee.

It's fine. I put in my order and join him at a table in the center of the room.

He's pale, with thin, fine hair in a corporate cut. He looked more outdoorsy on the app, kayaking with a helmet on. Probably an old picture. But compared to Mark and Jesse, he's awesome. Total dad material.

"So I guess you remember we hooked up almost a year ago," I say.

He nods. "I'm not on the app anymore. I only got your message because it was forwarded to my email. I deleted it from my phone, but I guess the app still sends notifications from old matches."

"I'm glad. It was rather urgent I talk to you."

"Is something wrong? Do you have a diagnosis or something I should be concerned about?"

He's worried about an STD. I draw in a long breath and unlock my phone. I pull up a photo of Rebel. I turn it to him.

"Who's this?" he asks.

"I had a baby two months ago. It puts conception in early October."

He stares at the image, the color slowly draining from his face. "He's mine?"

"I'm not totally sure. I'm hoping you'll take a DNA test." I quickly add, "I don't expect anything from you. I have a great family and lots of support. I just want to know for sure."

"But if he's my kid…" He can't take his eyes off the photo.

"We can work that out." Panic darts through me. Maybe he'll try to take Rebel from me. Have I misjudged? Was this the biggest mistake I could have made?

"Do you have other pictures?"

"You're asking a mama if she has pictures of her baby?" I laugh and try to lighten the mood, but my belly is tight.

I quickly zip past the trip and find a safe cache of images from Rebel's first six weeks. Brian watches them go by, rapt. "How long will the test take?"

"I brought a kit. It's a few days. Rebel is already done."

"That's his name? Rebel?" He can't take his eyes off the screen.

I nod. "Rebel Zachariah."

Brian finally breaks his gaze from the phone. "Okay. Where's the kit?"

I dig through my purse and pull it out. "Here. It's prepaid."

"Will I get the result?"

"I can send you the login."

"I'd appreciate that. It's not that I don't trust you."

I hold up a hand. "I get it. Honestly, you're taking this well."

He shakes his head. "I have to. We might have a long relationship ahead."

Relationship. I know what he means, a parental one and not a couple one, but he's right. If he is the dad, and the revised dates suggest he might be, we'll know each other for all of Rebel's life.

"I think that's your drink," Brian says. "I'll get it."

He stands up to head to the counter. So he's being polite. The baby has changed his tune.

He sets the drink in front of me. "Are you hungry? Can I get you anything else?"

I shake my head. This is a complete turnaround from Jesse the jailbird and disappearing Marco Polo.

He sits down. "You said you weren't sure. So there's someone else?"

I nod. "That's why I didn't contact you before. I thought someone else was the father. But it turns out my dates were wrong. So you became a candidate."

"How likely a candidate?"

I wrap both hands around my cup. "A highly likely candidate."

Brian lets out a rush of air. "This is a lot."

"I know. It was a lot for me when I found out. And you know, *had a baby*."

"I wish I could have been there to help. Did you go through it all alone?"

"I have an amazing sister. My family had a hard time with it at first, but now that he's here, they're in love with him."

"They don't ask about the father?"

"All the time. But I've put them off."

Silence falls between us, the music from the speakers filling in the quiet. The barista calls out, "Stephen! Mocha latte!"

Brian stares at his cup. "Were you scared?"

He does seem to want to know about my welfare. "Sure. I thought I was in labor once, but I was wrong. The second time I was in a restaurant when my water broke…" I trail off, deciding not to mention Donovan. "But my family surrounded me and we got it done."

"Will you need support? Can you afford him?"

"I'm not rich or anything, but my sister and I run a deli. We're getting by okay."

His eyes, a pale green flecked with brown, meet mine. For a moment, I pang with regret. If I told him at the beginning, if I knew, he could have been there for all the things he's missed. Maybe *we* might have had a relationship. Maybe Rebel would have been surrounded by a loving mother and father the whole time.

I shake it off. It could still not be him. There's dreaded Marco Polo. But something about the way Brian's eyebrows gather when he's worried reminds me of Rebel. I can see him in the baby.

Maybe it's wishful thinking. But as we say our goodbyes and Brian promises to meet me when we get the results, I can't help but wonder what might have been if my cycle was normal. If I'd known more about sonogram dating. If I told my doctor I was trying to weed out candidates, and he went over the information with me. I shouldn't have been so embarrassed and stupid about it.

But here we are.

Brian walks me to my car, carefully closing my door and waving as I pull out of my slot. A gentleman.

I feel like my whole life rests on that one little test.

32

DONOVAN

I manage to wrap up my Milan business on Monday rather than Tuesday, so I decide to fly straight to Boulder to surprise Havannah.

From our conversations, I already know she's more or less given up on doing much with the deli. She tried for a few days after her parents insisted, but something about the noise in the dining room set Rebel off into a storm of inconsolable crying. She thinks it must be a combination of the acoustics and some developmental phase he's in.

Since she can't bake or chop in the kitchen with him in the sling, she's back to doing social media work from home. She confessed during one conversation that she often feels like the new deli isn't even hers.

I want to give her the time of her life in her own town, so I book the biggest suite in one of the few luxury hotels in Boulder. I plan for massages and facials and mani-pedis, everything I can get on a flexible schedule to work around Rebel. It will be perfect.

I check in before heading out to find her, wanting everything to be in place. Champagne on ice. Cheese plates in the fridge. Fruit and chocolate. I picked up a silky robe in Milan that I can't wait to take off her.

When I'm done, I hop into the limo and text her, trying to get a bead on where she's at, schedule-wise. I assume she's at home.

She says she's about to head to Starbucks with Rebel, and I think—perfect. A public surprise is even better, because I can find her rather than knock on her door.

A quick search shows me over a dozen of them in town, but only three are likely candidates, closest to her apartment.

I head to the first one and pop in. Only a couple of customers are inside, students with headphones.

I move on to the next one. Busier, but no Havannah.

I wish I knew what car she drives. We stop at the third one, and this time I catch a flash of long blond hair inside a window. Could that be her?

I pause outside the door, checking the collar of my polo and squaring my shoulders. This is going to be great.

The music is louder inside than I expect. The place is busy. I step inside, and sure enough, there is Havannah, her back to me, Rebel waving his arms in his car seat.

But I'm frozen in place. There's a man sitting at their table. He pushes a piece of paper across to Havannah, and she nods, setting it aside as if she already knows what it says.

He turns to the baby and says, "I'm not sure what to do!"

"It's easy." Havannah unclips the harness and lifts Rebel out of the seat.

I step to the side of the door, not sure what to do myself. This must be the man Havannah thinks is the father. The computer guy.

In fact, based on this exchange, it looks like they've figured it out.

And he *is* the father.

She didn't tell me about this meeting, and I assume that was on purpose. I don't know exactly why, although I trust she has her reasons. The last thing I heard was that he agreed to take the test.

Havannah stands, and so does the man. She passes the baby to him. There's a look of wonder on his face. He seems totally fine with this turn of events. I can't see Havannah's expression.

The man stares at the baby, and my gut tightens. Rebel reaches up, and his fist connects with the man's chin. He smiles and takes the tiny hand in his.

He glances up at Havannah. "He's perfect," he says. "He's a little you."

I can't quite catch what Havannah says back to him. He drops in his chair, his hand on Rebel's chest. Havannah sits back down. She has no idea I'm here.

And I shouldn't be.

Because what is taking place looks perfect. Like what should be happening.

Like what is meant to be.

When the man turns to Havannah, his eyes full of

emotion, I know I need to give them their space. I should not intrude here. Maybe not ever. Because they have things to figure out.

And as an honorable person recognizing a difficult situation, I should remove myself from the narrative until they do. At least until Havannah tells me herself about the situation. Maybe the two of them are developing feelings. Maybe it's going to work out for Rebel that he has both a mother and a father.

So without a word, I ease back out of the door and to my limo. I cancel the room and the appointments. I have staff gather up all the food and drinks and pack my things to be sent by courier to the airport.

I ask Simon to submit a flight plan back to New York and have the limo driver take me out to the airfield.

At least until Havannah wants to share with me about the turn her life is taking, my relationship with her needs to go on hold.

33

HAVANNAH

Magnolia waits for me at home when I return from Starbucks, cross-legged on the sofa with a pint of ice cream.

"You look like you could walk on air," she says.

Rebel is asleep, so I set the car seat on the floor and flop onto the sofa beside her. "I'm feeling pretty good."

"So it went well?"

She already knows Brian is the father. We pulled up the results online together before I called him to meet.

"He was so amazing, Mags. Really took to the baby. We're going to have dinner tomorrow night. He wants to be involved."

Mags stares into her half-empty pint. "Dinner?"

"With the baby."

"Is there something happening between the two of you?"

"Oh, gosh. That's a question! I liked how he was with Rebel. He's a natural."

She presses her lips together. I can see the disapproval all over her face.

"What about Donovan?"

"He should be here this week if things go well," I say. "Maybe even tomorrow."

"But you're having dinner with Brian tomorrow."

I sit up. "Right! Oh, shit! I can reschedule with Brian if Donovan makes it."

Magnolia sets the ice cream on the coffee table as if she suddenly can't stand the sight of it. "Are you going to end up in some clichéd love triangle?"

"No! Of course not! I'm completely Team Donovan."

"Be careful," Magnolia says. "There's a lot of hearts involved."

"I know it."

My phone dings, and I dig it out of the diaper bag. It's Donovan.

My stomach falls as I read.

Sorry to reroute our plans, but my pit stop in Boulder has to be delayed. Rain check?

I type, *Of course,* and drop the phone to the cushion.

"What's going on?" Magnolia asks.

"Donovan can't come after all." My head falls back on the sofa. I focus on a water stain on the ceiling.

"I'm sorry." Mags nudges me with the pint. "It's a third full."

I take it from her and carve out a spoonful.

We sit for a moment, and I let the cold, creamy goodness slip down my throat. "It's not going to work out with him, is it?" I ask.

Magnolia kicks her feet up on the coffee table. "It's hard for him to get here, obviously."

"I'm not good with long-distance things."

"You're not good with short-distance things."

I nudge her again, and she laughs.

"It's true, though," she says.

"I know." I swallow another bite of ice cream. "Do you think it could be different with Brian?" As much as my heart screams Donovan, maybe I do have to face facts. He's a billionaire with a busy life.

Magnolia twirls her ponytail around her finger. "What was Brian like a year ago?"

"A little dull to talk to. But nice. Courteous."

"Nice and courteous. The opposite of what my sister normally goes for."

She's not lying. "I know."

"And in the sack?" She elbows me. "Because we know where your priorities lie."

"It was fine. Nothing wild, nothing terrible."

"Such a ringing endorsement."

I lick the spoon. I want to steer the conversation away from any potential involvement between me and Brian. "What's the wildest thing you've ever done?" I ask her.

"With Anthony?"

"With anybody."

"Well, it would be with Anthony."

I nudge her with my shoulder this time. "So Anthony's a wild child?"

Her cheeks go pink. "Sometimes."

"Tell your sister. What wild thing did you two do?"

"I shouldn't."

Now she has my interest. "Oh, you totally should."

"We might have used Dad's office."

I sit up straight. "*What?*"

She realizes she's managed to shock the queen of shock and sinks into the sofa. "He wasn't in town. He wasn't going to catch us."

"Wait. You have your *own* office right next door, but still you and hotcakes Pickle decide to use your *father's*? Dayum, Mags."

"He has a better chair," she says, her voice small.

I fling my arms out so fast that the ice cream spoon flies across the room. "*In his chair?*" I push myself off the sofa to pick up my spoon, shaking my head. My sister, banging her guy in my father's office chair. "You know I've got blackmail material now."

She shrugs. "Can't prove anything. And you have the ultimate proof of *your* transgressions about to start crying because he pooped his diaper." She gestures at the car seat, where Rebel is squirming in his harness.

The smell hits me. She's right. "A mother's work is never done." I pass her the ice cream and kneel down to free him from the seat.

"So what now?" Magnolia asks. "I thought you and Donovan hit it off."

Her words gnaw at me. "We did. We have. Oh, Mags, I don't know. He seems so far away. So impossible." I lay Rebel down on the changing pad. He's about to go at it, his eyes screwing up, face red. "You should have seen Brian. He was so excited about the baby. I think he fell right in love."

"Loving the baby isn't the same as loving you," Mags says.

"Donovan doesn't love me either," I fire back. "And now he can't even get to me."

Rebel starts to howl, so I swiftly get him cleaned and changed and bring him to my shoulder.

"Don't be in a rush as you go through this tough phase," Magnolia says when it's quiet enough to hear her. "Take your time. These decisions are a big, big deal. They affect everyone."

Rebel mouths my shoulder, so I move him down so he can nurse. As he settles on the boob, happy and content now that he's clean and getting fed, the whole situation falls over me like a heavy blanket.

What I do next will affect him most of all.

By the time my dinner with Brian arrives, I'm a wreck. Donovan not only canceled his visit, but he also skipped our usual phone call and has been super slow to respond to texts.

I know he's busy, and his work is important. But a tendril of doubt has invaded my happy memories. Maybe Donovan is only best at a fling. His lifestyle doesn't support a sustained relationship.

Brian, however, is in constant contact. I've sent pictures of Rebel and told the story of his birth, his name, and all the milestones since then.

I unload Rebel from the car in front of a modest restaurant near the Pearl. I immediately regret wearing my hair down when Rebel manages to capture a fist full of it and yanks. I spend long minutes in the heat trying to disentangle the strands from his tiny fingers.

I pause by the hostess stand, and she flashes a huge grin. "You must be Rebel's mother! Your party is over here!"

Party?

She turns, and my whole body goes on alert. A huge table lined with people is covered in balloons and packages. Brian stands at the end of it. "He's here!"

A great cheer goes up, and I plaster on a smile. "What a surprise!" I say, but nobody pays any attention to me. A mid-fifties woman and what appears to be her husband hurry over, peeking into the car seat at Rebel.

"He's the image of Brian when he was this age," the woman says. She turns to the man. "Isn't he?"

The man's eyes are shiny. "He is. Our first grandchild, Millie. Look at him."

I start to say, "He's two months—" but another woman butts in. She's younger, with short-cropped hair the color of Brian's. "Hi, Rebel! I'm your aunt Teddie! I'm going to spoil you rotten!" She turns to the older woman. "Can we take him out and hold him?"

I resist the urge to turn him aside and out of their clutches. They should be asking *me*!

Brian nudges his way forward. "Havannah, I'm so sorry to spring this on you."

"Are you?" My tone is harsher than I intend, and suddenly the party quiets, looking at me.

"They were all so excited," he says. "A new baby in

the family. I should introduce you. Why doesn't everyone sit down? We'll all get a chance to meet Rebel."

"What a name," Teddie murmurs, her gaze fixed on me.

I try to hold myself together. *Stay calm, Havannah. They don't know you, and this situation is pretty awkward.*

Brian leads me to his end of the table. There are about ten people total, and another young woman sits next to his spot. She's clearly not another sister, her warm olive skin and sleek black hair standing out from the others.

Between Brian's chair and my empty one, a sling is ready to hold the car seat. I set Rebel in it and sit down.

"Can we take him out?" Brian asks, and I'm relieved that at least he's respecting my role.

"I just fed him. As long as his diaper holds out, he'll probably be okay for a while."

Brian nods and makes a great show of unclipping the harness as if he's a master dad who knows all the moves. I sit upright in my chair, trying to be calm as he holds Rebel up for everyone to see, as if he's the monkey on the rock on *The Lion King.*

The table erupts in happy gasps, "Look at him," and "He's adorable."

"I'd like a turn," the woman next to Brian says. "If I may." She looks to me for confirmation.

I appreciate this. "Of course," I say.

She takes the baby and arranges him carefully in her arms. She's not practiced with babies and seems nervous, but she's game. I wonder who she is. Finally I lean over to Brian. "Should I be introduced?"

He tugs at his collar and his neck goes red. What's that about?

The woman glances up at him and lifts an eyebrow. "Havannah, it is nice to meet you. Brian told me about you yesterday. The news was quite a surprise."

"I'm sure," I say. I feel the penetrating judgment of the whole table as gazes shift to me.

"I'm glad you got the DNA test to confirm things," the woman continues. "That way the family can be confident going forward."

Going forward with what? Maybe this is a family lawyer. My belly quakes. Could they take him from me? Is there some legal loophole they can exploit since I didn't let him know before?

I wish I brought Magnolia, my parents, anyone in my corner. I feel at a sharp disadvantage.

Instead of speaking with her directly about whatever she might mean, I say to Brian, "We have a lot to work out. Rebel is nursing full-time, so visitations away from me aren't possible at this point."

"Of course," he says. "We're just glad to meet him."

Rebel makes a fuss, but when I move to stand and get him, the first woman hustles over. "Let me have that little guy. Grandma Millie has the touch."

The woman passes Rebel to her, and I have to practically sit on my hands to avoid snatching him back. Now free of the baby, she extends a hand across the table. "I'm sorry we haven't been introduced. I think Brian's nervous. I'm Delphine, his fiancée."

I barely register my hand reaching out to shake hers. I spot the diamond on her finger. His fiancée. Brian is engaged, and he didn't say a word about it.

The red creeps up his neck. "We didn't get around to all the relationships," he says. "It's been a lot to take in."

Delphine releases me, and I tuck my hand back in my lap. I have no idea what to say to any of this, but I manage, "Congratulations."

Rebel starts fussing harder, so I unclip his pacifier from the seat and walk it over to Millie, relieved to escape the latest surprise.

There's an extra chair next to her, and she pulls it out. "Please sit here, Havannah," she says. "We'd love to get to know you. We're all family now. I'm Millie, and this is Jared, Brian's father."

I pass her the pacifier and sit in the chair. It's probably easier to sit here than down there, next to the couple who no doubt have been shaken up by the news of the baby. It's been a solid year since my hookup with Brian, but that doesn't mean he met her after me. She might have just learned about him cheating.

There could be a lot more to their story and how it intersects with mine.

Grandma is definitely easier.

"Do you have family here in Boulder?" Millie asks.

"Yes," I say, relieved for an easy topic. "My parents are John Paul and Malina Boudreaux. They own the Tasty Pepper deli."

Jared turns to us, his pale gray eyes alight. "I eat there all the time! It's right next to my law office."

"I've met him there many times," Millie says. "It's a lovely establishment."

"My grandparents started it," I say. "My sister and I opened a second deli a few months ago."

Teddie leans forward from the other side of Jared. "I read about that. Tasty Mango. It's a pretty place. I saw the pictures."

They're not as horrible as my first impression. "I decorated it. I only got to work a week or so before this guy came along." I tweak Rebel's shoe.

He's in the outfit Donovan bought for him in Paris. A pang of need for Donovan to be here hits me hard. I had so much more confidence in his presence.

"We should have met there!" Millie says. "We'll make a point to stop in more, meet the other grandparents."

This is going better than it did at first. I relax my shoulders. This will work.

"Let me get a moment with that tyke," Jared says. "I haven't held a little one in twenty years, since Teddie was born."

Millie turns to me. "Is he okay being handled so much? He's quite small."

"He'll let you know," I say.

Millie passes the baby to Jared. "How did you come by his name?" Millie asks.

"It's my maternal grandfather's middle name," I say.

"And Rebel has Boudreaux for a last name, I take it?" she asks.

"Yes." I'm about to add that I didn't know Brian was the father, but think better of it.

"We have a lot of questions, of course," Jared says.

"And they can wait for another time," Millie adds.

Jared nods. I remember he's a lawyer, and my belly quakes again. We're not flush with money to hire someone if we have a fight. We sank everything we had into the second deli.

I pray I've done the right thing.

Millie reaches over to squeeze my forearm. "I can see your worry, Havannah. We're not here to make things harder for you. We are excited to meet this baby, no matter how it came about. The rest is between you and Brian."

I glance over at the end of the table. Brian and Delphine lean close together, talking quietly.

"How long have they been engaged?" I ask.

Millie glances over at Jared before answering. "Only a few months."

"This is a big deal," Teddie says. "They broke up about a year ago. Probably around when Brian met you. And while they were apart, they decided they were better together. Decided to get married but only made the engagement official in March."

That explains a lot. Or at least that's the story they're putting out there. Regardless, Rebel's here, and he's Brian's baby, and he'll be part of their story.

I stay at the grandparents' end of the table for the remainder of the dinner. A million pictures of Rebel are taken, me and Rebel, me and Rebel and Brian. Delphine declines to be in any of them, and I wonder if she's distancing herself.

Rebel conks out, so he's easy for family members to

hold. When it's time to feed him, I let them know we should go, with a promise for another meeting so everyone can get to know him.

"Havannah," Millie says, "when you're ready to leave him for longer periods, I will be happy to watch him if you want to work between feedings. I'm at home all day."

Wow, that would be a help. "Thank you."

She kisses my cheek. "I'm so happy to have met you and Rebel. Please let's get together again soon."

Brian walks me out to my car. "I'm sorry we didn't get to talk much," he says.

"It's okay. Your parents were lovely."

Brian opens the door, and I snap Rebel's seat into place.

We stand by the car. I glance back at the restaurant and see Delphine by the window, watching us from inside as the rest of the table gathers their things. I have a feeling she might not like how quickly her future mother-in-law took to me.

"I hope this hasn't caused problems with you and your fiancée," I say.

"I'm sorry I didn't tell you before. To be honest, I thought she might break it off when she learned about Rebel. She can be jealous."

"So were you two broken up when you got on that app?"

Brian looks away, his hand on the back of his neck. "We were. Sort of. She said she didn't want to marry me, and so I told her I needed to move on. It wasn't as clean as a breakup, but then we didn't speak for a few days. I got on the app as a dare to myself. I wasn't in a good place."

I hold up a hand. "Say no more. It's fine. You two have worked it out, and she seems dedicated to proving she can handle the baby."

"She does. We've got a ways to go on repairing this." He turns to the restaurant and also spots her watching. She holds firm, though, arms crossed.

"I think maybe it's best if we arrange things through your mom for a while," I say. "Until Delphine gets used to this whole thing."

"That's a good idea." Brian steps farther from me, as if trying to prove to Delphine that this isn't anything intimate.

"It will be okay. As long as we put Rebel first when we make our decisions, we'll be fine."

Brian's gaze meets mine. "You've changed since that crazy night last October."

"That's what being a mother does," I say. "I wouldn't change a thing."

He nods. "Did you get Mom's number?"

"I did. She'll let you know when we're meeting up again."

"Good, good." He ducks back inside the car, where Rebel sucks fiercely on his pacifier. I have about ten minutes before he goes full howl from hunger. "Goodnight, Rebel. See you soon."

When I'm finally heading home, my nerves start to calm. This night was completely unexpected. Probably

Brian is not the man I'd choose under normal circumstances. But his parents are going to be a blessing and a help.

So maybe it was even better than I thought.

34

DONOVAN

The door to my office opens, and I instantly recognize the wild curls of Arianna's head as she peers in. "Are you decent?"

Damn. I'm supposed to have changed for the charity event tonight.

She steps inside and tilts her head as she surveys me. "I know some of these balls have gotten casual, but I don't think that's black-tie."

I quickly round my oversized cherry desk and head for my private bathroom. "Three minutes. I'll change faster than Superman."

"I believe he does it in about three seconds!" she calls as I lock myself inside.

I can't believe I let this slip. My head isn't in the game. I kick off my shoes and quickly switch out from my business suit to the tuxedo. A whole week has passed since my aborted trip to Boulder, and I've spent the majority of it brooding over Havannah like a lovesick kid.

I've been following hashtag trails on Instagram and comments on Facebook, all connected to images of Havannah being welcomed into the rather prestigious Miller family, who own an established law firm in Colorado. The original founder is Rebel's grandfather.

Based on the images, they threw a party for her, and the most popular picture is one of her and Rebel's father, all cozied up with the baby between them.

They look great together. If they have more children, they will probably all be stunners.

She's taken care of. I can let go.

The thoughts of losing her completely have slowed me down in getting changed, so I speed up buttoning my shirt. I can do my cuff links in the limo. I'm still shrugging on the coat jacket as I exit the room.

In the meantime, Dell has also entered my office, looking anxiously at his watch. "I don't like to be late," he says.

I snatch my keys from my desk. "I thought Grace broke you of all those bad habits. Timeliness and worry."

Arianna fusses with Dell's bow tie. "I wish," she says. "But I think baby number two is going to be the one that fixes everything." She steps back and pats the bulge beneath her silver satin dress. She's starting to show more every day.

Dell glances around the room. "I thought you had a date for this."

I shake my head. "I gave my ticket to the new girl on staff. I assume she'll figure out how to get there."

He nods. "We should go, then."

"Give me that," Arianna says, taking my bow tie from me. "And don't forget your cuff links."

"Yes, Mom."

She whacks me lightly on the shoulder. "Someone has to keep you in line."

When we're in the private executive elevator, she works on my tie. "Speaking of which, how is Havannah?"

"Fine," I say, lifting my chin to give her room as she works the tie. I refuse to admit out loud that I haven't had any communication with her in a couple of days. It seems our affair has wound to its conclusion.

"I don't like the sound of that *fine*," Arianna says. "I like her. You seemed happy with her. And that baby was precious."

My eyes meet Dell's over Arianna's head. He lifts his eyebrows and shrugs.

"She's pretty tied up back in Boulder," I say. "Seems like she's connected with Rebel's paternal family."

Arianna pauses, her hands still near my throat. "Really? I thought she wasn't saying who the father was."

"She is now." I'm not going to elaborate. I don't know what Havannah wants known.

The elevator doors open, and I step away from Arianna. "I can finish this in the car."

The limo waits in the garage just outside the door. We load inside and speed into New York traffic.

When we're settled, Arianna leans over as if she's about to ask me another question.

Dell puts his hand on her arm. She tosses him a

look, but leans against his shoulder. They're good at this, the silent communication.

"I think this should be a fun evening," she says.

"That makes one of us," Dell says.

"Oh, Dell. You know we're doing this to get an opportunity to network with the Williamson family. I'd like to have them on my side if we're going to open that school."

"I know, honey. I'm game."

They continue talking about their strategy for the evening. I have none. We bought this table eons ago. The only reason I gave my second ticket to the new assistant is that it's important not to have an empty space when you're trying to make an impression. Dell and Arianna are.

I can't even remember the name of the young woman who will be coming. Susan? Sally? My assistant handled it. I should text him to ask, but I don't bother.

The driver is well versed in back streets, and despite my delay, we manage to make it to the venue while limousines are still pulling up and letting out other arrivals.

Dell and Arianna immediately find their mark and head over to schmooze. I aim for the bar.

With a brandy procured, I wander through the sea of tables to find mine. I will have to stay through at least the dinner. But once the mingling recommences, I can easily slip out and go home.

Only one person is seated at our table. It must be the girl from the office. She looks around nervously.

I plan to sit across from her, but realize that might

wreck the organization of the couples, so I take a spot beside her.

"You must be Donovan McDonald," she says, rather breathless. She's quite young, the low side of twenty-five, dressed in a simple black dress with only a plain gold chain for jewelry. She looks like a baby compared to the women who spent more on their facials than this girl's entire ensemble. Her hair is a curtain of dark brown, straight and unadorned.

"The one and only," I say. "I'm glad you could make use of the extra ticket."

"Oh, I love it. This is fancy." She glances at my drink. "Do you have to pay for those? I don't know how these things work."

I can't help but quirk a smile. It's always amusing to see the people who are unused to these affairs. "Completely open bar. No tipping. If you can see it, you can generally have it."

Only after I say it do I realize it might be construed as an invitation. I glance around, hoping nobody's watching and thinking I'm hitting on this young ingénue.

But my words seem to roll right past her. "I'm awfully nervous," she admits.

"Don't be. Can I get you something from the bar?"

"I would love some champagne. Should I come with you?"

"Sure. I can introduce you to some people." I stand up and pull back her chair. "I apologize that I didn't catch your name."

"Sylvie." She tucks a piece of hair behind her ear,

making her look even younger. Oh boy. I glance around, noting the positions of the event's official photographers. I will avoid them completely.

"All right, Sylvie." We head to the bar, and after procuring a glass of champagne, we wander through the mingled groupings. I'm looking for anyone I can introduce the girl to and then excuse myself.

"Is that a famous fashion designer?" Sylvie asks. "Oh my gosh. Is that the mayor?"

"Correct on both counts. Would you like to meet the mayor?"

She shakes her head. "No, no, no, no. I'm way too nervous."

"I'm sure you'd be fine." Despite my anxiety to offload her before anyone gets the wrong idea, I do find her amusing. I've forgotten what it's like to be around young people who can still get stars in their eyes over power and fame.

A photographer spies me. I plan to turn and duck, but he's too fast. As I take her arm to spin us around, he manages a quick shot.

Great. Exactly what I didn't want to happen.

I steer Sylvie back toward our table before anyone else gets any ideas. "Everyone will be sitting down soon. We should probably head back."

"Okay!" She takes my comment at face value.

We pass Dell and Arianna, and her eyebrows shoot up when she sees me with the girl. *I know. I know.* She's a baby. Good grief. I erred in my choice. I should have had her bring a date and bowed out completely.

Sitting alone is an even bigger mistake now that

we've been seen. I can feel the lenses aimed at us. This night will never end.

At last, the others settle around us. Sylvie talks very little during the dinner. Arianna asks her a few polite questions. Even though I know I shouldn't, as soon as people start wandering the room again after the dessert course, I ditch the whole lot of them and head home.

But the damage is done. Pictures of me and Sylvie hit some of the gossip sites by midnight.

Financial magnate Donovan McDonald returns to the society scene with a pretty young thing. Is she the reason he's been off the market all this time?

I read it ruefully and text my assistant to make sure the girl is given the heads-up about the publicity.

I pull up Havannah's name on my phone to explain the errant picture. I don't want her to get the wrong idea either.

But then I look at the date of our last message and realize it's been days. I've had relationships last less time than that.

The point is probably moot. She's spent much of her time with the Millers, based on the images popping up everywhere. The youngest Miller, Teddie, has devoted an entire new Instagram account to her nephew, so it's obvious how they've all taken to Havannah and the new family member. In the pictures, Havannah is always happy and smiling and dressed to impress.

It's probably best to let this fizzle out.

The decision done, I harden myself to the concept of wanting to see her or wondering how the baby is doing. I unfollow the Instagram account and clear my search histories.

She's part of my past.

I strip out of my tuxedo tie and jacket and head to my home office.

In fact, it's probably time to get my head back in the game.

And work.

35

HAVANNAH

I'm barely awake, nursing Rebel in bed, when Magnolia tiptoes into my bedroom in the last hour before dawn.

"Hey, sis," she says quietly. "You up?"

"Mostly." I shift the baby more securely against me. At this point, he can sometimes drain me so fast that I have to push him closer to get the rest.

She sits on the corner of the bed. "Have you checked your phone yet?"

"I forgot to charge it. It's totally dead. I was going to fetch it when Rebel was done."

She hops up again. "I'll get it."

"I thought you were sleeping over at Anthony's."

"I came back." She plugs the cord into the phone but keeps hold of it.

Now I'm more alert. "At this hour? Why?"

"You weren't answering your phone. I couldn't sleep. I was worried."

Now I'm alarmed. "Why would you be worried?"

My phone gets enough of a charge that it lights up. Immediately, tone after tone starts to beep through. Uh oh.

I sit up, bringing Rebel with me. "What's going on?"

"Remember when we saw that article about how Donovan must be off the market because he wasn't attending charity events with the society women?"

This is about Donovan. My body clenches. "Is he dead?"

"What? No!" Magnolia sits again. "Of course he's not dead. Why would I bring up the charity events if he was dead?"

"Sorry. That's where my mind went."

"Well, if that's what you're worried about, maybe this is nothing."

She passes me the phone, but I can't manipulate it easily with one hand. I set it on the bed. "I assume there's a new article? Am I mentioned? Did they get pictures from the wedding after all? Donovan said they had a nondisclosure contract with the photographers there. Maybe it was a guest who released something."

"It's not you."

"Then what?"

"He went to a charity ball last night. With some woman. A young one."

My heart falls. Even though we've been winding down, it's hard to know he's moving on. "Maybe he asked her before. He probably gets tickets months in advance."

"Maybe." Magnolia is no more convinced than I am.

I try to get to my messages, but my hand is at the wrong angle and I keep hitting the wrong buttons. I glance down at Rebel. I think he's close enough to done. "Here, take him," I say to Magnolia.

I dig into the notifications. The first message is from Dad. *What the hell is this?* It includes a link to the article about Donovan.

God. "Did Dad do a Google Alert on Donovan?" I ask.

Magnolia sighs. "He might have asked me how."

"Mags!"

"I told him it was a bad idea."

There are several from Magnolia. *Havannah? H? Hey, are you up? Don't jump to conclusions. I'm worried. Please answer me, H!*

Then one from Brian. *Delphine sent me this. Isn't this the guy you told Mom about?* I groan. I mentioned Donovan to Millie during one of our visits, when she seemed worried I was all alone in the world.

Boy, do I regret that now. I should have known she'd tell Brian and that Delphine would be watching.

I open Brian's message to reply to him first, but then realize I don't know what to say.

"There's a series of pictures in the link," Magnolia says.

I click on it.

It's Donovan in a tux, looking incredibly gorgeous. He's holding a brandy and sits next to a terribly young woman in a dress that doesn't quite fit.

In the next one, they're standing, and he's got his hand on her arm. Her hair isn't styled and her shoes probably came from a discount store. I know, because I've seen them when *I* shop. This is not his usual partner in crime.

I zoom in on his face. He looks miserable and very wary of whoever is holding the camera. He does not want to be photographed and seems tired of the whole ordeal.

"He's not with her," I say. "He doesn't want to be there." I click the photo away. "It's nothing."

"You sure?" Magnolia sounds skeptical.

"Completely."

I text Brian back now that I've seen the evidence. *Gossip rags make more money when it sounds like a juicy story. Happens to him all the time.*

I don't care that it's five a.m. I'll wake all of them up if they want to send me this crap. I text Dad too, for good measure. *Don't buy into the lies, Dad. You know better.*

I toss the phone down.

"You going to write Donovan?" Mags asks. Rebel is out cold in her arms.

"I'm not sure. We've been kind of quiet lately."

"Then how do you know this girl's not real?"

"I just do!" I don't intend to shout, but it comes out loud, startling Rebel. His arms fling out as a reflex, then he breaks into an unhappy cry.

"I'll change him," Mags says. "You pull yourself together." She heads for the living room.

It's seven a.m. in New York. Even on a Saturday, Donovan is probably up. He's an early riser.

I could text him. Or call him. Or request a video

call. That would tell me a lot more. If he turns it down, then I know he's with someone.

I don't care that it's been a couple of days since we texted or called. Our relationship has been sporadic from the beginning. Feast or famine. I need to know.

I hit the FaceTime button and wait for it to go through.

Waiting. Waiting.

He's with someone. They're sleeping in. Or maybe even doing other things.

I'm going to throw up. Despite what I said to Mags, how sure I was about this girl, I can feel the bile rising, crossing paths with my sinking heart. I was foolish to believe. I mean, how could this ever work?

Then suddenly, he's there, disheveled hair, eyes rimmed in red, like he's been on a bender.

My upset switches instantly to concern. "Donovan, are you okay?"

He nods. "Haven't slept. Decided to pull an all-nighter."

He's in the tux shirt, the top button undone. Is he at her house? Is this is a walk of shame?

I don't want to push him into a lie, but I have to ask: "What kept you up?"

"Nothing even that important," he says, rubbing his hand over his forehead.

"We haven't talked in a few days."

Something flickers across his face, something like— sadness? "Rebel keeping you on your toes?"

"No more than usual. And I'm getting a break today." I hesitate. Millie is taking Rebel to see how he does. I've already pumped the bottles. But I haven't talked much to Donovan about Brian or his family.

"That's great," he says. "What are you going to do with your freedom?"

He starts walking, and I study the scenes behind him. They don't look very feminine, all bold strokes in black and grays with the occasional flash of turquoise.

I realize I haven't answered. "Help out at the Tasty Mango. I haven't spent much time there."

He enters a kitchen, mostly black with stainless steel.

Finally, I can't stand not knowing any longer. "Is this your place?"

He glances around. "Yeah. I forget you've never been here." Another expression of regret crosses his face. "You want a video tour?"

"Sure." If he's willing to show it, then it must be his. Maybe he just got in from his wild night. Still seems odd he'd abandon her so early to be home by seven. He lingered in bed with me.

He videos his living room, the dining area, the balcony, a guest room, his bedroom, and he shows me the shower. His grin becomes mischievous. "I guess I could put on a show in here. I should get out of this tux."

"That might make me miss you too much," I say.

And just like that, we click back into our old ways. His lazy smile is back, the hungry look.

"Remember that huge bath in Saint-Tropez?" he asks. "The one with the water jets?"

"How could I forget?" Heat spreads through me. "What would you do to me there?"

This gets a genuine smile out of him. "What wouldn't I do? Remember the rose garden on the bench?"

"I do."

"That. For starters. Then that position on the chaise lounge on the balcony."

"I think about the balcony all the time." I can see it right now, in fact.

"Me too. You naked, my hands up in you. I liked the way you screamed when you thought dirty sailors were watching."

He's still standing in his shower, leaning on his arm, the phone low, aiming up at his face.

"Donovan, what are we doing?"

"I think it's called phone sex."

I laugh out loud. "I mean us. I hate that the press assumes everyone you stand next to is a dalliance."

His smile falls. "You saw it, then?"

"My dad sent it."

He shakes his head. "Good ol' John Paul. I'm sure he's glad to be rid of me."

"I'm not."

"But Rebel's dad. His family. Isn't it working out?"

"It might if his fiancée doesn't murder me."

Something flickers in his expression. "His what?"

"He's engaged. Not only that, they were only 'maybe' on a break when he found me on the hookup app a year ago."

"Oh, shit."

"'Oh, shit' right. But his mom is great. Because of the conflict, I'm mainly seeing her and the grandfather.

They're watching Rebel today. It's our first trial of him being over there without me."

"So you're not thinking of Brian as an option?"

I can't believe it. Is this why he stopped talking to me? To let me be with Brian?

I recover from my shock enough to shoot the accusation right back at him. "Are you thinking of that young thing in the picture as an option?"

"Point taken."

"Now that we're past that," I say, "where were we?"

"Phone sex," he says, and the intensity of his gaze tells me we really are past the hard stuff. We're getting the hang of this long-distance affair. There will be misunderstandings. But we will not make any assumptions.

"So, Mr. McDonald. I think you need to take that shirt off."

And he does.

Then a whole lot more.

36

DONOVAN

It's two weeks before I manage to cut loose of New York and get to Boulder for a weekend. But when the plane lands next to the mountains, a sense of peace comes over me. I'm in Havannah's world.

She suggested renting a house rather than a hotel so we can spread out, have Rebel part of the time, and send him to grandparents for the rest. I'm anxious as hell as I take the car that's brought out to the plane. I'm driving myself, another request of hers. She doesn't want limos or to show off.

I'm fine with it, and leave my business suits at home. We're going to eat burgers and hang out in parks. Be normal. I drive along the streets of Boulder toward the Tasty Mango, realizing I'm seeing so much more of the city from behind the wheel rather than distracted on my phone as a passenger.

I'm back to the Donovan who went to undergrad in Austin on scholarship, who used to work the greyhound race track by cleaning kennels. Who grew up without the insane lifestyle I've lived since taking over Dell's work.

I pull into the parking lot of Havannah's deli, impressed by how many spaces are taken. They're doing well. Havannah still feels distant from the family business, but she is getting to spend more time within its walls now that Rebel's grandmother is taking him for longer stints.

We've had long talks about her future. She feels a connection to the staff of the fairytale castle and wishes there was something equivalent near her other than Disney experiences. She wants classical majesty, not the cartoon version.

I want to buy a castle, hire a staff, and solve all her problems, but I recognize she has to work out some of them for herself.

I'm watching my brother as an example. Dell has helped in Arianna's dream of a school where children of wealthy, distracted parents are loved and nurtured rather than simply taught. He's figuring out when to step in, when to hold back. It's a balance between commerce and vision.

I broker big business deals every day. But for grand ideas to take flight, someone like Havannah has to have a dream. And that takes time, rumination, and learning. She's working on that.

When I pull on the door, I spot Havannah right away. She's behind the counter, greeting customers, cocking her head to listen to their orders. The line workers make the sandwiches, but she helps customers figure out exactly what they're after and suggests sides and additions. She's learned the value of the up-sell.

I catch her eye well before my turn comes. It's amazing to see her in real life rather than on the phone screen. She's different from when I last saw her in Milan. More sure of herself. Less harried. When she gives me a quick smile, the warmth in my chest tells me I'm exactly where I belong.

When I finally arrive at the end of the counter, I say, "So what's the best thing on the menu?"

She laughs and comes around, hooking her fingers on the belt loop of my jeans and pulling me close. "Me."

"I'll take it," I say, and lean in for the first kiss in weeks.

"I'll also take one of those," says a wavering voice behind me. Havannah and I turn to see an elderly man grinning up at us. His white-haired wife shrugs. "Happy to let her take him off my hands."

We can't help but laugh.

"I'll let the staff handle things," Havannah says.

"Oh no," I say. "I can't take you from work. I'll stand in line like everyone else."

Havannah flashes me a look, but returns to her position and tells me I'm going to get what I get. She explains my order to the line worker then moves on to the elderly man.

"I'll have what he's having!" the man says merrily.

Havannah leans on the glass cover over the line. "You sure about that? It's going to burn his face off."

Is it? I'm intrigued, but the elderly man seems concerned. "I guess I'll get my usual."

Ha. So he's a regular. Now it makes sense.

"Pastrami on rye, coming right up," she says. "Mrs. Whitestone, do you want your usual as well?"

"I think you should make him eat the new thing," she says. "Serves him right for treating women like it's 1952."

Havannah laughs. "Thankfully he's got a good heart, so we won't deal with him too harshly."

Mrs. Whitestone glances up at me. "Well, in that case, I'm up for a swap."

I almost choke, coughing through my own laugh.

"See, I can still make 'em react," Mrs. Whitestone says.

We move down the line, and Havannah greets the next group. There's a line to the door.

I get to the register, and a teen boy hands me a basket and a cup. "No charge," he says. "But I'd fill that cup to the top."

"Noted." I lift the basket, trying to scope out its contents. I fill my cup with tea and add cream and sugar, since plain water or soft drinks will be no match for anything with heat. Then I choose a table near the window with a good view of Havannah.

There's a side of some crispy, warm chips, and I choose one of those first. They're good, potatoes fried with sweet and spicy seasoning. I keep catching Havannah stealing glances at me, but I don't bite into the sandwich or even peek.

The line finally dwindles and she heads over, untying her Tasty Mango apron and setting it on the chair opposite me. She sits by my side. "You're not hungry? Or afraid?"

"Terrified. I'm game for eating it, but I like to know what I'm putting in my mouth."

She picks up my glass. "Tea with cream. You're a smart one. I wouldn't drink it, but I can see the benefit. Did you know my sister burned the inside of Anthony's mouth the first time they met?"

"The cooking show, right? Wasn't that an accident?"

"Or was it?" She grins at me, her chin resting on her linked fingers, batting her eyelashes.

I'm such a goner for her.

"Okay, let me see what is about to kill me." I lift the top bun on the foot-long sandwich. "I see pickles with an ominous red tinge, ham, I think, cheese with more ominous red bits, and an angry-looking spread. Did you add every item with a fire symbol from the menu?"

"Ding, ding, ding!" she says. "It's called the Fireball, and it's become more popular than Anthony's ghost pepper pickles. Both his deli and our deli serve it."

"The Fireball. Oh boy."

"Bon appétit!" She shoves my tea glass closer.

"The things I do for love." I lift the sandwich and shove the end in my mouth.

When I bite down, I see stars. Actual stars. The bun dissolves away into what feels like a ball of fire. They definitely named it right. I quickly chew and swallow, hoping to minimize the amount of time the hot lava inside this sandwich will spend in my mouth.

I snatch up the glass, trying to act casual but failing mercilessly, and gulp a third of its contents.

Havannah claps me on the back. "Surviving, Mr. McDonald?"

Much of the room has paused to watch. I cough a few times and say, "Did I pass the test?"

Havannah's smile is glorious. "With flying colors."

"Do I have to eat any more?"

She laughs. "Not a bit." She takes away the basket, and it's quickly replaced with a new one by the teen. "This one might be more to your liking."

It's a grilled cheese, oozing and flavorful. I take three bites before I can make myself stop. "It's amazing. What is it?"

She runs a finger along the table. "A little something we invented after I got back from France."

"Did you make this for me?" I ask.

She nods. "I didn't tell you about it because we weren't really connecting at the time. But it's called *Swiss You Were Here.*"

"It's fantastic." I reach for her hand. "You're amazing."

She glances around the deli. "I do like it here at the deli. But I have news. Big news. I wanted to tell you in person."

Now I'm intrigued. "What is it?"

"I applied for a French tourism program. If they accept me, I can do low residency and take the classes from here as long as I make one trip to France to do a two-week residency at a property there."

"That's amazing. Do I get to be the one to fly you to France?" I lift her fingers to my lips and press a soft kiss there.

Her gaze meets mine. "I was hoping so." She leans in, and her mouth on mine is like a feast after a long famine. I pull her close, my hands tangling in her hair.

"*Ahem.*"

We break apart to see Magnolia standing over us. She takes the apron from the chair as if she doesn't want her logo too close to us. "You guys get out of here. You're about to have sex on the table, and Millie only has Rebel for another hour."

We look at each other. "We can cover a lot of ground in an hour," Havannah says.

"I don't want to hear it!" Magnolia rushes off.

I take Havannah's hand. "The house isn't far from here. Stop by there first?"

"Totally." She picks up my basket as if she might toss it, but I rescue the sandwich first.

"I have to keep my strength up."

We hurry out to the car. The air is starting to cool in Colorado, and the view of the mountains in the distance proves how clear the air is. I shove the sandwich in my mouth and fire up the car.

As we drive along the pretty boulevards, I think, yes, I could probably take up part-time residence here. It's a beautiful place.

And I have a jet.

We can go anywhere we want to go from here.

37

HAVANNAH

Well, I can't say much more than *thank you* and *you're welcome* in French, but I'm getting by. Even Donovan's attempts to talk to me in French before I arrived for my low-residency requirement didn't stick. I'm officially too old to learn a new trick.

I hurry down the service hall of Demoor Castle, in awe of the stonework, the secret stairs, hidden rooms, and the history of the place. It's not nearly so massive or upscale as the one where Max and Camryn got married, but it has something even better—ghosts.

The haunted experience is the entire schtick, but it's not seedy or dumb. Guests learn the history of the castle in a welcome tour and get to know the tragic story of the original lord and lady of the manor, both of whom died in a fire two centuries ago.

The room where they died has been preserved, burn marks and all, and filled with paintings and household items from that era. The rooms are gothic and definitely set a mood. It's popular for honeymoons, God only knows why, but in the week I've been an intern here, I've learned a crazy amount about meeting guest expectations and managing a highly curated operation in an aged, complicated venue.

My mentor Felicity passes me in the hall. "After you greet the Weiss family, you're done for the day," she says. "They're German but speak enough English that you should be able to manage."

I nod. "Will do. Thanks."

"They have a baby. Make sure they have the setup they need."

The word *baby* makes my heart pang. "Glad to."

She nods at me, and we rush off in different directions.

Rebel will arrive tomorrow with Mom and Donovan. I can't wait to see them all. We agreed that seven days was long enough apart, and they would stay nearby for the rest of my residency requirement in France. He's ten months old and eating solids. He sleeps through the night, and everyone says he's doing fine without me.

Millie, Mom, and even Brian have taken turns keeping him. He apparently has a bazillion new toys and is getting terribly spoiled. I don't know where I'll fit everything when I get back. We're outgrowing the apartment I share with my sister.

But I spend a fair amount of my days with Donovan in a house he's rented in Boulder, and we're discussing if I might move into it full-time. My dad is freaking out about the idea, but I told him that if I can have a baby as a single mom, it's no stretch to move into a house with a man I've been dating for—well, for one day longer than my child has been alive.

The hall ends in a locked door that leads to the great hall. I pass my security card over it and buzz through to the grand room at the heart of the castle. Several guests have gathered in a cluster of chairs near the hearth.

The Weiss family is waiting by the check-in desk near the door.

"Welcome," I say. "I'm Havannah. I'll get you settled in your room."

They turn to me, two women and a baby about Rebel's age. "Hello," one woman says. "We are excited."

"Who is this?" I ask, looking at the baby.

"Fredrick," the other woman says.

"Nine months?" I ask. "I have a ten-month-old myself."

They smile at this. "Yes. Nine months."

"Follow me and we'll get you to your room and make sure you have what you need."

As we head down the halls, I describe the tour and the castle's history. The Weiss family has chosen the "quiet side" of the manor, with less risk of creaks or thuds in the middle of the night.

The various halls have different levels of paranormal activity. Much of it is an old house's bones in the wind, but there are plenty of events the staff can't explain.

The room is ready for them, a pack and play set aside for the baby, a bit out of sync with the dark furniture and red accents on the stone walls.

"This is amazing," one woman says. "Thank you."

I head for the door. "Call us if you need us. Come to the great room in an hour for the tour."

"Can the baby come? Is it scary?"

"Of course. It's only a walking tour. If you want to do a scary version, you might take turns. There are jump scares and flashing lights that might be too much for Fredrick."

The women nod.

This done, I head back to the service corridor to sign out and return to my hotel. I'm not sure what I'm going to do with this new certification that means almost nothing in the States, and I can't live in France with all the family in Boulder.

But I wanted to do it while I could. I have healthy grandparents happy to help. A boyfriend with a jet. And a baby who isn't old enough to give his opinions about my study time or jetting off to a haunted castle. Things will change soon. Life as a mother always does.

As I walk out to the road to catch a bus back to town, I glance back at the glorious structure. It stretches into the skyline, high, menacing, gothic, and eerie. I love it. It's not the vibe I'm going for in my own dreams, but I'm glad for the experience.

I spot the bus pulling up and take off at a run to catch it. I have to listen to two lectures tonight, turn in my notes, and take an exam, all before bed. Then I'll be mostly caught up and ready for my family's arrival.

By this time tomorrow, I will get to see my baby, my mother, and my man. I can't wait. Despite every hardship, my mistakes, and my missteps, my dreams feel very much within reach.

EPILOGUE: HAVANNAH

I clutch the handle of my car door as Donovan turns off the highway into nowhere.

"Where are we going again?" I ask, hanging on for dear life as we bounce over the rough terrain of an empty expanse of scrub brush and pine trees.

He mashes a button on the dash, setting the odometer trip counter to zero. As we lurch over rocks, clumps of low brush, and craggy outcroppings, I begin to wonder if he's lost his mind.

Donovan concentrates on maneuvering the Jeep. I understand why he rented it instead of his usual cars on his Colorado visits. "Almost there," he says.

I spot something flapping in the breeze up ahead. It's a squarish something. It's hard to see with the bouncing of the car.

As we get closer, I realize the strange object is an oversized canvas tent set with poles. It's easily as big as the living room of the apartment I share with Magnolia.

And sitting outside of it are two comfy-looking swivel chairs, a small table, and a rug.

A rug. In the middle of nowhere.

Donovan drives up to the tent and stops.

"I take it this is where we're spending the night?"

He grins. "Don't worry. I know how you feel about roughing it. This will be nothing like camping on a trail."

I open the door and jump down, now understanding his gift of my new hiking boots. I hope this expedition is not going to require any exercise. So not into that.

But the shoes are handy as we navigate the low brush to the cleared-off spot where the tent awaits.

I open the flap and peer inside. "Whoa."

It's like something out of a movie with an Egyptian prince. Tapestries line the walls, and silks cascade along the ceiling to soften the edges.

There's a wide bed in the center, a table on either side set with lamps. A small table with two chairs and two place settings fills a side wall, along with a small fridge next to a large box that looks like it contains a battery.

"Nice," I say. Cool air brushes against my cheek, and I turn to spy a freestanding air conditioner next to an ornate pedestal sink with a faucet. I turn the knob, and after a couple of seconds of chugging, clean water pours out of the spigot.

"Tell me where I'm going to pee, and I'll decide if I can camp like this," I say.

"There's a small privy behind the tent," he says. "You can check it out."

I wave my hands. "I believe you."

"Glamping services have gone upscale," Donovan says. "Do you like it?"

I walk up to him and wrap my arms around his waist. "I do. I like trying new things with you."

"Good." He leans down for a quick kiss. "There are some things I'd like to show—"

I shut him up with another kiss. "Less talking, more naked."

He hesitates, but then a slow grin comes across his face. We've been apart for three weeks, longer than usual. And today is the first anniversary of our first date. Tomorrow, of course, is Rebel's first birthday, and a huge party is planned.

Donovan will finally meet Brian—not that we've avoided it all this time, but it's never worked out. I don't see Brian all that much, spending most of my time with Millie and Jared.

Tomorrow will be very tied up.

Today is ours.

I pull his shirt from where it's tucked into his jeans. "Did you scout some friendly rocks?" I ask. "Because I'm willing to risk a sunburn in tender places for the full outdoor experience."

"You're always a step ahead of me," he says. "There's a river."

I hesitate. "Water? Outdoors? Like in movies?"

He grins. "Exactly."

I grab his hand. "How far? Do we drive there? Do we have to walk?"

"It's not far."

And he's right. He has the foresight to grab a couple of towels from a hamper near the chairs before we race across the field. There are no trails here, but we can navigate the bare patches in the brush easily enough. The lush green tree line tells us where the stream is, and soon we pick our way down a shallow hill to the gurgling crystal waters.

"How deep is it?" I ask.

"You can see the bottom."

I cock my head. "Do I hear a waterfall?"

"You do. It runs year-round as long as there isn't a prolonged drought."

I let out a squeal and move upstream. It's not far to get there, but I am hot and sweaty by the time we arrive. The waterfall is about fifteen feet tall, nestled in an outcropping of rock. The acreage looks to be at the foothills of Green Mountain, leading to the Rockies.

"It's breathtaking," I say. "It looks deep."

Anthony finds a flat bit of rock to set the towels on. "We going in?"

"Hell yeah, we're going in. Sex under a waterfall. That's a bucket list item."

He laughs. "Me too. Let's get 'er done."

We shuck our clothes and tiptoe across the rocks into the stream. It's only up to our knees until we start to approach the actual waterfall, where it quickly deepens.

"I think we can go around and behind it on that ledge," he says.

I take his hand, and we carefully approach the falls.

He's right, and we walk around it, all sound drowned out but the roar of the water over our heads. The ledge is a few feet wide, enough to walk along.

"Shall we see how deep it is?" I ask.

"Let's do it."

We lower ourselves down and find we can't touch the bottom. I dive below the surface, realizing at the last second I should've tied my hair back. It billows out behind me like a cloud.

We break through the surface of the water at the same time. "It's cold!" I shout. But I feel exhilarated, as if every cell in my body is electrically alive.

We find a lower section of rock farther down, water spilling across it before feeding into the pool beneath the falls. Donovan lifts me to sit on it and pulls himself up as well.

An occasional break in the falls allows sunlight to sparkle down and then is closed again. The roar is tremendous. The rock we sit on is cool, the flowing water a constant trickle over its surface.

"It's magical," I say.

"It's yours," he says.

I turn my head to him. "What do you mean?

"It's part of an eighty-acre parcel I purchased three weeks ago."

I clutch his arm. "Really?"

"You've been looking at properties. We saw a ton of them."

"Nothing like this."

"When I found it, I had to act fast. There were six

other bidders. The owner died and the family wanted to dump the acres."

"Donovan. Is this where…" I can't find the words to say it.

"It's your vision, baby. If you want your fairytale castle here, you have plenty of space and this beautiful waterfall to attract people to come."

I look up into the water flowing off the rock. "God. Donovan."

"You like it?"

"I love it. But the money. The funding."

He runs his hand down my arm. "We can worry about all that later."

"Okay. Right now, we need to break in this waterfall properly."

He leans down to kiss me, water flowing around our legs as if we are the force of nature that must be worked around. His hands are everywhere, following the curves he knows so well.

His skin is cool and wet from the water, and I follow the trails along the muscles of his chest, the indentions of his abs, and down to the part of him that is primed and absolutely ready for me.

We could be the only two people in the world, castaways in this wild, untamed land, finding a moment of respite, coolness, and ease in the water.

We lean back into the cool trickle of water along this hidden bit of rock, and I kiss down his body, following where my hands have led me, and take him in my mouth.

He lets out a sigh that disappears into the roar of the

water, gathering my hair in his hands to get it out of my way.

He knows I like that. I still like to run the movie in my mind of what we're doing, that exhibitionist streak alive and well. He always meets me where I'm at.

And this. This is next-level.

I work him with my hand and mouth until I feel the veins bulging, and the twitch that tells me I can finish here or move on.

I look up at him, his eyes closed, one hand thrown over his face.

The world is gray and green and wet and cool, the occasional dance of light creating dots on the walls of our hidden spot.

Donovan is part of it, all muscular man.

And he's mine. Neither of us has had a relationship last as long as this.

I crawl up his body, nipping bits of his flesh along the way up to his jaw.

"My biter," he says, drawing my face to his.

We kiss, his hands on my body, which has more or less recovered from pregnancy and childbirth, still a little softer in places, the pale streaks of stretch marks permanently etched here and there on my skin.

But my boobs are almost normal, Rebel only nursing occasionally, preferring his finger foods at this point. I feel alive, and in control of myself, ready for the next thing.

I ease back down his body until I straddle his hips. Then I lower myself on him, feeling my flesh give way, until he is buried inside me.

My knee shifts on a slippery bit of the rock, and he moves his hand to hold me steady.

"You got this?" he asks.

"Totally got this." I move up and down, easing him in and out. He clutches me, controlling our bodies and rhythm. I feel no hurry, despite the urgency I had before. Just like in that first fairytale, so long ago, in France, I don't want the fantasy to end.

I let the sounds penetrate, rushing water and cool air. My hair sticks to my back. I feel at one with everything around me, as if this is the most natural thing of all.

Despite these gentle, patient thoughts, the tension builds where we're joined. I tune back into it, listening to my body, feeling his inside me. We're in sync, taking our time, but letting the act find its way.

I suck in a breath. The tightness has begun to wind deep inside me. Donovan must recognize the change in my breath and moves his hand between us to find the nub that responds so well to him.

Then the cadence increases. I brace my hands on his chest and move with speed and power, crashing into him like the water on the surface below. My body tightens until I'm sure I will scream, I will never get there, I will simply collapse in on myself until I die.

But then it all releases, flashing out like a ripple on a lake when the surface tension is broken.

I collapse on Donovan's chest, our muscles pulsing, both of us gasping for air.

The warmth of him spreads in me, and his hand holds the back of my neck to press me tight. I lie flush on top of him, breathing hard, our hearts hammering against each other.

Nature takes no notice. The water continues its crash from high to low. The sun peeps through at the whim of the flow.

"I love you," Donovan says.

I rest my head on his chest. "I love you too."

"I'm glad you love this place."

"How could I not? The hardest part will be having to share it with others."

He laughs. "There might be a line to get back here."

"Maybe we can keep it a secret."

He laughs. "In the age of the Internet?"

"True."

I shift to the side, and we sit up.

"Want to take a swim?" he asks.

"Totally."

We slide off the ledge into the deep water. We push off the rock to pass through the waterfall, the power of it battering our backs as we cut through.

We surface on the other side, crystal droplets of water dancing on the surface.

"This is wild!" I call. "It's so perfect!"

We swim out for a bit and soon find our footing in the river.

"We need to monitor it during heavy rainfall and when it's dry," Donovan says.

I nod. "We can take our time. Visit in every weather extreme. Understand the land."

"And you can choose to never develop it. We can just own it."

I can't imagine doing that. It's too perfect.

We move slowly back toward our clothes. "We? I believe this is another great investment for you. I'm glad to be a part of it."

He shakes his head. "This property is in your name. Only yours."

I glance back at the waterfall. It's majestic.

Should I accept this? I remember the jewels my sister chided me for taking on that first trip to Paris. "Donovan, I'm not sure."

He searches through his clothes and extracts something from a pocket. It's too small for me to see at first, then he gets down on one knee, naked, cushioned by a clump of grass.

He holds up it. A diamond winks in the sunlight. "I'm hoping it will be *our* adventure," he says.

I look at the ring in his hands. It's a princess cut, and on each side is a deep purple stone, the birthstone for June. Both for Rebel's birthday and our first date. It's breathtaking.

"So what do you think?" he says. "Will you marry me? Can we make this merger official?"

I nod. I'm not sure if the wetness on my face is coming from my hair or my eyes, but I find it hard to speak.

He lifts my hand and slides the ring on my finger. I step closer.

He draws me to him, still on one knee, his beard tickling my belly.

"We're going to build a castle," I say. "People will get married here. Get engaged here. We will be the first."

He looks up at me. "I have to wait for the castle to be built to marry you?"

I laugh. "Well, maybe not completely built. Perhaps a nice gazebo."

"Good. Because a castle is going to take years, you know. We don't even have an architect. Or a plan."

It's true. "We won't wait that long." I run my fingers through his wet hair and lean down to plant a kiss on top of his head. "I'm so happy," I whisper.

His fingers tighten on my waist. "Me too."

I can barely breathe. For so long, I thought I would never be more than the circumstances of my mistakes.

But now I know that everything in life is what you put into it. And forgiving yourself is the first step. The next one is opening your heart to accept all the goodness that comes your way. To believe you deserve it.

My fairytale didn't end when I went a little crazy, or when I got pregnant.

And it didn't stop last year when I abruptly had to leave Milan.

This bold, brilliant life of mine has only just begun.

Thank you for reading *Tasty Mango*!

There will be more books in the Pickleverse! Cousin Sunny — I've got my eye on you! Sign up here to be notified whenever there is a new book!

This book is the bridge between two of my most popular rom com families! Learn about Donovan's brother Dell and how he ended up with baby Grace in Single Dad on Top and Single Dad Plus One.

And catch up on the Pickle family with Jason in Big Pickle, Max (whose wedding you just attended) in Hot Pickle, and Anthony (engaged to Havannah's sister Magnolia) in Spicy Pickle.

BOOKS BY JJ KNIGHT

Romantic Comedies

Big Pickle

Hot Pickle

Spicy Pickle

Tasty Mango

Single Dad on Top

Single Dad Plus One

The Accidental Harem

MMA Fighters

Uncaged Love Series

Fight for Her Series

Reckless Attraction

Get emails or texts from JJ about her new releases:

JJ Knight's list

ABOUT JJ KNIGHT

JJ Knight is one of the pen names of six-time *USA Today* bestselling author Deanna Roy. She lives in Austin, Texas, with her family.

To choose your next read from one of her fifty books, visit the web site **Read Laugh Swoon** to pick by book boyfriend, story line, heat level and more!

 facebook.com/jjknightauthor

 twitter.com/deannaroy

 instagram.com/deannaroyauthor

 bookbub.com/profile/jj-knight

www.ingramcontent.com/pod-product-compliance
Lightning Source LLC
Chambersburg PA
CBHW070430170726
48291CB00002B/430